THE CRYSTAL SKULL

The Crystal Skull

A Novel

Leon Arceneaux

iUniverse, Inc.
New York Lincoln Shanghai

The Crystal Skull
A Novel

Copyright © 2005 by Leon M. Arceneaux

All rights reserved. No part of this book may be used or reproduced by any means, graphic, electronic, or mechanical, including photocopying, recording, taping or by any information storage retrieval system without the written permission of the publisher except in the case of brief quotations embodied in critical articles and reviews.

iUniverse books may be ordered through booksellers or by contacting:

iUniverse
2021 Pine Lake Road, Suite 100
Lincoln, NE 68512
www.iuniverse.com
1-800-Authors (1-800-288-4677)

With the exception of the crystal skull, any similarity to persons living or dead is strictly coincidental.

ISBN: 0-595-34803-3

Printed in the United States of America

This book is dedicated to Margie, my wife, my love, my companion.
Together we've shared many adventures around the world.
Both exciting and harrowing.
Thanks.

"Sometimes, seemingly unrelated events
weave a web across time and
space—a web, which unless broken,
can ensnare millions of souls."

Captain Anthony Thompson, US Air Force

Contents

PROLOGUE: THE WEB IS SPUN 1
Chapter 1:   THE PYRAMID OF THE FEATHERED
             SERPENT 6
Chapter 2:   THE SELECTION 12
Chapter 3:   THE BLACK WIDOW 14
Chapter 4:   TDY 22
Chapter 5:   CROWS LANDING 26
Chapter 6:   THE CRYSTAL SKULL 33
Chapter 7:   MAGMA INTERFACE: THE DESTRUCTION
             THEORY 46
Chapter 8:   SUNRISE ON FIJI 51
Chapter 9:   HERON ISLAND 54
Chapter 10: THE PROPOSITION 61
Chapter 11: FATHER GORSKI'S WARNING 70
Chapter 12: THE SUB AND THE STRIGA 72
Chapter 13: HAWAIIAN INTERLUDE 81
Chapter 14: VAMPIRE OF PARIS: THE ATTACK 87
Chapter 15: REVELATION AT MONTMARTRE 103
Chapter 16: PREPARATION FOR MOUNT MISERY 108

Chapter 17:	THE VOODOO DANCE	116
Chapter 18:	MOUNT MISERY	125
Chapter 19:	TEMPLE OF THE FIRE GOD	132
Chapter 20:	THE DECIDING BATTLE	143
Chapter 21:	THE AFTERMATH	165
Chapter 22:	RETURN TO THE ISLAND	168
Chapter 23:	THE REPLACEMENT	175
AFTERWORD		181

PROLOGUE
The Web is Spun

Yucatan: 900 A.D.

"Quetzalcoatl is coming! The Feathered Serpent!"

Shouts echoed across the city. Excited chatter filled the air as the people gathered to line the main thoroughfare leading to the pyramid. This was the day they had been waiting for, bought with their labor and blood. Today they would celebrate.

While the excited throng waited, a deadly Evil was beginning to spin its web.

"It is done," the old high priest said to himself. Having risen early, he followed, as his warriors carried the throne to the base of the stone edifice. His face, deeply wrinkled, was the texture of leather from the many years of sun and wind. Long, white hair contrasted against his dark, sun-baked skin. As he walked, he adjusted the jaguar cape draped over his shoulders. A gold chain was placed around his neck. This was to be his day. He would now get the reward for his work. The Aztec god, Quetzalcoatl, promised him, through the god's messenger, that he would make him king over all the cities.

The day keeper, who marked the travels of the sun and the moon, had chronicled the time. The high priest ran his fingers lightly over the stone tablet he carried, feeling the marks. It took twenty summers, the season of the mighty storms, to complete the pyramid in honor of Quetzalcoatl, the Feathered Serpent. Each breath he took was an effort, but he now basked in his accomplishment.

The cost in lives had been high and he was now an old man, but he had built it exactly as the messenger had told him. He smiled as he thought of the final effort to complete his masterpiece. Grooves and valleys were gouged out on one of the faces of the pyramid. The messenger had told him, that on this day when the sun reaches the highest point in its travels across the sky, a serpent will be seen shining from the shadows, as if crawling up the pyramid. Its tongue will point to a hollow, which will be sealed with a stone facing.

An altar crowned the top of the pyramid. To get there, two hundred and forty steps graced the side facing the city. The old man thought in wonder, one for each time the moon went from dark to bright while we built the pyramid. He stopped to catch his breath and wipe the sweat from his face. How could Quetzalcoatl have known the exact time it would take?

The pyramid, at the end of the wide center street of the city, rose majestically from the green jungle behind it. The high priest admired its beauty, as the white limestone reflected the light from the sun.

"He will be pleased. Today is the day he will see his temple," The old high priest said proudly to the warriors near him. He had forsaken Kukulcan, his own Mayan god, and had turned to the Aztec god, Quetzalcoatl, the Feathered Serpent. The old high priest felt a slight tinge of guilt for leading his people to an Aztec god, but this god had promised power to him and prosperity to his people. He slowly lowered himself onto his throne.

Hearing the people cheer, the old man watched in eager anticipation, as an army of a hundred warriors marched up the street toward the pyramid. Leading them was Quetzalcoatl. He wore a large headdress made of the wing feathers of the great condor and was clothed in a robe of the white breast feathers of the heron. Approaching to within twenty paces of the high priest, he stopped. The old man's heart beat hard in his chest. He felt the pounding as he waited excitedly for the approval he knew was forthcoming. There was a hush as the people stood motionless.

Quetzalcoatl's face was the ashen gray of death and his eyes glowed red like coals of fire. He held something in his left hand. With his right hand he pointed at the people lining the street and seven fell dead. A gasp rose from the onlookers.

The high priest, trembling and straining every muscle, slowly and painfully stood up. Dragging his feet through the dust he approached the Aztec god. He will give me some of his power. He will make me king over all the cities. His mind raced as he struggled with every step.

Quetzalcoatl pointed a finger toward the throne and it disappeared in a flash of light. The high priest gasped. His muscles became like water. His knees buckled under him and he fell on his face before the god. Seeing this, all the people fell on their faces.

"I will have no thrones but mine."

He majestically walked through the smoke where the throne had been. "Bring the old man," he hissed, as he began climbing the steps toward the altar on top of the pyramid. Two of his warriors lifted the old high priest under his arms and carried him.

When they reached the top, Quetzalcoatl lifted his hands toward the sun. The high priest saw that he held a crystal skull. It pulsed red, like a beating heart filled with blood. The sun, reflecting on it, flashed in the old man's eyes, making the whole world seem drenched in blood.

While the Feathered Serpent stood with raised hands, a gasp went out from the people and warriors alike. For as the sun's rays reached an angle where they touched the stones of the pyramid, a shining serpent appeared to be crawling up the side. Its tongue pointed to a hollowed out stone. Lasting but a short time, the serpent then faded away.

He saw the serpent. I know Quetzalcoatl was pleased. He will now announce that he is making me king.

"Assemble the army of the city at the foot of my pyramid," ordered Quetzalcoatl.

When the city's fifty warriors had assembled, he stood in front of the altar on top of the pyramid and pointed down at them. There was a flash of light and a cloud of white, acrid smoke. When the smoke cleared, the city's entire army was no more. The people screamed in terror and tried to run, but the Aztec god's army surrounded them.

He placed the crystal skull in the hollow and commanded the high priest, "Seal the stone."

The old man, breathing heavily, struggling with shaking hands, placed a perfect fitting stone into the hollow, sealing it. *What is he doing to my people? He should be rewarding us for our good work.*

The two warriors seized the high priest and held him down on the altar. The old man didn't resist. He had no strength left in him. The Feathered Serpent raised a stone knife.

"Is this my reward?" the high priest whispered.

Quetzalcoatl plunged the knife into the high priest, ripped open his chest and pulled out his still beating heart. As he ate it, bright red blood ran down the sides of his mouth, contrasting with the ashen gray of his skin.

"The skull will be protected by the blood of the people until I return."

He stood at the altar the rest of the day as each of the people of the city was brought before him, their hearts ripped from their chests and their bodies sent bouncing down the stone incline. A grotesque offering of hearts was stacked at his feet.

On that day, when the sun rolled high across the sky, vultures circled in the hot, stagnant air, sickly sweet with the smell of death. Blood flowed freely from the altar of the Feathered Serpent, down the stone face of the pyramid and into the hungry earth.

When the last was sacrificed to him, he descended the steps of the pyramid. Down the wide center street that once was lined with curious people, but now empty, to the white powder beach, he slowly walked. The setting sun glowed scarlet, as though painted with the blood of the city. When the dull red orb touched the water, Quetzalcoatl, the Feathered Serpent, turned toward his warriors.

"Kill as I have taught you. Go from village to village and kill. Sacrifice their hearts to me. I will return to rule over you and all the people of the Earth."

After saying this, he walked into the sea, red from the setting sun, a sea of blood, and disappeared into the waves.

Siberia:
June 30, 1908 A.D.
7:16 A.M.

Father Gorski finished reading his morning prayers and walked out of the church into the mud of the street. His blond hair and long beard contrasted with his black cassock.

Had this really happened? Had God talked to me?

For some reason this morning he felt that he must renew his baptismal vows, and when he had said, "I renounce Satan…" he distinctly heard an audible voice saying, "I have chosen you."

The priest sloshed slowly through the mud, trying to understand. He felt that God had sent him there to serve, but he was open to whatever else God wanted him to do. Siberia was such a harsh and brutal land, yet he loved it, and this was where his people needed him.

Shopkeepers moved slowly and sleepily as they prepared to open for the day's business. He had heard of a revolution to overthrow the Czar, and hoped it wouldn't affect his village. He didn't know much about politics, and he didn't care about the outcome, as long as his flock was not adversely affected. But what did this voice mean? He hoped it had nothing to do with political turmoil. He just wanted to stay and tend his flock.

Through the corner of his eye, he detected a movement in the sky. Looking up, he saw a bluish-white ball moving rapidly from east to west, with a brightness that made the morning sun seem dark. Before he could even wonder what it was, there came a flash of incredible brilliance, which momentarily blinded him. Stumbling through the mud, he gasped, "My God! What was that?"

Before he could regain his sight, he heard a deafening roar and the force of a tremendous explosion threw him face down into the mud. His Bible flew from his hands. A hot wind tore at him, whipping at the pages of the book. Then came a deathly calm.

"My Bible," the priest mumbled, crawling through the mud to where it lay. Squinting, he tried to focus his eyes. It was opened at Luke chapter 10. The words of verse 18 seemed to burn from the pages: "And He said to them, 'I was watching Satan fall from heaven like lightning.'"

CHAPTER 1

THE PYRAMID OF THE FEATHERED SERPENT

Yucatan: Today

There was barely enough time to do it. If they missed this window, it would be another year before the pyramid would give up its secret. By then it may be too late. Could this terrifying secret be true? If it was, he must find and destroy it.

The air was hot and still. Moisture laden heat rose from the jungle floor. Professor Karolovitch bent slightly forward, laboriously plodded through the thick carpet of green and brown.

Sweat ran down his face and dripped off the end of his chin. His thick white hair hung wet and stringy. The smell of decaying vegetation was punctuated periodically with the sickly sweet fragrance of some unseen flower. A metallic purple and orange butterfly flitted by and a bird darted through the green vines with a flash of red. In the oppressive, steamy heat, the jungle was ominously silent, save for the crunch of vegetation underfoot and the hacking of the machete.

Leading the way, Carlos, a young native, bare to the waist, swung his machete at the thick tangles. With every stroke, muscles rippled under skin shiny with sweat. Now and then he would stop, slap at a biting insect, and mutter a curse in Spanish.

Professor Karolovitch looked back at his granddaughter, Natasha, to make sure she was all right.

Natasha, her long black hair tied behind her head, wiped her face with a handkerchief. Her dark brown eyes always seemed to have a gleam of excitement in them. Even though she was wearing no makeup, her face had a smooth softness to it, with just a touch of pink in her cheeks to highlight her high cheekbones. At the age of twenty-five, with a master's degree, she was already more knowledgeable in the field of Archaeology than many Ph.D.'s twice her age. She went with her grandfather on all of his expeditions and was eager to learn from him.

Professor Nikolai Karolovitch had defected while attending a conference at UCLA where he was presenting a paper on the writings of ancient civilizations. He had taken his granddaughter, who was five at the time, with him.

One month before Natasha was born, her father had disappeared after speaking out against the government and had not been heard from since. Her mother had died during childbirth so Natasha had no family but her grandfather.

After his defection, Professor Karolovitch was granted asylum and subsequently received a research grant to study the works of the Mayan. In the course of his research, he kept finding stone carvings of hieroglyphics depicting a legend of a crystal skull. Little by little he pieced together a collection of knowledge so awesome that he dared to share it only with Natasha. If what he had pieced together was true, the terrible power of the skull must never get into the wrong hands.

For years they had been searching for the Pyramid of the Feathered Serpent. They had to find the crystal skull before the Feathered Serpent returned to claim it.

When it seemed imminent that they were close to finding the skull, he had contacted the CIA who had assigned one of its agents to investigate. Although the CIA bureaucracy did not take it seriously, the assigned agent, Karl Farmer, was very interested. The professor, however, had revealed only very sketchy information.

"Be careful, *Señor*. You may not know there are large vipers here on the Yucatan."

"Yes, I know," the professor said, wiping his face. "Natasha, are you all right?"

"Yes, I'm fine, but I'd be much better if it weren't so hot."

Just then, the native stopped as he came upon an opening in the dense growth.

"There it is, *Señor*, the pyramid of Quetzalcoatl, the Feathered Serpent. I can go no further. I have been told that one will die if one approaches his temple. I will leave you now. If you do not die, follow the trail back. But I must warn you that if you do not die, he will find you. You cannot hide from his curse."

Natasha looked out onto the clearing. There, at the end of a wide stone avenue, stood the pyramid, rising majestically from the jungle floor. It was not like the other pyramids they had come upon in the jungles of Mexico and Central America. Instead of a layer of soil and jungle growth covering it, this one appeared to be as clean and white as the day it was completed.

Silently she considered every detail. The sun, reflecting on the white limestone, made the smooth and polished blocks seem as though they were radiating a light of their own. On the side facing the avenue were steps ascending to the top. A pink stone altar crowned the flat crest. She noticed that one of the sides of the pyramid was different from the others. Uneven and ragged, with pieces of stone jutting out, and deep gouges cut into the blocks, its surface gave the appearance of being unfinished.

"Isn't it beautiful, Natasha?"

She began taking pictures and experimenting with various speeds and exposures.

"Yes, it is." She was trying to capture every detail on film. "But why does it look like it's not finished, and why isn't it covered with vines and jungle growth?"

"I wish I knew."

She looked at her watch. It was only fifteen minutes before the sun would be at the proper position in the sky. The writings suggested that when the sun crossed the zenith, the first day of the Mayan year, the Feathered Serpent would reveal the hidden place of the crystal skull. This was the only day of the year the pyramid uncovers its secret, and they had almost missed it.

She thought about how they had quickly organized this trek as soon as they realized the drawings in the temple of the moon goddess at Tulum were showing them the location of the pyramid of Quetzalcoatl. Working against time, they searched until they found someone who would guide them to the location. They could not find anyone who would admit that it existed, until they found one young man brave enough to lead them here. Her heart beat faster thinking of how her grandfather, even at his age, had unmercifully driven the three of them, since before dawn, so they would be here at the right time. They had not arrived any too soon. This was what they had searched for, for so long. This was what they had suffered so many hardships to find. Her grandfather had paid the price in years, to be where he was now.

"The sun will soon be at its apex," the old man said breathlessly. "The Feathered Serpent will tell us its secret. We must not forget why we are here and we must remember that beauty sometimes hides the evil within."

As she watched, suddenly the rough portion of the pyramid became a glowing serpent coiling up the side with its head near the altar. The sun, shining on the jutting rocks and crevices, made a glistening white serpent of the highlights and shadows. Its forked tongue pointed to a spot on the side of the stone altar.

"That's it, Natasha! That's it!" he said excitedly.

She looked on in awe, not moving a muscle, hardly breathing as they watched the spectacle. The serpent slowly faded away until it could no longer be seen, and became a jagged, uneven surface once again.

"Yes!" Natasha exclaimed excitedly. "Yes, the serpent pointed to it with its tongue!"

When they arrived at the base of the pyramid, the professor sat to rest before they started to scale the steps. Natasha noticed a place where the rock appeared to have been melted.

"That's strange," she commented. "The rock in this spot must have been subjected to intense heat, but only a laser could have produced that much heat in such a concentrated area."

The professor wiped the sweat from his face. "Remember what I told you, Natasha. If we find the skull, you must never touch it. Not even through the leather satchel."

"Yes, I remember," said Natasha, smiling. She felt like jumping up and down with excitement, like when she was a little girl.

"Did you write down the name of who you were to contact if something should happen to me?"

"I can remember. The policeman in the village, Raul, will contact Karl Farmer of the CIA and tell him we have it." Natasha answered. "After I pay him off." She smiled and continued. "But nothing will happen to you. Are you rested enough?"

"In a minute." The professor took a deep breath. "It's all arranged for Farmer to take the skull to a safe place until it can be destroyed. You must impress on him the importance of this. The skull must never get into the wrong hands. The fate of the world could be in the balance. Remember, tell no one, except Farmer, what we've learned. He'll decide who else must know in order to destroy it."

"Grandfather." Natasha looked patiently at him. "You've told me all this a million times. We both know the importance. But nothing will happen to you, so don't worry."

"I've rested enough. Now help me up the steps to the altar."

She took him by the arm, and laboriously, step-by-steps, started the climb to the top.

"Do be careful, Grandfather."

Natasha carried the satchel and backpack with the tools, at the same time carefully helping her grandfather to climb each step. Her slight figure was deceiving. She could hold her own with any man when it came to endurance.

It was a long and arduous climb for the Professor. Every few steps he had to sit and rest. Finally they reached the top.

The altar, which from the ground, appeared to be made of pink stone, was of the same white stone as the rest of the pyramid, but it was stained with something red that had permeated the porous rock. Natasha touched it with her finger. It felt slimy and she quickly pulled back. There was a red substance on her finger, like blood. She wiped it on her pants.

Natasha watched her grandfather on his hands and knees, as he looked closely at the side of the altar. "Is this the spot the serpent's tongue pointed to?"

"Yes, I think so," said Natasha. She continued wiping her finger disgustingly on her jeans.

She watched intently as he ran his hand across the smooth surface of the rock until he felt a very slight unevenness. "This is the place. Quick, hand me the hammer and chisel."

Slowly he chipped around a square area, and as he cut into the rock, a thick red fluid oozed out as if the altar were bleeding.

"What's that?" Natasha asked as she backed away.

The professor dropped his tools, drawing back from the thick, oozing fluid. "I...I don't...looks like blood. Like the rock is bleeding."

When the oozing stopped, he slowly, with trembling hands, picked up his tools and started chipping again. "Have to get the skull. Have to get the skull," he kept whispering over and over.

"Be careful," Natasha said haltingly. "We don't know what that fluid is. It could be some kind of poison. Try not to touch it. Wait." She took a spare shirt from her knapsack and gingerly wiped the fluid that had oozed from the stone.

Finally the seal-slab loosened and the professor was able to remove it. Inside the hollowed rock was the crystal skull. "Hand me the tongs."

Natasha watched him as, with trembling hands, he carefully reached in, grasped the skull with the tongs, and slowly pulled it out. He then placed it on top of the altar.

Natasha gasped at its beauty. The skull, about six inches in diameter, was made from a single piece of perfect colorless crystal. There were no imperfections whatsoever. It was smooth and no tool marks were evident. It had every detail of a human skull. As she watched, it seemed to fade away until she could barely distinguish its outline, and then it appeared to harden into a solid shape again. The skull seemed to be on the verge of being dissolved into the air, repeatedly fading and returning. Was it the way the light hit it, or was there a faint flicker as of fire deep within it?

"It's beautiful!" She was so awed by the sight that she momentarily forgot her grandfather's warnings and reached to touch it.

"Stop! Don't touch it, whatever you do! Here, hold the leather bag."

She quickly drew her hand back, feeling foolish. "But why does it seem to fade away at times?" Natasha asked as she took hold of the leather bag.

The professor carefully picked up the skull with the tongs, placed it into the bag and pulled the drawstrings tight. "It must have almost the same refractory index as air. That's very strange. I wonder what the composition of the crystal is. Get the leather satchel."

Natasha put the satchel on the altar, holding it open. The professor held the leather bag by its drawstrings, placed it into the satchel, and then zipped it closed. "Here, Natasha."

She took hold of the handle and raised it from the altar. The bottom of the satchel was stained with the red fluid.

Going down was very slow. One mistake could send them careening forward to their deaths. Natasha held the satchel in one hand and her grandfather's hand with the other.

In the shadows, a black, furry evil waited, crouching, ready to spring. As the professor was slowly feeling with his foot for the next step, a large black tarantula, in one giant leap, landed on his neck, sinking its fangs into the soft flesh. He yelled, grabbing at the mass of fur and legs. Tearing from Natasha's grip, he plunged headlong down the side of the pyramid.

A scream of horror escaped Natasha's throat and the jungle echoed back her terror. The professor's body tumbled, rolled, and twisted down the stone steps, coming to rest at the bottom, in a grotesque position. He lay still—unseeing eyes staring into eternity.

She screamed again, and this time her echo, returning from the endless reaches of the steaming jungle, reverberated into a laugh as from the bowels of hell.

Chapter 2

THE SELECTION

"Let's review them again," Karl Farmer said with a sigh. "Too bad we had to annihilate the Navy Seal. He was a good candidate."

He squinted at the computer screen. "I hate to put you through this, Natasha, but we have to be sure."

Natasha sighed deeply. "I know. I wish it wouldn't have to be this way."

"Let's use a different approach," Karl said as he typed on the keyboard. "What do you think of this?"

"What?"

"What if we were to select two candidates who fulfill all the other requirements, but also work closely together as a team?" Karl looked at Natasha and smiled.

"How will that be better?"

"If one doesn't pass the test and has to be annihilated, we still have one and we don't have to make another selection. But if they both pass the test, we have the two working together as a team, which should enhance the project."

"I guess so…but I hate this annihilation. They're human beings. I wish there'd be another way. What if they both fail?"

"Well, then we have to start over. But when you consider what hangs in the balance, it's not too high a price to pay."

"For us, maybe." Natasha again sighed deeply. "But not for them."

"We have to look past this toward the ultimate goal." Karl squinted at the computer screen again. "Here's a fit." He pressed a key.

Natasha picked up a sheet of paper that spit out of the printer.

"What do you think about this," Karl asked?

"Two test pilots from Edwards?" She scanned the page.

"They fit the profile to a tee," Karl said as he looked over Natasha's shoulders.

"But test pilots? Shouldn't we be looking at someone like Army Special Forces or Navy Seals?"

"Think about this. These people are in danger every day. They handle crises all the time as a matter of course. They live on the edge. I think these two fit the bill."

Natasha stood up. "I hope you're right and I hope their will is strong enough to pass the test. Sure would hate to see two more good men annihilated. But I guess this is the only way."

She handed the sheet to Karl. "Okay, lets give it the go-ahead and start the process."

Chapter 3

THE BLACK WIDOW

General Stone read the communication again, then ran it through the shredder. He poured himself a drink from a bottle in his desk drawer, downed it, and then left his office, walking briskly toward the control center.

✳   ✳   ✳   ✳

Tony pulled back on the stick and firewalled the throttle. The Mach meter read .95! *I'm going to push through compressibility and go supersonic on a vertical climb without afterburners! This aircraft is as good as they said it was going to be.*

As he reached Mach one, there was a slight shiver, and then it smoothed out again. The velocity stabilized at 1.5 and he couldn't shove it any faster.

"Come in. Tony." Mac's voice crackled in Tony's earphones.

"Tony here. Over."

"How do you like her?" Mac asked.

"Fine as wine," answered Tony on the scramble channel to the evaluation control room. "Is the vendor rep there? Over."

"He's sitting right next to me at the monitor."

"Hey, Rep. Are you reading me on the monitor? Over."

At ninety thousand feet, Tony noticed the sky had turned a deep purple and he could see a few stars as silver points of light.

"Roger, Tony. You can level out, now. Ease up on the throttle and pull her over slowly. Go easy on the negative G's. Over."

"Wilco."

Tony slowly pushed the stick forward and felt his body lifting against the harness.

"Okay. Now firewall her. Got your velocity on the monitor. We'll be watching the combustion turbine temperature and tell you when to start easing back on the throttle."

Tony looked at the sky again. It was dark blue velvet, almost black. The same color as that velvet dress she used to wear. He remembered the way it clung to her and how it felt as he moved his hands along the curves of her body. Tony could almost smell the perfume she wore—soft and faint like the smell of magnolias in the moonlight. After making love, she would snuggle in his arms.

Damn, I loved that woman! A wave of grief surged over him as he remembered the telephone call about the automobile accident and the kiss on that beautiful, cold face just before they closed her casket. Tears filled his eyes and he had to blink hard to be able to see. It was a year now and he still missed her.

"Tony. Come in, Tony." It was Mac. Tony had let his mind drift. Even a moment of distraction could mean death to a test pilot.

"Roger. This is Tony." He looked at his Mach meter. It registered three and still accelerating. "Everything's A-okay here."

Tony and Mac had been through test pilot training together and were inseparable. They had been selected to evaluate the XXF. Tony was chosen to make the first evaluation flight for the Air Force.

Captain Anthony Thompson, Tony, as his friends called him, was five foot nine with light brown hair and blue eyes. His hair was close cropped in the manner of military pilots.

Things always came easily to Tony. He went to the best boarding schools and was able to obtain a congressional appointment to the Air Force Academy. He was soft spoken with an air of self-assurance. Now that Sherri was gone, flying and science were his life. Everything had to have a scientific explanation. Although he was brought up attending church, after Sherri's death, he turned his back on religion. He did not believe in the spiritual. He had to be able to see, feel, and measure it to accept it as real.

Tony came from a small town in Mississippi. He had stopped telling people the name of the town because no one had ever heard of it and no one seemed to care when he did tell them. It was important only to his family because they were important there.

Captain Charles MacPherson, Mac, on the other hand, was six feet tall with brown eyes and black hair. His close-cropped hair lay flat in every direction. His complexion was ruddy and he had a deep tan.

Things never came easily to Mac. He was raised by a single mom on the wrong side of the tracks. He got a job while in public high school to help out at home, and had to devote long hours of study to maintain good grades. No one except his mother seemed to have faith in his success in life. In an effort to show everyone he could do it, he took a competitive test for the Air Force Academy. He was surprised and overwhelmed when he was selected.

Mac was boisterous and loud, trying to overcome a feeling of inferiority. He had never married and was too busy trying to impress women to ever have a serious relationship. Mac wasn't gifted with polished speech, and what flowed from his mouth came straight from his heart.

Mac, like Tony, also didn't bother to tell his friends where he was from. "I don't give a damn where I've been. It's where I'm going that's important."

"Who's in the control room, Mac?" Tony asked.

"Besides all the vendor reps…let's see. We got four Majors, Colonel Martin and General Stone himself. You're playing to a full house."

The Mach meter now read 3.7.

"Okay, now," the rep's voice came over his earphones. "Start easing back on the throttle to about fifty percent thrust."

"Roger, fifty."

"Okay, take her down to a thousand feet and let's take that vertical climb again. We didn't get all the data.

"Roger, wilco."

As he started his descent, Tony looked about the cockpit in awe. This was truly more than just a piece of equipment, it was an extension of himself. The old time pilots who flew by the seat of their pants only controlled a machine, but today's pilots were part of the machine. They were a link to close the loop between man and man's creation.

In addition to testing the XXF, Tony and Mac were also working on the CYBER program—Cybernetic Interaction of Humans and Machines. The other two members of the CYBER team were a flight surgeon, Captain Mike Bloom, who they called "Doc," and an engineer Captain Bob Berretti, who specialized in Cybernetics. Tony was excited to be working in this program because he knew that this was an important first step into further integrating man and machine.

"There is nothing that science can't achieve in due time," Tony often said. "Everything has a scientific explanation, even those so-called miracles that the religious nuts claim."

"Okay, I'm starting the vertical climb," Tony said as he pulled the stick back. The aircraft responded beautifully until the meter reached Mach 0.99. There was a shudder, a piercing alarm and a flashing red light.

At that moment Tony saw a face looking into the cockpit. It was not really a face—just a black hood and blackness where a face should have been. He didn't have time to think about it.

He pulled the stick toward him to lay it on its back, and then rolled it over to straight and level. At the same time, he pulled the throttle back to fifty percent thrust, while he flipped the guard up from the ejection button.

The alarm and the flashing red light stopped, so Tony relaxed somewhat as he pressed the "FIRST OUT" button on the alarm panel. He waited while the computer searched then flashed "COMPRESSOR HI TEMP" on the screen, and then the words "CONDITION STABILIZED".

"Emergency! Emergency, Blue Base!"

"Come in. Tony. Status." Mac sounded anxious. "Compressor stage high temperature alarm. Stabilized."

"Roger, we got the alarm here. We'll clear you with the tower for an emergency landing."

Tony dropped his landing gear, made a ninety-degree turn to his right and lined up with the long white ribbon of runway at Edwards Air Force Base. He eased the throttle to twenty percent thrust and lowered his flaps.

The rep had told him, "You got to fly this baby all the way down. Don't cut your throttle until you're firmly on the runway then pop your drogue chute."

Tony felt contact. Then as his nose wheel touched, he cut the throttle and released the drogue. "Touchdown. See you in debrief, Mac."

"Roger, Tony. See you there."

When the adrenaline stopped flowing and he had time to think, Tony remembered the face. *Everything happened so fast. But I saw it.*

Tony didn't mention it in debriefing. They would have thought he was off his rocker. He imagined it. With that thought, he put it out of his mind.

After debriefing, he went to his room and took a cool, leisurely shower.

The sun was setting as Tony left the bachelor officer's quarters. The hot desert wind no longer blew across the Mojave. It was calm, with just a slight breeze, now and then, to stir the air against his face. He thought of the cool beer waiting for him at the club. The oxygen rich environment in the pressurized cockpit, and now the dry desert air, had depleted his body of moisture and he craved liquids.

Tony walked slowly toward the Officer's Club. He loved this time of day, twilight, just before the dark, when all the world was hushed. As a child, he would sit on the porch with his mother and watch the light fade in the west. She used to recite a poem for him. Something about "sunset and evening star." He wished he could remember it.

He would rather have stayed outside to enjoy the quiet of the evening, but he knew that his friends were waiting for him, so he entered the club.

"Hey, Tony. What the hell took you so long? Finished the first pitcher already. Need a refill," Mac yelled from across the room.

"Hi," Tony said as he pulled up a chair and opened a newspaper he had picked up at the door. The waitress placed a full pitcher of beer on the table.

"Tony, pay the lady. That'll teach you to be late," Mac loudly proclaimed.

"Wow! The last of the big spenders," Bob chided when Tony laid the money on the table.

"That poor woman," Tony said as he opened a newspaper.

"Put that paper down and talk to us," said Doc.

"It says here, this young woman was with her grandfather on an archaeological expedition in the Yucatan. He fell down a pyramid. Killed him. She had to drag his body back through the jungle," Tony said as he folded the paper and dropped it on the table. "I really feel sorry for her. It must have been tough."

"Heard you had a wild ride today," Doc said to Tony. "We've been waiting for you so we could celebrate your first encounter with the Black Widow."

"You mean the XXF? Why the Black Widow?"

"Well, she's like a black widow spider. She's black, right?"

"Yeah, she's black."

"And like the spider, if you're the male she can give you a hell of a ride, but you gotta be quick on your toes or she'll kill you. So you're somewhere between screwing and death."

Tony grimaced. "That's a hell of an analogy," he replied, as he reached for the pitcher of beer.

"Wait, get your cotton-picking hands off that pitcher. I'm about to create a super-duper celebration drink," Doc said as he reached into a brown paper bag.

"What are you doing? It's the middle of the week." Tony watched as Doc unscrewed the cap from a bottle and poured some medicinal alcohol in the pitcher of beer.

"That figures. The three of you been drinking boilermakers. You guys get obnoxious when you do heavy-duty drinking. Are you crazy, Mac? I flew today. You might have to fly tomorrow?"

"Don't have to worry about flying tomorrow. Tell him, Mac," Doc said as he shook the last drop from the bottle.

Tony looked at Mac. "What's he talking about?"

"Well, General Stone wants to see both of us tomorrow."

"Does it have anything to do with the flight today? If there's any chewing to do, it should come from Colonel Martin, not General Stone."

"Don't get shook," Mac answered. "He told me he wanted to see us before it happened, so it's not a donkey barbecue."

"What the hell is a donkey barbecue?" Bob asked.

"A donkey barbecue's an ass eating."

"Oh."

"Don't know what it's about, Tony," Mac continued, "but one thing's certain. We're not going to fly 'til the evaluation team comes up with the reason for the hot box. In the meantime, drink up, me lad."

Bob held up his glass. "A toast. May Tony and Mac screw the Black Widow without getting eaten."

"Hear, hear." Doc said as he held his glass high. He took a swallow, then put his glass down, cleared his throat and said, "Did I ever tell you guy's about the time when I was doing my residency? One Saturday night this guy brings in his buddy with a light bulb up his…"

"Hold it," Tony interrupted. "Not the light bulb story. I don't want to hear it."

"Let him tell it," said Bob.

"Wonder what the General wants?" Tony said while looking at his glass as he swirled the liquid.

"Who cares," Bob piped up. His words were beginning to slur.

"Yea," Mac chimed in. "Forget the general. Right Doc? Everybody chug-a-lug the Doc's famous prescription boiler makers." Mac topped the glasses, overflowing each one as he poured.

"Tell us the light bulb story," urged Bob.

Doc finished downing his drink and wiped his mouth. "Sorry Bob. Maybe some other time when Tony's not here. He doesn't appreciate my stories."

Tony stood up. "I missed the evening meal. Man, I hate to drink on an empty stomach. This drink is already getting to me. I'm going to see if I can find something to eat."

"This is pretty good stuff, Doc." Mac's tongue was getting a little heavy. "Did you learn this prescription in med school?"

"I'll let you in on a little secret if you promise not to tell anyone." Doc's speech was starting to slur also.

"Promise I'll take it to my grave."

"I spent three years in the Navy before med school. Three years as a swabby. Used to drink depth charges. Fill shot glasses with vodka and drop 'em in a mug o' beer. Finish the beer. Get the shot. Lots of guys ended up with broken teeth. Started just pouring vodka in the beer. This is called boilermakers. Don't know why they call it that, but that's what it is."

"Don't know when to believe you, Doc. But this is good stuff. It will zap you, that's for sure. Wouldn't want to do this every night," said Mac.

"I think he learned to make it in med school," mumbled Bob.

"You got anything to eat?" Tony asked the bartender as he walked up to the bar.

"Peanuts or potato chips. You got your choice. And tell the guys to cool it. I wouldn't want the general to walk in and see them making boilermakers."

Tony returned to the table and sat down.

"You find something to eat?" asked Mac.

"Potato chips," Tony said as he opened the bag. "What happened to Doc and Bob?"

"Hell, Bob started to get sick so Doc took him to his quarters."

"Well, I guess that's the end of the party. Bob knows every time he drinks those boilermakers he gets sick. A couple more and I would of been shit-faced. Fact is, my head's spinning now. Guess we ought to hit the sack."

"Yeah, have to see old stone face in the a.m.," Mac said.

Tony and Mac staggered out into the moonlight. The air was cool and refreshing, as the nights are in the desert. In the distance came a staccato of barks, then the trailing howl of a coyote.

"Listen to that coyote," Tony mused.

"Yea. This is the wild west."

"You know any western songs?" Tony asked Mac.

"Maybe."

"Something from an old western. Remember Gene Autry? Trigger?"

"Hell, Trigger's a damn horse. Never once heard him sing."

"All right, forget about the singing."

"Okay. Let's sing, then. You start it off."

"What about this one? Do you know it?"

Arms around each other, they staggered together in the soft moonlight singing an old western song while the coyote flung his lonesome call to the dessert wind.

Chapter 4

TDY

"'General Stone will see you now."

Tony and Mac slowly got up and walked into the large, austere office.

"Wish I hadn't drank so much last night," Mac whispered to Tony. "Tastes like the whole frigging Chinese army walked through my mouth…bare foot."

"Don't act cute in front of the general," Tony whispered through the side of his mouth. "You'll get us both in trouble."

"Come in, gentlemen," the general said between puffs on a large cigar. "At ease. Have a seat."

"Yes sir." Tony said stiffly. "Thank you, sir."

Tony and Mac took their seats in straight-backed maple chairs across from the General's huge maple desk.

"Gentlemen," the general said, slowly forming each word. "I have a top secret request from the Central Intelligence Agency, through the Joint Chiefs of Staff. They want two volunteers by the names of Captain Anthony Thompson and Captain Charles MacPherson. I have no information on what the mission is, but they were very clear about who they wanted."

"You said you don't know what it's for, sir?" Mac asked.

"Like I said, I have no information on what you'll be doing, but somebody wants you real bad," the general slowly said while intently looking at them with steel gray eyes.

"Pardon me, sir," Tony asked. "How long would this be for and where would we be stationed?"

"Well, son," the general was now doodling on a piece of paper. "I don't know how long or where you'll be, but I suspect that by the time the investigation on the malfunction of the XXF is completed and the modification installed, you'll be back. This isn't a transfer. It's only temporary duty, TDY. It's a good time for this to come up. It'll keep you busy. The CYBER project can wait."

"But sir," Mac protested. "Just for the record. What if we didn't volunteer?"

"Well, son..." The general looked at Mac while squinting his eyes. "It would not make me look good with the Joint Chiefs, now would it? I would not be happy."

What is he doing? Tony thought as he shifted uneasily in his chair. He's going to get us in trouble.

"Furthermore," the general grunted, puffing up like a toad. "That would be a definite career limiting move. You'd be doomed to duty that you don't want to think about." He paused for effect, and then continued, "For the rest of your career, which wouldn't be very long. But it would seem like an eternity."

"I understand," said Mac.

"Good," the general answered. "Pack some civilian clothes like you're going on leave. You have reservations at the Valley Inn in Bakersfield. Stay there tonight. Let everyone know you're going to San Francisco. But, instead of going all the way to San Francisco, you'll turn off Highway 5 at Crows Landing and report to the commander of the Naval Air Station."

"Excuse me, sir," Mac asked. "What's at Crows Landing? Every time I fly by, all I ever see is an old tanker plane flying around and that's all. It's weird that a naval air station would be back in the hills like this one. What are we going to do there, sir?"

General Stone's face turned red. "Don't ask questions, damn it! Just do it! Dismissed!"

Tony and Mac quickly stood up at attention, saluted, turned as one and started toward the door.

"Just a moment, Captain MacPherson."

Mac stopped. "Yes, sir."

"Come back here and close the door."

Tony stood and waited outside the door. What the hell's going on in there, he thought. I hope Mac's not in trouble.

After what seemed like an eternity, Mac strolled out of the general's office smiling.

When they were safely out of the building, Tony looked at Mac and said, "I don't believe you. Next time you want to make a career limiting move, deal me out."

"Shit, Tony. The old son-of-a-bitch puts his pants on one leg at a time just like we do."

"And what was that all about? Are you in trouble?" Tony asked.

"Hell, no," Mac replied with a grin from ear to ear. "When the time is right, I'll tell you. But don't ask me 'till we get back from TDY."

"Okay, I guess I can wait." Now, what the hell is going on, Tony thought? But I'll respect his wishes. He was quiet for a few moments and then continued, "I wonder what the CIA wants with us?"

"Hey, Tony. This could be exciting. Haven't you ever read spy novels? They always have beautiful women who like to screw."

"Get serious, Mac. This could be dangerous."

"Bullshit!" Mac was now smiling broadly. "Get with the program, Tony. If there's beautiful women involved, make the best of it. It's time you got out of your shell. Can't keep living in the past. She's gone, Tony. You have to look to the future."

Tony glared at Mac.

"Sherri is dead, Tony," Mac continued. "Accept it. You haven't been able to say her name since she died. Say it, Tony. Say, 'Sherri is dead.' Say it."

Anger flashed through Tony like a lightning bolt. "This is none of your damned business! Stay out of my private life. What I do and what I think is my business."

Mac's smile faded. "Not true, Tony," Mac said while looking straight into Tony's eyes. "Your mental state could very well affect what could happen to me. Remember, we're a team. There are times when your support or lack of it could mean my life. Remember gunnery training? You saved my ass from that flaky student who almost shot my tail off. If you hadn't been looking out for me, he might've gotten me. Can't be looking toward the past, Tony. You can get your ass killed. What's more, you could get my ass killed, too. Don't know what we're getting into, so we got to keep on our toes."

Tony looked directly into Mac's eyes, "Sherri is my business. Lay off, will you?"

"Hey, I'm sorry if I got you pissed. But don't you see what I'm trying to say?"

"Well, I guess," Tony grudgingly admitted. "But lay off about Sherri."

"Right on!" Mac flashed a smile.

"What are we going to tell Doc and Bob?" Tony said thoughtfully. "We got to tell 'em something. We can't just walk away."

Mac rubbed his chin. "Well…the General said to make people think we're going to San Francisco for fun and games. Doc and Bob are people, so that's what we tell 'em."

"They're going to think it's awful strange, just taking off like this."

"We'll tell 'em we pissed the general off and he told us to get the hell out of here."

"Yeah, Mac. Better not tell 'em that. Knowing those two, they might try it and end up in the pogy," Tony said, with mock seriousness.

"Yeah," grinned Mac. "Wouldn't that be fun?"

"You know. Come to think of it, no telling what they might do if they start drinking those boilermakers," Tony said.

"Yeah," Mac replied. "Those things are dangerous. Good thing Doc saves that concoction for special occasions."

"Who's car are we going to take?" asked Tony.

"Let's take my Jag. Might look more like we're going on a fun trip in a sports car, than in your big ol' tank."

"If you want to take your car, that suits the hell out of me. I'll just pull the cover over mine to keep the dust off and have Bob start it every few days."

CHAPTER 5

CROWS LANDING

The wind whipped across Tony's face as he and Mac sped westward in the open convertible, over the mountains toward Bakersfield.

"Doc and Bob weren't too happy when we told them we were going on leave today," said Tony, speaking loudly over the sound of the wind. "I hated to pull that on them. They think we didn't want 'em to come."

"Nope. They bought the story. Got a phone call from two girls from my hometown. Wanted us to show 'em around San Francisco. Two girls. Two guys. No more." Mac yelled back.

"Hey, slow down, Mac."

"Don't sweat it. Enjoy life while you can. May not be a tomorrow."

"There damn sure won't be a tomorrow if you go over the side. I saw a wrecker pull a car up a couple of weeks back. Not a very pretty sight."

"Don't chew a hole though my seats with your ass. Relax. We'll soon be out of the mountains. Look at it this way. The faster we go, the sooner we'll be out of the mountains and the safer we'll be," Mac said with a laugh.

"Great logic, Mac."

As they drove out of the mountains and onto the broad, flat floor of the San Joaquin Valley, Tony breathed a sigh of relief. A pall of dust hung in the atmosphere, and the setting sun was a red ball over the coastal range in the western sky. Hot air, blowing in his face, smelled of freshly plowed earth. Tony licked his lips. "The air felt good up in the mountains. Nice and cool. But this sure is hot. It'll be nice to dive in the pool at the hotel."

While checking into the hotel, Mac kept proclaiming in a loud voice, that they were on leave. He also made sure everyone heard that they were on their way to San Francisco for a well-deserved R&R of fun and games.

"Let's get our bathing suits on and go for a swim," said Tony as they walked to their rooms.

"Suits me," answered Mac as he fumbled with his key. "See you at the pool."

* * * *

Mac was already waiting for him as Tony walked through the iron gate to the pool area. "Time for some serious swimming," Tony said.

"Don't see any bathing beauties," Mac lamented as they dropped their towels on a deck chair. "Fact is, I don't see anybody…no women."

"Come on," Tony chided as he dove into the pool ahead of Mac. The cool water slipped around his body. They swam to the other end and hung on to the side. "This feels good. You dried me out with the top down. I could soak up this water by osmosis."

"You're too conservative, Tony. You'd rather ride around in your big clunker with all the windows up and the air conditioning on, instead of a sports convertible with the top down."

"I like my comfort, Mac. I'm not trying to impress women." Tony pulled himself out of the pool. "I'm going into the spa. Need some relaxing after riding with you."

He lowered himself into the hot, bubbling water, while Mac stayed in the pool. The bubbles caressed his body as he laid his head back against the edge of the spa and looked up into the night sky. Two palm trees reached over him, while a silver moon shone through the fronds. A balmy breeze, heavy with the sweet perfume of Oleander blossoms rustled through the palms. *If only she were here with me tonight*, he thought. *If only I'd taken time to do things with her—like spending a weekend here—while I had the chance. Too busy to take time off. Thought I'd make points with the general. Lot of good that did. Railroaded into whatever this is, with the CIA yet. Probably get my ass killed.*

"Isn't it romantic?" A soft female voice startled him back to reality. He looked for the source of the voice. She smiled at him with perfect white teeth and brushed her blond hair back from her face.

"Yeah, I was just thinking the same thing," Tony answered.

"If you want romance. I could be Sherri tonight."

"What?" Tony gasped in disbelief. "How'd you…"

"Hi!" Mac almost fell as he jumped in. "I'm Mac. How do you like me so far? What's your name?" Mac pushed between the woman and Tony. "What's your name?" He repeated as he turned his back on Tony and faced the woman.

"Marilyn. What are you guys doing here? Are you on business?"

"No, we're test pilots from Edwards," Mac answered as he puffed up.

"Oh! Test pilots. I'm impressed. Are you on furlough?"

"Well, we've been working pretty hard making all those test flights. The danger keeps you on edge, you know, and you have to take time off every once in a while or you'll go bonkers. The general himself told us to take a rest," Mac boasted.

"Are you going to be here for a few days?"

"No, we're going to San Francisco tomorrow."

"Where are you guys from?"

"Around."

"Mac, I think…" Tony tried to speak but was interrupted by Mac.

"I graduated from the Air Force Academy."

"Do you have a girlfriend?" she asked.

"No, I don't. Where are you from?" asked Mac.

"Vegas."

"Ever been to Frisco?"

"No." She was silent for a while, and then excitedly continued. "Hey, I was here for a seminar but we finished today and I'm going to take a few days vacation. I always wanted to go. Maybe I could go with you and you could show me around."

Mac grinned widely. "Hey, that would be great!"

The whiteness of her teeth shined as she smiled. She brushed her blond tresses back behind her ears. "Okay. Let's go to my room, have a drink, and make plans on what we'll see and do in San Fran."

"Sorry. You can't come." Tony said emphatically.

"What? Why?" The young lady sounded confused.

"I said you can't come," Tony continued. "Mac's my boyfriend. Mac, you promised it would just be you and me. You didn't tell me you liked girls. No, young lady, you can't come. Three's a crowd."

Mac stood up. He had a look of both abject horror and disbelief. For once in his life he was speechless.

The young woman hurriedly left the spa without saying a word or looking back.

"Have you lost your frigging mind?" Mac said, his voice trembling with anger. "What the shit did you do that for, anyway?"

"It was weird. Had to do something to throw her off track."

"You dumb shit. What are you talking about?"

"I think she wanted to find out if we really were going to San Francisco."

"You're a frigging nut, Tony."

"I don't understand. She knew about Sherri..." Tony was silent for a moment, and then continued, "Like she could read my mind."

"You imagined it. I think you're going off your rocker."

"Look, Mac. We can't take any chances. She might have been a spy trying to get information. You'd have had to tell her we weren't going to San Francisco."

"Bullshit, Tony! Bullshit!" Mac was furious. He slammed the water with his fists. "Now she thinks we're gay! She'll probably tell everybody in the hotel. I'll never be able to come back here! Do you know you just ruined me?"

"Calm down, Mac. We don't know what we're getting involved in, so we have to be cautious."

"Come on! Let's get the hell out of here!" Mac climbed out of the spa and grabbed his towel. "Can't believe this shit! Damn!"

Mac walked swiftly back to his room while mumbling under his breath. Tony followed. "I thought you had better sense than that, Mac. Calm down. Pull yourself together."

Later that night, Tony lay in bed thinking. How did she know about Sherri? Did she really say it, or did I just think so? Maybe I was so wrapped up in my thoughts about Sherri.... Maybe Mac's right. Maybe I am going off my rocker.

* * * *

The highway stretched ahead of them like a white ribbon, up and down the golden hills. Neither talked. Tony was deep in thought. Finally Mac spoke.

"Sorry about last night. Guess I lost my temper. What were you saying about her reading your mind?"

"I don't know. Maybe I imagined it. I thought she said if I wanted romance, she could be Sherri."

"Getting worried about you, Tony. Think you need a rest," Mac said as he thoughtfully stroked his chin.

Tony replayed the happenings of the night before in his mind, thinking that perhaps he had misunderstood the woman. But it was unmistakably clear in his mind. That was what the woman had said. "I don't understand it," he said, half aloud.

"Well, here comes the Crows Landing turnoff," Mac said as he turned onto the off ramp.

"I don't see any air base," Tony mumbled.

"Hang on. There has to be at least a runway for the tankers to take off," Mac answered.

"There it was, Mac. The sign to the base. You just passed it up."

Mac slammed on his brakes and spun around in the road.

"Way to go, Mac. If I can only live until we get assigned to a safe spy mission, I'll have it made."

Mac turned down the narrow asphalt road that led to the air station. "Still don't see anything, Tony. Hey, what's that sign say?"

"It says not to go any further unless you have government business."

"Well, what do you know. A guard shack. I can even see a hanger and some buildings."

Mac pulled up to the guard post and stopped as a Marine stepped out. "Can I help you, sir?"

Mac and Tony showed him their identification. He saluted stiffly and they acknowledged with a halfhearted salute.

"Captain MacPherson and Captain Thompson, we're expecting you, sir. Just a moment." He went back into the guard shack, picked up a phone and held a hurried conversation, then hung up. "Sir. Do you see that hangar? Proceed to it and someone will meet you there." He saluted stiffly again.

Mac gunned the car and headed toward the hangar. "Well, I wonder what's next on the agenda?"

As they approached the hangar, a man in Navy dungarees motioned them to enter. Inside was a Lear Jet. A man in civilian clothes walked toward the car.

"Take your gear with you and get into the airplane."

Tony started to get out of the car but Mac remained motionless.

"What the hell's going on here? Who are you to order us around?" Mac asked.

"Excuuuse me, sir," the civilian said with a sneer, as he flashed a CIA identification card. "Just leave your keys in the car. We have valet parking and your car will be well taken care of. Do you want me to call a porter to unload your bags, sir?"

"A smart ass," Mac answered. "That's all we need."

"Mac, just do what he says," Tony cut in. "They're just doing their job."

Mac got out of the car and grabbed his bag as the Navy enlisted man in dungarees climbed into the driver's seat.

"You better take damned good care of that car," Mac said as he recorded the mileage on a piece of paper.

The Navy man smiled. "Yes, sir." He then drove the car to a corner of the hanger well out of sight.

Mac watched intently then yelled, "Hey, there's a cover in the trunk. Keep the dust off."

Tony and Mac carried their bags to the Lear. Another Navy man loaded the bags into the baggage bay. Upon entering the airplane, they were met by a short red-faced man.

"Good morning. I'm your pilot. Make yourselves comfortable. There's hot coffee and donuts. The other gentleman you met outside is my co-pilot. He'll be coming aboard as soon as he's sure all is secure."

"Where are we going?" Tony asked.

"Yeah, where the hell are we going? Mac echoed.

"Look. You don't worry about that," The pilot said rather sharply. "You'll know when you get there. In the meantime have a seat. There are also some sandwiches and soft drinks for later if you get hungry. They're in the box behind you."

Tony and Mac buckled their safety belts. Several navy men pushed the Lear out of the hanger while the co-pilot walked alongside.

"Why a civilian airplane?" asked Tony to the pilot.

"Because we're civilians, right?" the pilot answered sarcastically.

"For some reason or other, I don't like either one of those bastards," Mac mumbled under his breath. Tony agreed.

The co-pilot climbed aboard, sealed the door and took his place next to the pilot. The engines started and the Lear took a position at the end of the runway.

"Hope these guys know how to fly this thing," Tony commented.

"Yeah," Mac answered. "The Black Widow could chew up this little shit of a plane, spit it out, and ask for more."

When they reached altitude, Tony poured himself some coffee. "Want some, Mac?"

"No thanks," Mac replied as he lay his seat back and closed his eyes.

"Wonder where we're going?" Tony mused. "I know we're heading east, so it's not Hawaii."

Mac sat bolt upright. "Damn. No use dreaming about hula girls." And then he laid back again and closed his eyes.

Tony slowly sipped his coffee and looked out of the window. Soft, billowing, cumulus clouds slipped past. He gazed at the shades of lights and shadows. They seem to have such real substance, Tony thought, but when you get into them they turn to nothing. The only real part are the thermals tearing at your ship. Life is a lot like these billowing cumulus.

He took another sip of coffee. Like my life with her, it was so beautiful, but suddenly it all dissolved around me, like the vapors of the clouds. All that's left are the thermals tearing at me, trying to rip me apart.

"Ah. This is the life," Mac mumbled as he reached down and struggled to remove his brown flight boots. "Might as well get comfortable," he said to no one in particular as he lay back in his seat. "It's like having a chauffeur. But in this case, we don't tell him where we want to go. The bastard takes us where he wants to. Don't even know where the hell we're going. Oh well, might as well just sit back, relax, and enjoy the ride. Not often we get to just ride."

"Yeah," Tony mumbled in reply, as he adjusted his seat. "Might as well enjoy the ride." He laid back and closed his eyes trying to relax, but questions kept racing through his mind. Why were they chosen to work with the CIA? What was the project and why was it so secret? Did the weird happening at the hotel have anything to do with the mission, or was it just his imagination?

The muffled drone of the engines put all thoughts from his mind and he was soon deep in sleep, but not a restful sleep. He kept seeing the face of the woman at the hotel. Each time she appeared, she would change a little. First, her blue eyes changed to glowing red coals, then her beautiful smile changed to a serpent's mouth with poisoned fangs and a forked tongue. Finally, her hair became writhing snakes, and her smooth, white skin turned to scales—a nightmare, halfway between asleep and awake. He tried desperately to awaken as fear gripped at his very soul, but he couldn't. The face disappeared, and Tony drifted into the kind of sleep where one's mind strives desperately to solve unknown problems that have no answers.

Chapter 6

THE CRYSTAL SKULL

Tony didn't know how long he had been sleeping when he was jolted awake as the wheels touched the runway.

"Well, I guess this is our destination," he said as he sat up blinking his eyes at the bright sunlight. I wonder where we are? I wonder what's next?

The Lear turned onto a taxiway, and proceeded toward the hanger area where a car was waiting. The co-pilot unsealed the door and dropped the ladder. He walked to the car and talked to someone inside.

"All right, you two. You can come out now," the copilot yelled toward the plane.

Tony and Mac unbuckled their safety belts. "Well, la de da," Mac said. "We are allowed to deplane. Isn't that nice of him. The son-of-a bitch."

Tony looked out of the door, stretched and took a deep breath of jet fumes before climbing down the ladder.

The copilot met them at the bottom. "Okay, you guys. Into the back seat of the car."

The driver, dressed in a charcoal gray suit, smiled and extended his hand to them. "Hello, I'm Karl Farmer, CIA. Just bear with me for a little longer and I'll explain why you're here."

There was a tap on the window. It was the copilot again. "Hey, you guys want your gear? It's out here." With that he turned and walked away.

"Real nice zombie you have there," Tony commented. "Hope he's not representative of the CIA."

"You'll have to overlook his personality. He's not used to being nice," Karl said as he stepped out of the car and opened the trunk.

Hearing the whine of turbines. Tony looked up and saw the Lear taxiing away.

"There they go," Mac mumbled.

"I hope they take the course on how to win friends and influence people," Tony said under his breath. "Especially the co-pilot."

Karl started the engine, and slowly drove toward a road at the end of the hanger.

"Can we ask you a question?" Tony asked.

"Sure," Karl answered.

"Can you tell us where we are?"

"Oh, didn't they tell you where you were going?"

"Those two buzzards?" Mac chimed in. "Hell no. They wouldn't give us the time of day."

"My apologies, gentlemen, but it really doesn't matter."

"Well, I'll be," said Mac as they entered the freeway. "Hell yes. I know where we are. Came here once. Spent a couple of months at the air base. Met a fine girl here. Maybe I can give her a call."

"I don't think you'll have the opportunity to do that," said Karl.

"Are we going to the base?" Tony asked.

"Yes."

"Why didn't we just land there?"

"Didn't want to cause any undue attention by landing a civilian airplane at an Air Force base. It was Okay at Crows Landing because it was in the boondocks and no one was around to notice.

"What the hell are we doing here?" asked Mac.

"You'll have to wait until we get there," replied Karl.

"I remember this," Mac commented. "This road takes you to the air base. It's all coming back to me. I'll bet I could find that babe's house."

Tony heard the roaring whine of an airplane low over their heads and saw it line up with the runway and disappear behind the trees. A highway sign said "Air Force Base two right lanes." Karl pulled all the way over into the left lane.

"Didn't you see the sign?" asked Tony.

"Yeah, I saw it," replied Karl as he continued on his way.

"Where the hell are you taking us, then?" Mac asked. "Aren't we going to the base?"

"You'll see in a few minutes."

Soon they passed the family housing, the golf course, and then there were fields of corn. Karl slowed the car, turned off the highway, and stopped in front of a gate in the fence.

"Would one of you please open the gate? Here's the key," Karl said. Tony took the key and got out of the car.

"What do you want us to do, Farmer," Mac said, laughing. "Pick corn? Should of known, with a name like Farmer."

"Hang in there, MacPherson. You'll soon find out what you volunteered for."

"It's a joke, but let's get something straight, Farmer. We didn't volunteer. We were shanghaied."

Tony opened the gate. Karl drove through and then stopped. He looked at Mac. "I have a piece of paper that says Captain Charles MacPherson and Captain Anthony Thompson volunteered for this mission. You are now working for me, and unless your attitude improves, and I mean fast, I'll send you back to the General, and he will not be very happy. I apologize for our two friends who flew you here. We're not all like that, so let's work together."

"Okay. Fair enough. But my so-called friend, Tony, got this trip off to a bad start by a shitty deal he pulled on me at the hotel last night. But, hey, I shouldn't let that gnaw on me. Let the good times roll," Mac said with just a hint of sarcasm in his voice.

"Come on, Mac. Let's go pick corn," said Karl as he stepped out of the car.

"Oh, what the hell," Mac commented nonchalantly. I'll try anything once."

Karl led the way, pushing through the field of cornstalks, with Mac and Tony following at his heels.

"Where are we going?" Tony asked Mac.

"How the hell do I know," answered Mac. "Just follow and smile, or we get sent back to General Stone."

"What are you talking about?" Tony asked.

Just then they came to a clearing. The cornstalks made a circle, hiding an area overgrown with weeds. A ventilator barely extended above the tops of the tall grass. Karl walked to the center of the clearing and took a numeric keypad from his pocket, punched in numbers and a hatch swung up revealing a ladder.

"Follow me, gentlemen," Karl said.

"Well, I'll be dipped!" commented Mac as he climbed down the ladder. Tony followed close behind.

When they reached the bottom, the hatch slowly closed and sealed. They proceeded down a long narrow hall. It was cool and damp and had the stale, musty smell of a tomb. Karl opened a door into a small room. "Have a seat, gentlemen. Would you like some coffee?"

"Yes, thank you," Tony said, as he looked around the room. There were a few folding chairs facing a table. He sat in one. It wasn't very comfortable.

"I'd really like something stronger," Mac added, smiling.

Without a comment Karl left the room, the door slid closed behind him.

After the door closed, Tony and Mac looked at each other. "Wonder what we're waiting on," Tony said. He had an uneasy feeling. "What were you and Karl talking about in the car? Did you find out anything?"

"Not a thing, except that I have a bad attitude."

"So what's new?" Tony grinned.

"Screw you, Tony. You and the horse you rode in on."

Just then the door opened and an Air Force sergeant entered, carrying a tray with two cups of coffee.

"Hey, there is life in the nether world," Mac beamed. "Tell me, sergeant, what brings you to never-never land?" The sergeant didn't acknowledge. He put the tray on the table and left. The door closed behind him.

Tony thought he heard a locking mechanism click. He took a sip of the hot, black liquid. "I'm not sure that guy was alive or not. Damn! No cream or sugar."

"Good. Don't like to ruin my coffee with cream and sugar, anyway," Mac said, stretching and yawning.

"What's going on here, Mac?" Tony was by now beginning to feel really uneasy. He didn't like being locked in a room that seemed like a prison cell.

"What the hell. Hang loose. We'll find out sooner or later. In the meantime, relax and enjoy the suspense. We got roped into this, so I guess we should make the best of it. With all the zombies around here, maybe the next person to walk in that door will be a beautiful vampire who'll want to bite my neck." The door opened and Karl walked in. "Shit," mumbled Mac, "Can't win 'em all."

"Gentlemen," began Karl, "you've been carefully selected for a very important mission. Your psychological profile, service records and ability to work together have been carefully scrutinized. You'll be doing your country a great service. In fact, you'll be doing the world a great service. Please keep an open mind to what you're about to hear and see. Don't discard a concept just because you don't understand it."

"Why did you pick us?" Tony asked.

"We wanted someone who had nerves of steel—someone who could look danger in the face and not flinch. Also we wanted team players, because this will be a team effort."

"Okay, stop blowing smoke up our ass," Mac said. "Just give us the bottom line."

"Just have patience. I'm coming to that. I've asked two people to come into the room to explain everything. One, who will remain un-named at this time, is foremost in his field. The other is a young woman named Natasha Karolovitch, who has a very important task to define to you."

Mac elbowed Tony. "Here it comes, Tony. The beautiful spy."

"Cool it, Mac. Cool it." Tony whispered through the side of his mouth. This whole thing was creeping him out and he didn't feel like playing games.

A tall man, graying at the temples, entered the room. A young woman in her late twenties followed him. Her long black hair was tied behind her head.

"Gentlemen," Karl Farmer said crisply, motioning toward the gray haired man. "This is a very distinguished person. He has a Ph.D. in Parapsychology. The doctor has been studying and performing experiments in this field, especially with Psychokinetics, for the past thirty years."

Motioning toward the woman, Karl continued. "This is Natasha Karolovitch. Natasha's grandfather, Professor Nikolai Karolovitch, was a renowned archaeologist. He met with an unfortunate accident recently. Professor Karolovitch spent many years studying the ancient Mayan civilization. Natasha accompanied her grandfather on all his expeditions. She is considered an authority on the Mayan culture.

"Both of these people know your records and your history. They are in agreement on your selection.

"Again I ask that you keep an open mind to what you are about to hear, see, and experience. First, the doctor."

Why does he keep saying to keep an open mind, Tony thought?

"Gentlemen, may I call you Anthony and Charles?" asked the tall gray haired man, as he stood behind the large table. Natasha stood beside him.

"It's Mac and Tony," Mac answered. Tony nodded his head.

"Mac and Tony it is," said the doctor with a smile. "Let me tell you a little about myself and my work.

"As Mr. Farmer said," the Doctor continued. "I have a Ph.D. in Parapsychology. I would like to add that I also have a Ph.D. in Clinical Psychology. Parapsychology is not a true psychology, and is not a science in the truest sense of the word. The results of most of these experiments are non-repeatable. Parapsychology, as you may know, is the study of what many people refer to as the supernatural. I prefer to refer to it as the study of phenomena of a non-familiar source, be it of a hidden dimension or the redirection and concentration of a natural but non-physical force."

Okay, Tony thought. Let's get the show on the road.

The doctor continued. "I became interested in Parapsychology while doing clinical research with inmates at a hospital for the criminally insane. I was involved in a case that I could not explain from known scientific standards. Although the records showed that this man was ninety-seven years old, he, at times had almost superhuman strength. His skin was that of a twenty-year-old, and he walked straight and tall. But it was his mind.... He had the knowledge and intelligence of a genius. Not in one field only, but in math, geography, history, science, you name it. However, that was not the most interesting aspect."

He paused, giving Tony the impression that he was savoring an especially good memory. Then he continued with an eager anticipation in his voice.

"When he got angry, he could move large objects with his mind-force. I tried to get him to cooperate with experiments, but he would not. It was as if there was another person living within him. I could feel a presence when I was near him—something that exuded from his body—a kind of force. In the old days they would have called him demon possessed, or would have killed him as a warlock."

The doctor paused again as if to let what he just said sink in, and then continued.

"Much of my research in Parapsychology has been directed at Psychokinetics, or the movement of objects with mind-force. My experiments have been with the directing and focusing of this force. I would like to demonstrate so that you will better understand what you will be dealing with.

"Tony, if you wouldn't mind, please place your coffee cup on the table before me. Mac, please also come forward and stand by the table with Tony."

Tony slowly stood up and took the cup to the table where he cautiously placed it before the doctor. Mac followed. What the hells going on here, Tony thought?

The doctor dropped his hands at his sides and closed his eyes. Slowly the cup started to move to the right. It moved about two feet and then slowly moved back to its original position. The doctor stood with his hands still at his side but now his whole body started trembling and beads of sweat broke out on his face. His eyes were still closed, but Tony had the eerie feeling that he could see through the closed eyelids.

For about ten seconds Tony felt as though the room was filled with some kind of energy, and then the cup started vibrating. Suddenly it shattered into a pile of dust. The doctor opened his eyes.

Tony stared at the table and the pile of dust that had once been a cup. He was at first amazed, and then he became suspicious. "Wait a minute. You brought us all the way out here just to show us a magic trick?"

"Hold it, Tony," Mac said. "I read about stuff like this. Just because you can't explain it in scientific terms, doesn't mean it can't happen. Go on," he continued, looking at the doctor. "Tell us more."

"In the first phase of the demonstration, I used the power of my mind to push and then to pull the cup. In the second phase of the demonstration, I focused and concentrated the mind-force much as a magnifying glass focuses and concentrates the rays of the sun. It is conceivable that something could be developed that would act as an amplifier and could direct pure amplified mind-forces." He paused for emphasis, and then continued. "Such as a laser does for light waves or photons." He paused again. "Please be seated, gentlemen."

Tony and Mac slowly backed away from the table and sat in their chairs.

"I know nothing about Parapsychology," the young woman began. She had a slight Russian accent. "I'd like to tell you of a Mayan legend.

The ancient Mayan had a very advanced civilization. On the Yucatan, in the ruins of Tulum, was found an observatory where the Mayan studied the stars, the moon, and the planets. Calculations on the wall of this observatory showed a distance from the earth to the moon. It was not until after a radar beam was bounced off the moon and the actual distance measured, that it was realized these calculations were closer to the actual distance than any calculation before. Only an advanced civilization could have built the cities of the ancient Mayan. The construction of the pyramids would be a feat of technology even today. The Mayan civilization flourished and then it died almost overnight."

She wiped a strand of stray hair from her face, and then continued. "The writings and hieroglyphics found in the ruins of deserted cities that once were busy trade centers and seats of knowledge, tell a story. The Mayan worshiped the sun and the moon as gods. One day Quetzalcoatl appeared on the scene. He told the people he was the Feathered Serpent, the moon god. His skin was the color of the moon. Although he was an Aztec god, the people worshiped him."

Tony watched as she moved with a supple, liquid movement while she talked. She is a beautiful woman, he thought. He quickly pushed the thought from his mind.

"Wherever he went," she continued. "He left behind a crumbling civilization of hate, discord and death. He had with him, at all times, a crystal skull, which he carried in his hands. As long as he held this crystal skull, he had tremendous power. He could destroy whole armies with one look. He conquered the entire Mayan nation almost overnight with only a small band of followers. His power was awesome.

"Legend has it that he had a pyramid built in his honor, and after placing the skull in a secret place in the pyramid, sacrificed all the people in the city. He then told his band of followers he would leave them, but one day, when the time was right, he would return and rule the world. He then disappeared into the sea. This was why, when Hernando Cortez landed in Mexico from the sea and his skin was light, the Aztecs remembered the Mayan legend and many thought he was Quetzalcoatl, The Feathered Serpent, and worshiped him as a god.

"My grandfather…" She stopped and wiped what looked like a tear from her eye, and continued. "My grandfather spent many years of his life searching the jungles for Quetzalcoatl's pyramid and the crystal skull. He found it just before he met with a fatal accident. My grandfather entrusted me with the safekeeping and delivery of the skull to the CIA so that a suitable method to destroy it would be decided upon. This power must not be unleashed on the earth. It must not fall into the wrong hands."

Hey, this must be the girl I read about in the paper, thought Tony. He felt sorry for her after what she had been through.

Karl spoke. "We have kept the people who know about this to a very small number. Only those who can contribute to the project have knowledge of it. This is what is known as a Black Project because no information leaves the project. Not even the president of the United States knows of it. He may never know, so don't start looking for medals. The only satisfaction that you'll get, if you live, will be the knowledge that you kept an awesome power from enslaving the world."

"What do you mean, Farmer?" Mac interrupted. "If we live?"

"Well," Farmer answered. "I had to tell you that. Anyway it's a worst case scenario."

"I don't know," Tony said hesitantly. "It's hard for me to believe. I'm sorry, but I'm not convinced."

"You will be," answered Farmer.

"What if it were in the right hands?" asked Mac.

The doctor answered. "What are the right hands? No human, or even a being that is not human, could have that much power and not be tempted to put himself above all other beings in the world. This power is more suited to destroy than to build. This is the ultimate amplifier of the mind-force that I was telling you about, gentlemen. A thought is all that is needed.

"Stop and consider. Look at that other coffee cup. Which is easier? To think about destroying it, or to think about creating it?" He paused then continued. "I rest my case."

"We have the crystal skull here in safekeeping," Karl said. "We tried to shatter it with a five ton press, drill into it with a diamond tip drill, and burn it with a plasma arc, but we couldn't faze it. It's virtually indestructible. At the present time it's in a vault made of high chrome steel twelve inches thick. It's constantly monitored by video cameras. Twenty-millimeter machine guns with explosive shells are placed at random locations within the vault. At the push of a button, any person inside would be disintegrated."

He was silent as if to let the thought sink in, and then continued. "So that you may have an idea of the forces that you're dealing with, we're going to ask you to enter the room individually and the door will be sealed. We will direct you to pick up the skull that will be on a table made from a solid piece of granite. Also on the table will be two six-inch cubes of tungsten steel and two-six inch cubes of hardwood. After you pick up the skull, we will direct you to melt one of the steel cubes and then to destroy the wooden cube. We will then tell you to place the skull on the table and back away.

"You will then wait until someone leads you out of the vault. We will be monitoring you with the video camera. If at any time you hesitate too long when given a command or do not obey a command, the button will be pressed and you will be annihilated.

"Tony will be the first to go and then Mac. Come with me."

"Poor choice of words," Tony mumbled under his breath.

Karl led them down a long hall. It made a ninety-degree turn to the left, and about fifty feet further, dead-ended at a steel door. Karl pressed a buzzer and the door opened.

The group entered a room with four video monitors on a control panel. Men in Air Force fatigues sat, one at each monitor. In the middle of the room, where he could see all four monitors, a fifth man sat at a table with a large red button. The monitors showed a huge block of granite with what appeared to be a crystal skull resting on it. There were also four cubes on the block, two on one side of the skull and two on the other.

Tony's mind was racing. He couldn't make sense out of what he had been told.

"All right, Tony," Karl said. "Follow me."

They went through a narrow passageway that opened into a large room. In the center of the room was a square steel structure.

"There it is," Karl said.

It had a door with a wheel lock, not unlike a bank vault. Karl turned the wheel and pulled. The door slowly opened.

"Just stand inside and don't do anything unless you're directed to do so," said Karl, stressing each word.

Tony hesitantly walked in and the door closed behind him. He heard the wheel turn and the door seal. *Whatever this is, it's too late to back out now, even if I could,* he thought. He felt trapped. A feeling of curiosity changed to a feeling of dread.

He looked at the large block of granite. In the center was a skull about six inches in diameter. The skull was a clear, flawless crystal that at times appeared almost to dissolve in the air and then re-crystallize. A red fire seemed to flicker deep within it.

Tony could not take his eyes off of it. He felt, as he looked at the flickering within the crystal, that he was looking into a deep, deep hole. It seemed as if something were drawing him toward this flickering glow, drawing him to the very gates of hell. Tony was brought back to his senses by a voice from a speaker.

"Walk slowly toward the table."

"Now, slowly pick up the skull with both hands."

Tony reached toward the skull and cupped his hands around it. With each beat of his heart, the crystal filled with what appeared to be a glowing red substance, making it look as though it were engorged with blood. It retreated to the deep center then filled the skull again at the next heartbeat. As he lifted it, Tony felt a surge of energy fill his body. He experienced a euphoria of such magnitude that he felt he could stand on top of the world and turn it with his feet. He wanted to run through the steel wall and fly through the clouds.

"All right, now," the voice was slow and emotionless. "Look to your right. There are two cubes of steel. Think about melting one of the cubes when I tell you to. It does not matter which one. Do it now."

Tony thought about the cube getting hot. It glowed red, then white, and started to melt like butter on a hot stove. Soon it was a liquid that flowed over the granite table and ran down the sides onto the floor. A powerful surge swept through his body. He felt as though his body were filling with a force that had to be released.

"All right," the voice continued without emotion. "Destroy one of the wooden blocks. Do it now."

Tony looked at one of the blocks and before he had time to consciously think, the block vaporized in a flash of light. Another powerful surge of energy enveloped his body. He wanted more! He wanted to destroy! To destroy! Tony fought back the urge to annihilate the room, the facility, the air base, the city! The power, the energy, the force, whatever it was, encircled his body like a steel spring. It was almost as if he were having a sexual experience. He wanted to lose himself into, as well as to become this force.

A voice brought him back into reality. "Slowly place the skull back on the table and back away."

Tony didn't want to give up the skull. He wanted it forever. He wanted it to be part of him. He wanted to destroy everything around him so that he could keep the skull and then no one could take it from him. With every ounce of strength he could muster, he slowly released his hold on the skull and moved his hands away from it. The skull stopped pulsing and the dull red flickering glow retreated deep within.

Tony's mind was filled with screams. "Let me live!" Immediately he felt as if energy had been drained from every cell in his body. He felt a deep, dark depression descend upon him and envelope his body. He wanted to grab the skull again.

The voice from the speaker was deliberate and clear. "Slowly back away from the table. Now stop and wait until we enter the room and lead you away."

Tony stood waiting for the door to open. Please hurry, he thought. He didn't know how much longer he could keep himself from lunging forward and grabbing the skull. He was glad when he finally heard the door open and felt a hand on his arm. He breathed a sigh of relief when the door was sealed behind him as he was led away.

"It was almost like I was being drugged," Tony mumbled as he sat in the control room, trying to regain his strength and clear his mind. "Like my body was being taken over by a force. I can see now how it could be a very real threat if it got in the wrong hands. But I still don't understand."

"You don't need to understand," said Farmer. "As long as you see the threat and the power. Now you know why it must be destroyed. Would you like to watch Mac on the monitor?"

"No. I know what he's going through. Don't want to relive it. Suppose he doesn't make it?"

Tony sat quietly and waited, hoping he wouldn't hear the sound of bullets ripping Mac apart. He felt as if his body was an empty shell and he didn't have the strength to move. It seemed like an eternity before the door opened and Mac was led into the room. Tony was relieved when he saw his friend.

"You made it. I didn't want to watch. Didn't want to go through it again. I know what you went through, buddy."

"What a trip." Mac's voice was almost a whisper. "Shit, I felt like I could rule the frigging world."

"Gentlemen," The doctor spoke in a quiet but excited voice. "Gentlemen, do you realize that you were at the very edge of your psychological endurance? Most people would have succumbed. That's why you were scrutinized so carefully. Even so, we were afraid that we might have had to destroy one or both of you, but your discipline, your training, and your psychological makeup pulled you through."

"I apologize for having to put you through this," Farmer said. "I know it was traumatic, but we had to be sure. You've now passed the test and you're qualified, in our minds, to take on the responsibility for the project. Our team will be kept to a minimum. The fewer who know, the more secure it'll be for all of us. At the present time there are the two of you, Natasha Karolovitch, the doctor and I. Natasha is on the team because she has a vested interest in seeing that the skull is destroyed. The doctor is on the team as a consultant. Now that you're officially on the team, let me introduce Dr. Aaron Slaughter."

Tony mumbled under his breath. "Dr. Aaron Slaughter." Then he continued out loud. "Weren't you in the news a few months ago about some kind of government project that was canceled?"

"Yes," Dr. Slaughter answered sadly." Congress was not ready for what I was proposing and would not fund the money."

"Wasn't it a proposal to train astronauts to leave their bodies and travel through space by the power of their minds? Astral projection?" Tony stumbled on his words. "It seemed far fetched to me at the time." He stopped in thoughtful silence and then continued. "But then, after this…I don't know…"

Karl Farmer interrupted. "It's a moot point, now that the Congress rejected Dr. Slaughter's proposal. That's in the past. What's important is that Dr. Slaughter is on this Project. He has one of the most brilliant minds in the world."

Dr. Slaughter smiled. "Thank you. Please do not call me Dr. Slaughter. Call me Aaron. We are all part of a very vital project. We each have our part to play."

"Tony and Mac, you two have been chosen because of your dedication, discipline, and calmness under fire," Karl said. "You're an important part of our team.

We'll need nerves of steel in the days ahead." Karl paused, then continued. "There will hopefully be a sixth member of the project team. You'll be briefed on that tomorrow. In the meantime, you'll be confined to your quarters. Your meals will be served in your rooms. Rest, gentlemen. You deserve it."

"Wait," Mac said. "What about the Air Force guys? They know about the skull."

Farmer smiled. "I'll take care of the situation. They'll be given an injection that will erase any memory of it. But you, my friend, need to rest now."

Tony was escorted to his room. As the door was closed, he heard the grinding and distinctive "clunk" of a bolting mechanism. He tried the door. It wouldn't open. "What the hell's going on?" At first he felt fear, then anger. But then, he was so drained of emotion that he didn't care.

He looked around. The room was small. The ceiling, walls, and floor were white and the area was flooded with indirect lighting. A metal bed was on one side of the room. In the far corner were a commode and a lavatory. It reminded him of a prison cell, or maybe, except for the commode and lavatory, the inside of a crypt. The room smelled of stale dampness.

His mind was still foggy. He hadn't had a chance to talk to Mac and discuss the recent happenings with him. Anyway, he couldn't intelligently discuss it at the present time. He had doubts that he could ever discuss it with anyone. He tried to find the light switch to turn off the light but couldn't. Just then the light dimmed to a pale blue glow. He dropped into his bed without taking his clothes off and fell into a deep sleep. Even if he had noticed the video camera scanning his room, he wouldn't have cared.

Chapter 7

MAGMA INTERFACE: THE DESTRUCTION THEORY

The locking mechanism clicked and the door slid open. Tony awoke with a start and sat bolt upright. As the door opened, the light came on in bright mode. The same sergeant, who had brought the coffee the day before, entered the room and placed a tray on a shelf he pulled out from the wall. Without a word he turned and walked out. The door slid shut behind him.

Tony closed his eyes and savored the familiar smell of bacon and coffee, even though he wasn't hungry. At least the stuff on the tray was familiar. Nothing else was. His mind was struggling to make sense out of his experience with the skull, but nothing made sense. How could it be real? Could it really have happened? Was his mind made to think that it had really happened?

Periodically throughout the night, he had awakened in a cold sweat, shivering, fear gripping at his soul, yet this fear was without a face, without a name—a fear without form, without substance, yet it was real.... It was real—as if his soul wanted to hide but did not know what to hide from. Then he would fall back into sleep, only to experience the same terror again and again. Once during the night he awakened calling his mother. Thinking about it now, it seemed absurd.

Slowly getting out of bed, Tony walked to the shelf, picked up the cup of coffee and took a sip. He spit the lukewarm coffee back into the cup. The bacon was soggy. The fried egg was cold. He didn't even want to touch the toast.

He noticed his bag near the door. Someone must have brought it in during the night.

After he dressed, he sat on the edge of the bed, and idly looked around the room, waiting for what would happen next. A damp coldness radiated from the concrete block walls, seeming to suck life-energy from his body. The musty smell reminded him of a tomb. He shivered. What had he gotten himself into? If he had known, could he have refused the assignment? But that was a moot point now. It was too late. There was nothing to do now but to charge ahead, even though he didn't know what he was charging into.

He tried to clear his mind by shaking his head. Then the thought hit him. We must be part of a government experiment—a tactical, physiological experiment. But then why the feeling when he held the skull? How could they accomplish that? Were they using some kind of radiation to make him feel that way? Were those 20 mm cannons aimed at him real or mock-ups? He had to believe that this was some kind of manipulation. He only believed in the physical world. That was the only thing that was real.

As he was trying to sort out all his questions, his eyes rested on what appeared to be the lens of a video camera.

"Damn! I wonder how many people have been watching me? This is ridiculous!"

He tried to throw a hand towel over it but the lens didn't extend far enough for it to catch. Just then, the door slid open with a grinding sound and Karl Farmer entered.

"Good morning, Tony. Did you sleep well?"

"No! Lousy! What gives with the television camera? I kind of enjoy having a little privacy and not having the whole world watching me."

"It was for your protection. After what you experienced with the skull, we didn't know how you might react. Dr. Slaughter monitored both you and Mac. Would you come with me, please?"

"How's Mac, by the way?"

"Oh, he's quite well," Karl said with a laugh as he walked down the hall. "He noticed the camera while sitting on the commode. Picked up a shoe and threw it. His aim was quite good, I might add. We haven't been able to monitor him since."

As they walked down the hall Tony noticed moisture glistening on the walls. How could anyone stay down here for long? I need to get out of here into the sunshine. I joined the Air Force to be in the sky not under the ground.

"Well, here's his room, now." Karl stood at the eye scan and the door slid open. Mac was waiting for them.

"What the hell are you doing, Farmer? Selling tickets to watch me take a crap?"

Tony laughed. "Yeah, Mac. You were on prime time."

* * * *

In the meeting room, Dr. Slaughter and Natasha were waiting at the conference table.

"Morning," Tony said.

"Hi, babe," Mac echoed, smiling at Natasha.

Natasha nodded her head in acknowledgement.

"Cold bitch," Mac mumbled to himself.

After they settled down with a cup of hot coffee, Karl began speaking. "We've been in quite a dilemma about how to destroy the skull because it appears to be indestructible. But Dr. Slaughter has proposed a plan we think may do the trick."

Dr. Slaughter cleared his throat. "There are convection currents in the magma within the earth. A slight cooling takes place where the molten magma interfaces with the earth's crust. This magma, being cooler and therefore slightly denser than the magma which interfaces with the molten metallic core of the earth, is pulled by gravity toward the core where it reheats and rises, thus setting up convection currents."

"Okay," Mac interrupted. "Cut all the fluff. What's the bottom line? How do we fit in?"

Slaughter cleared his throat again and continued. "There are fissures in the earth's crust where the magma rises to the surface and, if it exerts enough pressure, spews out as a volcano."

"We know about volcanoes," Mac interrupted again.

"Just cool it. Play along." Tony whispered out of the corner of his mouth.

Slaughter looked at Farmer as if to say, how do I handle this?

"That's all right. I'll take over from here," Farmer said.

"The bottom line is…" Farmer looked directly at Mac, "The bottom line is, somewhere there is an accessible place where we can deposit the skull."

Slaughter interrupted eagerly. "Anything deposited in this magma would be carried to the core of the earth."

This seems far-fetched, Tony thought. But let's see where this is going. He stood up. "So you're saying that if we drop the skull in just the right place it would be carried to the core of the earth?" He motioned with his hands in a downward motion.

"Yeah," Mac said rubbing his chin as if in deep thought. "For all practical purposes it would be destroyed. It would be irretrievable." He looked at Natasha and smiled. She looked away.

Tony was feeling uneasy about the whole set up. Why are we here? We're not geologists. How do we fit into the experiment?

"How are we going to find this honey spot?" Mac asked.

"You aren't. Sandra Kay is," Farmer answered.

"All right," Tony said. He felt that there was something wrong with this whole picture. "Another person added to the mix," he continued almost under his breath.

"Yeah, Farmer," Mac injected. "Who the hell is Sandra Kay?"

Farmer continued as if he hadn't heard. "Our computer has completed a personnel profile data search, or PPD." Karl Farmer reached into his pocket and pulled out a sheet of paper. "There is a person who has done research in this phenomena and who may be able to help us. Here is the print-out of the profile." He unfolded the paper.

"She's thirty years old, an American citizen—Ph.D. in Geology. Did research on *Magma in Equilibrium* and *Convection Currents in Sub-mantel Magma*.

"Seems to fit the bill, doesn't she?" continued Karl.

"I'll say," said Mac, rubbing his chin. "Where is she now?"

"Well," Karl said, looking again at the piece of folded paper. "Intelligence Scan indicates she resigned a teaching position from Scripps Institute of Oceanography in San Diego where she taught a course in sub-surface volcanoes. She got tired of teaching and wants to do more research on magma but hasn't been able to find a sponsor."

Natasha cleared her throat. "She's on Heron Island off the east coast of Australia. Part of the Great Barrier Reef, about ninety miles off the coast from the town of Gladstone."

"Well whataya know," Mac said. "She can talk."

"All right, Mac," Tony said with a grimace, feeling sorry for Natasha. After all, she had gone through a lot with her grandfather's death in the jungle.

Natasha rolled her eyes, took a deep breath and continued. "The island is very small. It's holds a resort and a turtle research station. She's working for the resort, taking people on walking tours of the reef during low tide and assisting the dive master on scuba. If she ever hoped to save enough money to finance her own research, by now she must have realized it's impossible with the salary she makes."

"Sounds like she's ripe for the picking," said Mac rubbing his hands together. "Who's going to recruit her for the project?"

"You are," answered Karl. "You and Tony and Natasha. I know you and Tony scuba. Natasha has taken the course at our request. She just completed her open water dive. So you can go to Heron Island on a dive vacation and get to know Sandra Kay."

He coughed and then continued. "This afternoon you'll take a commercial flight to San Francisco where you'll board a plane to Sidney, Australia, then on to Heron Island. Might as well enjoy yourselves. You don't mind mixing a little pleasure with business, do you?"

"Hey, that sounds like a good deal. I'll buy that," said Tony, smiling.

"Yeah," Mac said. "You're not such a bad guy, after all, Farmer. I could almost like you." Then whispering in Tony's ear. "Hope Sandra Kay's more fun than this one."

"Karl," Tony asked, "is it safe to use our own names?"

"Sure. If anyone was following you, the trail was lost at Crows Landing. You were supposed to be going to San Francisco. As far as anyone knows, you'll be leaving San Francisco with a girl you met there."

Well, lets get this over with so I can get back to flying, thought Tony. *I don't know where we go from here, but I guess this is where the fun begins.*

Chapter 8

SUNRISE ON FIJI

The airplane droned on through the dark, starry sky. Natasha sat in the seat next to Tony. Mac sat behind them. The flight to Honolulu had been uneventful and now they were airborne again on the leg to Sidney. Natasha was sullen, and except for an occasional yes or no, had not spoken a word. She was now staring out the window into the blackness.

If this was only an experiment, thought Tony, why were they going to such lengths? But then, Natasha seemed sincere. She was not acting. And she had lost her grandfather on the expedition supposedly to obtain the skull. His mind was at a dead end.

"Hey Tony. What's the movie?"

"Don't know, Mac. Think I'll just sleep." He looked at Natasha.

"Are you going to sleep? We have two plane connections to make tomorrow."

"Maybe later. I have a lot of things to sort out."

Tony was soon fast asleep. It seemed like he had been asleep a very long time when the voice of the pilot came over the speaker.

"I would like for everyone to wake up. I have an announcement to make. We have some good news and some bad news. The good news is, we're right on schedule. The bad news is, the Sidney air traffic controllers have called a wildcat strike and have shut the airport down until daylight. We're going to land at Nadi on Fiji until Sidney is operating."

"That's just great! What about our connections?" Tony exclaimed.

"Relax," Mac replied. "There's nothing you can do about it. Enjoy. Have you ever been to Fiji?"

The airplane rolled to a stop and the engines shut down. The flight attendant's voice came over the intercom. "You may leave the plane but stay nearby because when we receive word from Sidney we will leave immediately. It is three o'clock local time. The souvenir shop will be opened for your convenience."

Mac stood up, stretched, and looked at Tony. "Getting out?"

"Yeah, I need to walk around. Are you getting out, Natasha?"

"I don't think so."

Tony and Mac stepped out onto an elevated outdoor wooden walkway, which was the same height as the door of the airplane. The walkway teed onto another, with the souvenir shop and passenger lounge at one end, while dead-ending at the other.

The shop had everything from jewelry and luggage to fine cameras and knickknacks. After browsing around, Tony decided to return to the airplane. Mac stayed, looking at a selection of wooden carvings.

Instead of going to the plane, Tony continued walking. A lone figure stood at the end of the platform. As Tony approached, he recognized it to be Natasha and stopped next to her without saying a word. There was a faint glow in the sky, a harbinger of the coming dawn.

After a while, Tony said softly, "I'm sorry about your grandfather."

"He devoted so many years of his life and just when he found it…" She spoke softly, almost in a whisper. "At least he was able to look at its beauty. It seems a shame to destroy it. What if…?" She stopped and was silent for a while, then spoke again, her voice shaking, "Now I have all the responsibility of keeping it out of the wrong hands."

Tony put his arm around her shoulders. "No, you don't. We're here to help you, but what do you mean, wrong hands?"

"Oh, Tony." Tears filled her eyes and slowly rolled down her cheeks. She stifled a sob. Tony pulled her closer to him. She pulled away and wiped her eyes. "I'm sorry."

"You don't have to be. Look at the sunrise. It's a new day."

The scattered fluffs of purple turned to light pink then slowly changed from salmon to red. The soft, warm breeze of early morning carried a faint perfume of tropical flowers.

"Have you ever seen the sun rise on Fiji?" Tony asked.

Natasha took hold of his hand and squeezed it. "Thanks," she said softly.

"Hey, Tony." Mac came strolling toward them. "Hey, Tony. The plane's getting ready to leave. Well, I see the babe's come to life."

"Did you get any souvenirs?" Tony asked.

"Yeah, but something weird happened in there. I was looking at the carvings, minding my own business when I heard this voice right behind me. 'Mac, you bastard. We'll chew you up and spit you out.' Just as plain as anything. I turned around ready to deck someone. One of the native clerks was standing there. I said, 'What did you say?' He just stood there and smiled. I asked him again. This time he answered. 'Do you want a folding basket? We'll wrap it up and ship it out.'"

"Yeah, Mac," Tony said. "You should have taken a nap on the plane. You sure you didn't smoke something in there? Anyway, what the hell's a folding basket?"

"Guess this traveling must have scrambled my brain. Could have sworn…. Oh well, look what I got." Mac pulled a wooden warrior from a paper bag. "See that shield he's holding in front of him? When you take the shield away, you can see what he's hiding. Look."

"Mac!" Tony said. "Sorry, Natasha, but that's Mac." He turned to Natasha. She was pale and trembling.

"Sorry," Mac said. "Didn't think it would bother you that much."

"No. It's not that. Are you sure that's what you heard?"

"Plain as day, but then…."

Natasha's voice was shaking. "Let's get back to the plane."

Chapter 9

HERON ISLAND

The plane's late arrival in Sidney caused the trio to miss their scheduled connection. But as luck would have it, they caught the next flight to Brisbane and arrived in time to board the puddle jumper to Gladstone. The last leg of their journey was by helicopter to Heron Island.

It was late in the day when Tony climbed into the helicopter. He leaned back in his seat, took a deep breath, and slowly let it out. Might as well enjoy it. Don't know what this whole exercise is about but might as well enjoy it, he thought. He stretched and said, "I'm tired. It'll feel good to stretch out in a bed."

Mac grinned. "This'll be good duty. If there's a watering hole on the island, that's where I'll be tonight with my dancing shoes. You can have your bed."

Natasha sighed and rolled her eyes upward. "Get serious. I'll be briefing you two tonight."

"Loosen up, babe. Enjoy life," Mac retorted.

"Look. You were chosen 'cause we thought you could do the job. If you want to play, we don't want you. You can go back now and nothing will be said."

"Damn it, girl. We can do what we gotta do and still have fun along the way," Mac snapped back. He was silent for a moment as he composed himself, then looked at her, smiling, and said softly, "Stick with me, kid, and I'll show you how to have fun. I'll show you how ol' Mac does it."

Natasha rolled her eyes again. "Incurable," she mumbled under her breath.

"That's just Mac," Tony said. "The bottom line is, when things get tough, you can count on Mac."

Natasha didn't answer.

She said she'd brief us tonight, Tony thought. Maybe now we'll find out what this is all about.

Just then the pilot climbed aboard, closed the door, and pulled himself into his seat.

"G'day, mates. Would anyone like to sit up here with me?"

"Why don't you?" Tony asked Natasha.

She climbed forward and settled into the seat next to the pilot.

The engine was started, and with a wop, wop, wop, lifted off and headed out over the sea. Late afternoon sun sparkled like diamonds on the green water. The shoreline receded behind them and the sea took on a deep blue color, intermingled with the dark shadows of reefs fringed with green.

Mac leaned over to Tony. "That sure is a cold mama. She's no fun at all."

"Look, Mac, give her the benefit of the doubt. She's real serious about this whole thing. She's not here to have a good time. She knows more then what she's telling us. Let's just keep our eyes and ears open, do what we got to do and get it over with. I don't feel good about this whole setup. Don't understand it, and don't like it."

"Hey, don't worry. We'll do it. But I might never have an opportunity to come here again, so I'm going to enjoy it."

Mac's a great guy, Tony thought, but he sure can be hard to deal with at times.

"Okay, Mac, but let's play this cool. Just don't screw things up."

"Who, me? Never let it be said I screwed things up. I may screw things, but I never screw things up."

Tony chuckled under his breath. Natasha was right. He was incurable. He looked at Natasha. She was staring intently at the scene unfolding below her. Long black hair softly cascaded down her neck and across her shoulders. Her nose turned up ever so slightly. She's a beautiful girl, Tony thought. He wondered how it would be to hold her in his arms—to kiss her. But then the thought of Sherri came to mind and he was filled with guilt.

He laid his head back and soon was dozing. He dreamed that Sherri was leaning over him, just about to kiss, when the pilot's voice brought him back to reality.

"Heron Island, dead ahead."

A green gem, like a piece of jade in a silver setting of white sand, lying flat on an azure sea, was Heron Island. As they approached, Tony could see a lagoon with several small boats tied to a wharf extending into the crystal clear water. A sunken ship lay at rest in the shallows of the entrance. The helicopter hovered over the beach and settled onto the sand.

The trio checked in and a receptionist escorted them through an incredibly green jungle to their building at the end of the trail. It was twilight and there were birds everywhere, screaming and croaking and whistling.

Tony and Natasha each had an upstairs suite and Mac had one on the ground level. A young man was unloading their bags when they arrived.

"Sure glad Farmer sprang for this nice setup," Mac said as he opened his door.

"See," Tony answered. "Farmer's Okay after all."

"Don't know why, but for some reason or other I still don't like the son-of-a-bitch," replied Mac.

"Let's freshen up and meet in Tony's room in an hour," Natasha said. "I'll brief you then."

"All we have to do is get Sandra Kay to agree to join us," Mac said. "What else is there to do?"

"Just meet in Tony's room. One hour," said Natasha.

"Tony, I am going to the bar," Mac spoke his words slowly and distinctly, pronouncing each word, all the while looking at Natasha, "to see if there is anything interesting and bring back a bottle of booze to help us unlax before we hit the hay."

"Be back in an hour, Mac," Tony stressed.

The living area of Tony's suite looked out through glass louvers onto a balcony facing a green tangle of vegetation. The sunset and evening faded into darkness. Through openings in the branches he could catch glimpses of moonlight reflecting on the water.

Tony sat in the darkness. The air was balmy and tasted fresh and clean. The myriads of birds that inhabited the island began jockeying for the best roosting branches, and the screams, croaks and cries were almost deafening. Every now and then the noise would quiet down to a few squawks, then a loud cry would start the ruckus again.

During the periods of quietness, he could hear the far off crash of the waves on the barrier reef. Tony looked up at the sky. The number of stars he could see was incredible. The Milky Way stretched like a bright belt across the blackness. I wonder where the Southern Cross is, he thought.

There was a knock on the door. "Who is it?" he yelled from the balcony.

"It's Natasha. Are you busy?"

"No. I was just sitting on the balcony. Hold on a minute. I'll let you in."

"May I sit with you?"

"Sure."

She followed him to the balcony.

"Do you mind if I turn out the lights?" Tony asked. "I was looking at the stars."

"No. I'd enjoy that too."

They sat in silence for a while, and then Tony spoke. "Have you ever seen stars like this before?"

"When I was on expeditions with my grandfather, we had time to talk together in the evening as we rested. He made me realize how insignificant we are when you consider how these untold numbers of planets and stars and galaxies extend into infinity."

Tony sighed. "Humbling, isn't it?"

"Tony, I studied your psychological profile but I know nothing of your private life. Maybe it's none of my business, but are you married?"

"I was, but she was killed in an auto accident about a year ago."

"I'm sorry."

"Still can't accept it. Seems like she'll be there when I go home." There was a long silence, and then Tony continued, his voice choked up. "On nights like tonight, I think of her. We used to sing a song together: 'I'll be seeing you in all the old familiar places…'" He couldn't go on and stifled a sob.

He was silent while he got his emotions under control and wiped a tear on his cheek with the back of his hand. "Yes, that song is so true. Never thought much about the words then." He took a deep breath that ended in a sigh. "She was so beautiful. When I close my eyes I can see her—moonlight shining in her hair."

Natasha looked up into the starry sky. "When you lose someone you love, it leaves such a void, doesn't it? I miss my grandfather." She was quiet for a while and then continued. "Had to drag his body out of the jungle and carry the skull out, as well."

"I'm sorry." Tony looked at her and saw her eyes in the moonlight, glistening with tears. He reached out and touched her hand.

There was a knock on the door.

"That's Mac," Tony said as he got up. "I can tell by his knock".

Mac strolled in carrying a bottle of wine. "This Australian vino is supposed to be fine stuff. Where's the glasses?"

After two swallows and a deep sigh, Mac smacked his lips and said, "This is good stuff." He took another gulp. "While you two were sitting here wasting your time, I met Sandra Kay. Asked around. She was in the bar."

"Well?" Tony asked.

"Thought I'd get the jump on things, put on my charm and get things started. Win her over."

"Oh boy, here it comes," Tony said.

"Well, she won't be easy to work with," Mac commented as he poured himself another glass of wine.

"I'm afraid to ask," Tony said slowly. "Why?"

"She's a bitch. A mean, smart-ass bitch."

"What do you mean?" Tony asked.

Natasha's jaw dropped, her eyes widened with surprise.

"Went up to her, introduced myself, and asked if she was Sandra Kay. Said she was, and wanted to know why I asked. Well, I started putting on the charm. Then she asked if I wanted to get laid. I was surprised, but thought maybe my charm had overwhelmed her. She asked again if I wanted to get laid. Well, I couldn't pass up an opportunity, so I said, sure. And she said, go crawl up a hen's ass and wait. That pissed me off, so I told her to go screw herself, got my bottle of wine and left."

Tony looked at Mac in disbelief. After a long period of silence, he blurted out, "Damn, Mac! I don't believe this! You really screwed things up royally this time! What a dummy!"

"What were you thinking about?" Natasha blurted out. She paused, taking a deep breath that ended in a sigh. "That's Okay," she said calmly. "Damage control. We can handle it. Mac will have to stay out of the picture when we approach Sandra Kay."

"Hell," Mac grumbled. "Didn't do anything any red-blooded American boy wouldn't have done."

"Not red blooded. Hot blooded," Tony replied. "Try to cool it."

"Look," Mac said, sounding dejected. "Not used to this spy stuff. I'm a test pilot. Remember? And a damn good one, I might add. But when it comes to women, sometimes I lose it."

"All right," Natasha broke in. "Here's the plan."

"Okay, babe, we're listening," Mac interrupted. "Lay it on us."

"The plan is, we came here as scuba enthusiasts to dive the Great Barrier Reef. We go on a dive tomorrow morning. Sandra helps the dive master on the morning dives. When there's a low tide in the afternoon, she conducts the reef walking tour. Low tide tomorrow is at 2:37 p.m., so she'll be there."

Mac broke in with a look of mock admiration. "Hey. How do you know all that, babe?"

Natasha ignored his comment. "Tony and I'll get friendly with her. Mac, act like you aren't part of our group when we're around Sandra. At the first opportunity, we'll tell her we can help her in her research. Then we'll meet with her, you too, Mac, and tell her it's an important mission, and explain the details. We're to disappear from the island together without arousing suspicion. We have just two days after today to do what we have to do here."

"How are we going to disappear from the island together without arousing suspicion?" Tony asked.

"Yeah," Mac said, still looking intently at Natasha. "I'd like to hear how we're gonna do that."

"I'll tell you all at the same time. And Mac, it's not that I don't want you to know. For security reasons, the least said, the better. If we're bugged, we want minimum time for someone to react. With the forces we're dealing with, our lives are only valuable to them as a means to find out what the plans are for destroying the skull."

"Okay, I'll buy that," Mac said. "I think we can work together, if you can put up with my kidding. But what are these forces? Are they human or not? If they're not human, why do they need to bug us? Can't they just read our minds? How can we deal with an enemy we know nothing about?"

"...I...I really don't...but they're not human as we know it."

"Well, I don't believe in the supernatural," Tony said.

"You've got to keep an open mind, Tony," said Mac, rubbing his chin. "Maybe they're human and maybe they're not. Anyway, you can count on me to work with you, babe. Sorry about the screw-up with Sandra."

"That's okay, but don't pull anything like that again," said Natasha smiling.

"Hey, look at that," Mac said. "The babe has finally cracked a smile. Everything's gonna be all right."

"Natasha," Tony asked skeptically. "If these are supernatural forces we're dealing with, why don't they just appear and take the skull? Bullets wouldn't hurt them."

"We're all tired," Natasha said, ignoring Tony's question. "Let's go to breakfast together at seven. But Mac, don't sit at our table. The dive boat leaves at nine. We'll have time to eat, go by the dive shop, sign up, and get our gear before nine. Let's all get some sleep."

"Sounds like a winner," Tony said.

After she left, Mac looked at Tony. "You know what? She didn't answer your question. Wonder why?"

Tony poured some more wine for himself and Mac. "I don't believe in the supernatural, but there is something to that skull. We experienced it. Couldn't have been just smoke and mirrors, or could it?"

He sat and looked Mac in the eyes. "Mac, I don't believe this is on the up and up. I think they're using us in some kind of experiment, or something. But I don't know how this all fits together. There are too many pieces and none of them fit together. It seems too elaborate."

"I don't know, Tony. Take it at face value. That's what I'm gonna to do."

Tony picked up the wine glasses. "Natasha seems sincere. I don't know what to think. She makes it sound like some kind of spooky supernatural thing. I can't believe that. What are these so called forces or wrong hands she's talking about?"

Mac rubbed his chin. "Well, I believe there's forces around we don't know about. Call it spirit world, supernatural, whatever. Maybe they're somewhere between natural and supernatural. Tell you what, though, I really don't like the idea of pissing something off I can't see."

Chapter 10

THE PROPOSITION

Tony awoke with the first hint of light in the eastern sky. He stretched, and breathed in the pure, sweet air. There's not many places left in the world where the air's as pure as this, he thought, as he took another deep breath.

He dressed and went out onto the balcony. Glimpses of blue water sparkled through the thick, green foliage.

Tony heard a movement on the balcony next to his. A wall shielded the view.
"Is that you, Natasha?"
"Yes."
"Are you dressed?"
"Yes, why?"
"It's only six. We have an hour before breakfast. Want to walk on the beach?"
"Sure."

They met behind the building, crossed through the thick ground cover on a board walkway, stepped onto the sand, and kicked off their shoes. Tony felt the cool, soft sand between his toes. In silence they stood side by side looking out over the water that had turned to liquid gold before the rising sun. The water's edge was alive with gulls and terns. Running before each wave and retreating back with its return to the sea, the birds seemed to be a virtual part of the wave itself.

Tony spotted a small, fluted, purple shell and picked it up. "Look at this. Isn't it pretty?"

Natasha held out her hand and Tony placed it in her palm. As he did so, he touched her soft skin and slid his hand into her's. She let the shell fall. Holding her hand, he led her to the water's edge and they ran laughing before the waves, like the terns. Suddenly, he felt guilt, like he was betraying Sherri.

"Hey, Tony!" Mac called from the walkway. "What are you guys doing out there? Let's go eat. I'm hungry."

The dining room lived up to the name of the island. It was open to the wildlife, and all kinds of birds wandered in at their leisure, looking for crumbs dropped on the floor. There were walking birds and hopping birds, large birds and small birds. Long-legged herons wandered among the tables, hoping there might be something they could steal when no one was looking.

Because they had agreed that Mac would not sit with them in case Sandra saw them, Mac sat at the next table. He tried to shoo away a persistent heron that kept looking at his plate. "If that bird makes a move for my bacon, I'll have him for supper tonight."

Tony laughed.

"This is their island. We're the intruders," Natasha said. "They were here long before people moved in on them."

"Yeah, but when it comes to my food, he's crowding the territory," Mac replied.

After breakfast, each went separately to the dive shop to sign on.

Upon boarding the boat, Tony and Natasha found a place to stow their gear while they surveyed their surroundings. A tall, blue-eyed woman, with short, straight blond hair and a golden tan, was checking the air tanks. A blue tattoo bracelet adorned her right wrist and left ankle. Although she was slightly muscular, it only enhanced the natural curves of her body. She looked up and smiled at Tony and Natasha. That must be Sandra, Tony thought.

"Hi, I'm Tony. This is Natasha," he said.

"I'm Sandra. You from the States?"

"Yeah," Tony replied.

"So am I. Welcome to Heron Island. You'll love the diving here."

Just then, Mac swaggered on board. "Oh, shit," she whispered under her breath, turned and started checking the tanks again.

As the boat made its way through the channel from the harbor, the dive master spoke: "This morning we'll be doing a drift dive from Pam's Point to the Bommie. We'll be diving at about sixty feet. The reef drops off to your right. If you keep the staghorn coral on your left, you'll be going the correct way. When your air pressure gets to five hundred pounds, surface. It'll take about thirty minutes and the skipper knows where we'll be. Does everybody have a dive buddy?"

"I don't," Mac said.

"Sandra, you be his dive buddy."

Sandra took a deep breath and Mac grinned broadly.

"Okay, so what's your name?"

"Mac."

Tony assembled his gear, slipped his buoyancy compensator vest over the tank and connected the air hose. He checked the air pressure—two thousand pounds. Putting the regulator into his mouth, he took a couple of breaths. It worked fine.

"Need any help, Natasha?"

"Just check to see if I do everything right."

Natasha removed her terry cloth cover up and put on her weight belt. She was wearing a bathing suit cut high on the thighs. Her breasts traced their shape beneath the stretch fabric. Damn! Tony thought. This woman really turns me on. As he looked at Natasha, a warm feeling flooded his body. He never thought he could ever feel this way again, but it was happening. And yet there was still this feeling of guilt. Tony helped Natasha put on the tank and Buoyancy Compensator. He slowly slid his hand down her arm. She looked up at him and smiled.

One by one, the divers stepped off the stern of the boat and disappeared beneath the blue water with just a few bubbles now and then to attest to where they were. Tony waited for Natasha. They let the air out of their BC's and sank into the world beneath the waves. In all directions were fish of every size and color.

Keeping the staghorn coral on their left, they soon came upon large bommie coral heads and plate coral with ledges and grottoes. A huge coral head appeared on their right just as a cloud of small silver fish enveloped them and swam on. Brightly colored parrotfish grazed on the coral while a large turtle swam by. A black tipped shark swam toward them, turned and swiftly swam away. Brightly colored soft coral in reds and purples and yellows swayed in the current.

The dark, shadowy shape of a huge manta ray descended from above, and drifted slowly over them with a crew of remora accompanying it. Natasha grabbed Tony's arm.

The manta ray, with wingspan of about thirty feet, slowly looked them over. Its eyes appeared to be glowing. Must be my imagination or the light playing tricks on me, Tony thought. It turned, and then gracefully flapping its bat-like wings, the ray disappeared into the blue void. Another name for the manta ray is devilfish, Tony thought. A chill surged across his body and was gone, as if a cold current had swept by.

Tony and Natasha swam to the stern of the boat, took off their tanks and handed them to the deck hand. Removing their fins, they climbed on board and sat together sharing their experience. Tony always felt invigorated after a dive. He was happy to share his experience with Natasha. She was excited about the manta ray, but she didn't mention the eyes. Must have been my imagination, he thought.

Sandra climbed aboard, followed by Mac. "That was a great dive. Sandy. Thanks a million." Then Mac continued in a lower voice, "I apologize for last night. I guess I came on too strong."

"Well, you did hit on me last night, but you're a good diver, so I guess you can't be all bad, Sandra said with a grin and then added. "And my name is Sandra, not Sandy."

"Did everybody see that manta?" Mac yelled out excitedly.

*　　*　　*　　*

"Hello again," Sandra said that afternoon as Tony and Natasha stood looking at an enormous pile of sneakers of every size and description. "Find a pair that fits and leave your own shoes here. You'll need these to walk out on the exposed reef."

During the walk, Natasha stayed close to Sandra and tried to impress her by being extra friendly, while expressing interest in the natural life on the reef.

When the tour ended, Sandra encouraged the group to wander around on their own. Natasha walked alongside Sandra, talking.

"My grandfather was an archaeologist," Natasha said. "I used to go with him on his expeditions."

"Well, la-de-da. Don't go any more?"

"No. He died in the jungle."

"Oh. Well, shit happens."

This remark tore at Natasha's heart. She felt like walking away and not having anything else to do with Sandra. How can somebody be so heartless? Natasha sucked in her breath and composed herself.

"Sandra, I know you're very interested in doing research in the study of magma."

Sandra stopped suddenly and turned toward Natasha. "How do you know that?"

"You have a Ph.D. specializing in volcanism. You can't find a sponsor to back you for further research, but I can help you."

"How do you know all that?"

"Meet me at my place tonight. I'll tell you about it."

"Oh, no. What's this, some kind of scam? You trying to set me up?"

"Please trust me."

"Why?"

"You can help us and we can help you. You'll have all the money you need to do your research. It'll be deposited in a trust fund."

"What is all this crap?"

"Just hear me out."

"Look, I don't know what you want me to do, but I'm not getting into anything illegal." Sandra ran her fingers through her hair in a backward motion. She was silent as if thinking and then continued. "And I damn sure don't plan on selling my bod."

"This is strictly legal. Just hear me out. You can make up your own mind."

"Well…shouldn't waste my time, but might be fun listening to your bullshit. But I won't go to your room. If you want to tell me about this wonderful plan of yours, buy me a Mai Tai. We can walk on the beach and you can tell me all the bullshit you want to."

The beach was deserted and they slowly walked sipping their drinks.

"Okay," Sandra said after she had taken a few sips. She pushed her short hair back but it fell on the side of her face again. "It's your nickel. Don't make it too long or you'll have to buy me another Mai Tai."

"Look," Natasha began. "It's all on the up and up. I have a sum of money at my disposal. All you have to do is to locate a magma pool that's in equilibrium. After you locate it, a large sum of money will be deposited in a trust fund for you to continue your research. Call it a research grant."

"Why don't you use an infrared satellite to scan for magma?"

"You know why, Sandra. I want you to locate magma in equilibrium. A satellite could find the magma pools but not know which ones are—."

"Okay, okay. Just checking to see if you did your homework." Sandra kicked at the sand, brushed back her hair then shook it back like it was before. "Why is this so damned important to you and why do you want this info?"

"My team is doing a research project. We want to place an object in this type of pool so the convection currents will carry it down into the earth."

"What research group are you with and who controls this research grant? The reason I left the university was that some old bastard professor wouldn't let me use my own protocol and do what I wanted to do. And he wanted to get all the credit." Sandra kicked hard at the sand sending sand into the air where the wind picked it up and blew it into Natasha's face.

Natasha wiped her face and spit some sand out of her mouth. I think Mac was accurate in describing her, she thought. I wish we didn't need her. I wonder if we can rely on her to be a team player?

Natasha took a deep breath and then said, "We're an independent group. You will have complete control of the grant money to use as you please." Natasha was getting nervous. What will it take to convince this woman, she thought?

"How do I know this isn't some scam and you're not bullshitting me."

The wind blew Natasha's hair in her face and in her mouth. She wiped it back. "You don't. We're not going to ask you to donate money or whatever, so it's not a scam. But it's a chance to make big money. If you don't join us, the rest of your life you'll wonder if you passed up a once in a lifetime opportunity. It's up to you. You can take it or leave it. I have two other people I've recruited to be on the team. They'll be in my room tonight to hear what I've got to say."

Natasha finished her drink and then continued. "Nobody's forcing you. You can stay here and never get anywhere, or come with us and be independent to do what you want to do."

"Well, damn. It's against my better judgment. But hell, buy me another drink and I'll come by to see what it's all about."

"Seven? Okay?"

"I'll be there, but I'll be bringing my brass nucks just in case there's trouble."

*   *   *   *

Tony, Natasha, and Mac sat in Natasha's suite, waiting for Sandra to arrive.

"Let me do the talking," Natasha said. "We have to be careful not to spook her, she's very skittish right now. Besides, you have just as much to learn as she does about the plan for leaving the island. We won't tell her anything about the skull. We'll just leave it as an 'object'. She thinks it's a research project. We'll play it by ear, but let's leave it on a need-to-know basis."

There was a knock and Natasha opened the door. Sandra suspiciously looked in. She saw Mac sitting on the sofa.

"Uh-oh. He's in on it, too? Forget it." She turned to leave.

"Wait. Just hear us out. Then you can make up your mind," Natasha said. "I promise it will be well worth your while."

"Well, I don't know…."

"Have a seat. Would you like some wine?"

"No thanks. I'll just stand at the door. Just get on with it." She stood just inside the opened door with her back to the wall.

"Sandra, this is Captain Anthony Thompson, Tony, and Captain Charles MacPherson, Mac, of the U.S. Air Force. Tony, Mac and I are part of a team working on a project for the U.S. Government."

"Wait a minute," Sandra interrupted, "You told me it was a private research project. What's the government doing in it?"

"The project is backed by the government. But just listen."

"Okay, but it better be good." Sandra ran her fingers through her hair in a back sweeping motion as she fingered her brass knuckles.

"It's a top secret project. We have to destroy an object so it can never be retrieved."

"You didn't tell me you wanted to destroy something. But wow, sounds like you been smoking some good shit. I'd like some, too. Pass it here."

"As I told you, we want to place this object in a lava pool that's in equilibrium and allow the natural convection currents to carry it down. We think this'll put it out of anyone's reach. We'd like you to find the perfect spot. You won't have to deal with anything except finding the right place. We'll do the rest."

"What is this so-called object and why do you have to destroy it this way?"

"The only thing you need to know is, you'll be doing your government, no, the world, a great service."

"You've been sniffing the white stuff, or mainlining? How do I know you're not feeding me a line of bullshit?"

"Like I said, in return for the use of your expertise, we'll set up a trust fund for you. You'll be able to continue your research. But it's up to you. You can take a chance for a once in a lifetime opportunity or you can walk away."

"Bullshit or not, I'm just spinning my wheels here. Never let it be said that Sandra was too chicken to take a chance. What the hell. What have I got to lose? If this is true, I stand to gain. If not, I haven't lost anything. I was going to quit here soon, anyway. Are you sure this is legal?"

"Backed by the U.S. Government."

"Yes, but is it legal?"

"It's as legal as you can get," Natasha said with a laugh.

"Everyone's got their price…Oh, what the hell. If all I got to do is find the magma, you can count me in."

"Welcome to the team!" Mac jumped up, smiling and extended his hand.

Sandra looked at his extended hand with a disgusted look, without reaching for it.

Mac stopped smiling and slowly backed toward his chair.

"Okay," Natasha said. "Here's the plan. Tomorrow night, the four of us will go on a private night dive where the reef drops off. To the right of where we dove today. Think you can arrange it, Sandra? Just the four of us?"

"Sure, I can do that. The dive master and I are real good friends. But why?"

"A sub will be waiting for us, submerged in deep water."

"A sub? What are we doing with a sub?" Sandra said. "And what the hell are they doing in these waters?"

"They have clearance. They'll have a radio beacon buoy on the surface. I have a miniature radio direction finder, an RDF. We'll zero in on the signal. When we reach it, I'll drop the RDF into the water. The water will activate a transmitter that'll send a short burst of signals, letting the sub know we're there. Then we'll go in with our scuba gear." Natasha took a breath and brushed back her hair.

"Hold it." Sandra interrupted. "You're going too fast for me. Now what the hell are we gonna do? Go in the water with a sub?"

Natasha continued. "A transportable, connected to a modified escape hatch on the hull of the sub will be released. It'll have an opening on its underside. With the air inside equalized to the water pressure, we'll be able to swim up into it like an air lock. After we're in, the hatch will be sealed."

"Hell, I don't know if I want to do that," Sandra said hesitantly. "I don't do subs."

Mac cleared his throat like he was going to speak. Natasha shot a sharp glance his way. Cool it, Mac, she thought, almost saying it out loud. She then continued.

"It'll be safe."

"Well, I'm not chicken," Sandra said, while looking at Mac. She threw her shoulders back and held her head erect. "Sounds interesting. Tell me more about this sub deal."

"The transportable will be piloted by a one-man crew," Natasha continued. "It will latch onto the escape hatch, and we'll be able to enter the sub. Next morning they'll find the empty boat still anchored and the world will think we're all dead."

"Why do we want people to think we're dead?" Sandra asked.

"Only so we can do what we have to do undetected," Natasha answered.

"Who are we hiding from? And wait a minute. Will we stay dead, or will we come back? I need to be alive to do my research," Sandra said with a nervous laugh.

Mac laughed.

Natasha fired a look at him again and then continued. "Oh, we'll return."

"How long will we be gone and how will we explain it?" asked Sandra.

"I don't know for sure how long it will take, but it shouldn't take longer than a month, two at the most. Depends on how long the research takes. When the mission is over, we'll return and be put ashore on a deserted island some distance from here. We'll say we drifted too far from the boat and when we came up, couldn't find it—that we got caught in a strong current and when daylight came were nowhere near Heron Island. We'll say, we drifted with our buoyancy compensators and finally made it to the deserted island. There are rain pools and fruit on the island that could sustain life." Natasha poured a glass of wine and held it out for Sandra.

"How will we get off the island?" Sandra inquired as she took the glass.

"It'll be arranged for someone to alert rescuers."

"Well, like I said, I'm not chicken. I got more guts than a certain blowhard son-of-a-bitch who's all mouth," Sandra said, looking directly at Mac. "Besides it sounds exciting." She held her glass up. "Shit, let's do it!"

Mac grinned broadly at her. "Okay, let's do it!"

CHAPTER 11

▼

FATHER GORSKI'S WARNING

Tony awakened during the night with the feeling of a presence in his room.

"Who's there?" Tony asked, sitting bolt upright.

No answer.

"Who's there?" he repeated. He reached for the lamp switch and turned it. Nothing happened.

Tony saw the faint outline of a shadowy figure in a long black robe and hood.

"Who are you?" Tony asked. A wave of fear washed over him and he stiffened, ready to protect himself.

"I am Father Gorski," came the answer in a hoarse whisper.

"What do you want? How'd you get in here?" Tony slowly slipped out from under the covers, all the while keeping his eyes on the figure. He stood next to the bed, fists clenched.

"Hear what I must tell you. You are in great danger. The Feathered Serpent has returned. I was in Siberia when Satan lost the battle with Michael and was cast from heaven. Satan is now roaming the earth as a roaring lion seeking whom he may devour. He started his spread of evil with the advent of Communism. Used this as a training ground for his minions. Satan is about to take a giant step. He is setting up his principalities. Now, he is ready for his prince, the Feathered Serpent, to control the world." There was a long silence and then he continued.

"The Feathered Serpent sent his minions out to retrieve a crystal skull that he will use as the instrument of evil to accomplish this end. He had hidden and protected it with the blood of the innocent. His pyramid is empty. Someone has desecrated it." There was another long silence.

Tony's heart pounded in his ears.

The dark figure continued. "The instrument he needs to bring the world under his thumb has been stolen. His minions have orders to deliver the crystal skull to him. They know where it is and are waiting for the right time and place. One of his minions is on your team. One of you belongs to him. Beware. You are in great danger." He was silent again.

Tony was aware of his own breathing, which came in short quick breaths.

It spoke again. "Remember, its strength is in the fire. I have been commissioned to help you. Remember, its strength is in the fire."

Tony stumbled over the words, "What…what do you mean, its strength is in the fire?"

The apparition slowly faded away until there was only the moonlight shining through the window, and now and then the cry of a bird that sounded like a little child in pain.

He rubbed his eyes, and shook his head. Was this a dream? It had to be a dream. If this was not a dream, then what was it? If this was not a dream, then he would have to accept the reality that they were not dealing with natural forces. Sometimes dreams seem so real. Still, he had to talk to Mac about it. He hurriedly dressed and started toward the door. As he put his hand on the doorknob he heard a knock.

"Who is it?"

"It's me! Open up. Tony! Hurry!"

Tony opened the door. Mac stood in his shorts, he was pale and he had a look on his face of abject terror.

"Tony, I just had one hell of a dream."

Chapter 12

THE SUB AND THE STRIGA

Tony looked at Natasha. This was her first night dive and she was afraid. He knew she was afraid because she avoided his eyes but she would never admit it. He squeezed her hand reassuringly, and then rolled backwards off the gunwale of the boat into the inky black water. Natasha gripped his hand tightly as they proceeded to dive toward the transportable, thirty feet beneath the yellow marker buoy. Its single headlight beam acted as a beacon to show the way.

They swam beneath the vehicle to enter up through the open hole. The narrow portal proved too narrow to allow entry with the bulky scuba gear, so they had to remove their equipment. Being a new diver, Natasha balked. Tony squeezed her hand gently to reassure her, and then let her breathe from his spare octopus regulator, while he helped her shed her gear. He then guided her through the opening. Tony stayed at the entrance to help the other two in and then he pulled himself through the opening. The hatch was closed and sealed. He looked at Natasha and smiled. "We made it."

Natasha smiled at Tony and said nothing.

The whirr of the electric motor let them know they were moving.

Mac looked at Sandra. "What do you think of this?"

If Sandra was afraid, she didn't let on. "This is cool shit," she said while looking at Mac. "But I wish they would have given us something to dry ourselves."

Soon, they heard a clanking sound as the transportable latched onto the sub. The hatch opened and they climbed down into the sub.

A nervous looking officer greeted them. "Good evening. I'm Lt. Commander Cummings, the executive officer. Welcome aboard. I'll show you to your quarters where you can dry off. You'll each find one set of civilian clothes. At zero seven hundred hours you'll eat at the officer's mess. Until then, you're requested to remain in your quarters." He paused, clenching his teeth and pulling his lips back in a nervous grimace.

"Captain Thompson and Captain MacPherson, the skipper wants to see you as soon as you get into dry clothes. I'll wait in the passageway for you."

"Well, let's get in high gear," Mac said impatiently. "These women are freezing. Instead of staring at these bathing beauties, let's get them to their quarters.

"Hey, Tony. Wonder if Farmer picked out our clothes. No telling what they might look like."

The group followed the officer down a narrow passageway. Heads peered around corners curiously watching them. He stopped and opened a door to a small room. "You two gentlemen bunk here. The two ladies will be in the next cubicle."

"This is cozy," Mac remarked with a laugh. "Don't know if I like being this close to you—just barely enough room to get in. What do you want, top or bottom rack?

"Hey, I've got an idea. Why don't we switch. You bunk with Natasha and Sandy can bunk with me."

"Get serious, Mac." Tony looked around to make sure there wasn't a television camera or microphone around before continuing. "What do you think we ought to do? Tell Karl about our dream, or whatever it was?"

"Hell no. He might be the enemy. Don't trust that son-of-a-bitch." Mack struggled to put on some dry clothes. "Look at this crap he got for us to wear. I look like a nerd. I'll be ashamed for the crew to see me." He looked around and sniffed the air. "Boy, it sure smells stale in here."

"Focus, Mac. You're right about Karl. We can't take any chances. Maybe we ought to discuss this with Aaron Slaughter. He's an expert on this kind of stuff. Maybe he can make sense out of it."

Mac shook his head slowly and sat on the bunk. "The trouble with you, Tony, is you're too damned trusting. We can't trust anybody. We don't want whoever or whatever to know what we know. If they don't feel they're under suspicion, they might make a slip, and we'll be watching."

"Well, I can't make any sense out of it. And who the hell are 'they'?" Tony commented.

"Well, until we find out who the hell 'they' are, we need to keep on our toes," Mac replied. "Besides, we don't even know what it is we're dealing with."

Tony nodded his head. "Yeah, you're right. But Natasha's not one of them. Remember, she had the skull all to herself after her grandfather died. Also, she's too nice a girl."

"I've been meaning to talk to you about that," Mac said, rubbing his chin. "I think she's getting to you. See, you're already saying she's not guilty because she's a nice girl. I'm the one who's supposed to lose control over a female, not you."

"You know what, Mac? I really like Natasha and I think she's great, but I feel guilty when I'm around her because…well…because of Sherri."

"Look. Don't unload your guilt complex on me. You really do have a problem, buddy. Do something about it. Screw Natasha and forget about Sherri, or keep your hormones in check. If that don't work, see a shrink when we get back, but keep your mind on the project."

There was a knock at the door. "The skipper wants to see you now."

"Screw you and the skipper," Mac mumbled under his breath.

Tony opened the door and the two followed Lt. Commander Cummings down a long, narrow passageway.

"Come in, gentlemen." A tall man with graying sideburns, wearing an opened collar khaki shirt, stood in front of a blue fiberglass desk. His height made him seem incongruent with the cramped quarters of a submarine. "Come in, gentlemen." He looked at the executive officer who stood idly by, nervously clenching and unclenching his teeth. "You may leave." The officer saluted, closing the door behind him.

"Good evening, gentlemen. I'm Commander Hawkins. It's a dubious honor to have flyboys on my tub. You'll see what it's like to be under rather than over." He smiled showing perfect white teeth. "I'm not privy to the details of your mission, but you have Alpha One clearance. My ship is at your command. There's a gentleman waiting to talk to you on ULF through the scramble box here in my office."

Tony and Mac looked at each other.

"ULF, sir?" Tony inquired.

Commander Hawkins smiled again. "You Air Force guys don't use ULF, do you? Ultra Low Frequency. Carrier of one cycle per second with audio superimposed on it. The Navy recently perfected the superimposition of audio. We are one of the first to get it. ULF can travel through water and earth the same as high frequency waves travel through air. The Navy is far ahead of the Air Force.

"In your dreams," Mac said with a superior tone.

The skipper flipped a switch on a speaker on his desk. "Hello, Commander Hawkins here. Would you like me to leave the room?"

"No, you can stay," said a familiar voice from the speaker. "This is Karl Farmer. How are you? Did you accomplish the task?"

"Roger, Karl. Mission accomplished according to plan," Tony replied with a hint of pride in his voice.

"Yeah, Farmer," Mac broke in. "We now have a new member of the team. Fine looking broad."

"Congratulations. I knew you could do it."

"Thanks," Tony answered. "But Natasha really was the one the credit should go to."

"Is she with you?"

"No, she's with Sandra."

"Give her my congratulations."

"I will."

"Commander Hawkins. Thanks for your cooperation. You're to proceed to coordinates 5 and L section CM20 on your G5 charts. You'll rendezvous with an aircraft carrier in the area. She'll send a helicopter to transfer your four guests."

"We'll proceed immediately." The skipper snatched up the piece of paper he had been writing on. "You gentlemen can stay and finish the conversation." He then hurriedly left.

"Boy, Farmer. I'm impressed," Mac spoke with mock admiration in his voice. "You sure got that skipper hopping. How does it feel to be so powerful?"

A short laugh came from the speaker. He cleared his throat as if embarrassed, then after a moment of silence, spoke. "As soon as you transfer to the carrier, you'll be flown to Barber's Point on Oahu. A sum of money will be given to each of you. Buy some clothes and whatever you need. Are you alone?"

"Yeah," Tony answered.

"By the way, there'll also be new identifications for the three of you. Remember, you're missing and presumed dead. I also went ahead and got identification for Sandra. I knew the three of you could pull it off."

"All the research facilities of the University of Hawaii will be available to Sandra. She'll have her new I.D., but, if she runs into someone she knows, she can say she married and her husband died or she divorced, and kept his name. Aaron

Slaughter will meet you there and go into detail with Sandra on what his theory is and what he's looking for."

"Hey, are we going to fly the birds? I always wanted to fly off a carrier," Mac said as he leaned over the speaker.

"Afraid not. The Navy doesn't want you practicing with their aircraft. Besides, I need you alive for the project."

"Thanks a lot," replied Mac. "You're a real buddy."

"Hey, Karl, I resent that," Tony interrupted. "You're talking to the two top test pilots in the country."

"Well, pardon me," Karl said sarcastically. "But like I said, the Navy doesn't want a couple of Air Force jockeys screwing around with their equipment. Maybe after the project is over, we can arrange it."

"Okay, if that's the way you want to be," Tony answered, "but when are we going to get our new names?"

"Your new I.D. cards and passports will be given to you at Barbers Point. Only the last names will be changed so you won't mess up and say the wrong name talking to each other."

"Hey, Farmer. I'll bet you came up with some doozies for names," Mac said.

"Not bad," Karl answered. "The names are not bad at all. Mac, your new name is Charles Shagnasty."

"Shit! I quit! There's no way I'm going out in the world with a name like that. Farmer, you're a—"

"Hold it, Mac," Karl interrupted. "Just kidding. Your new name is Charles Smith."

"You really put some imagination into that one, Farmer."

"I try to please. But, you know what? We can't call you Mac because you're not MacPherson any more. We'll have to call you Charlie."

"Bullshit. I'm still Mac."

"Yes, I guess we'll still have to call you Mac. You probably wouldn't respond to anything else."

"What's my name?" Tony asked. "Probably Anthony Lipshits."

"No, Anthony Brown."

"That shouldn't be hard to remember."

"There's a reason for calling you Smith and Brown. It's like vanilla ice cream. No one will notice if you have vanilla ice cream, but if you have chocolate fudge swirl or walnut cream, people will take note. So you have plain vanilla names."

Tony smiled. "You're making me hungry. What about Natasha and Sandra? What's their flavor?"

"People pay more attention to men's last names than women's. Natasha will be Natasha Kirst and Sandra will be Sandra Andrews."

"Hey," Mac chimed in. "We can call her Sandy Andy."

"Cute," responded Tony.

"All right, guys. Have a good night's sleep. Like I said, Dr. Slaughter will be meeting you in Hawaii. I wish I were going, but somebody has to stay and watch the store."

"That's the way it goes," Mac retorted. "Sometimes you win. Sometimes you lose."

"Talk to you later," Tony said.

As the speaker clicked off, the skipper walked in.

"Did you gentlemen get your business taken care of?"

"Yes sir," answered Tony. "I think we'll hit the sack now."

Later that night while Mac's snoring resounded across the close space of the small room, Tony pulled the sheet up around his chin and closed his eyes. There's got to be a logical explanation for all this, Tony thought. I don't believe in ghosts—but, the skull, the dream—all of it. My mind can only think in logical terms. I'll just have to accept it and let my reasoning bypass it. I just hope we're not caught up in some grandiose scam.

It's amazing how quiet the sub is, he thought. He couldn't feel any vibration or hear any engine noise. These nukes are really something. He relaxed his body and soon drifted off into sleep.

He hadn't been sleeping long when he felt a hand on his shoulder. He awoke with a start. Although the room was dark, he could see a shape in a long black cassock with a black hood, bathed in a soft green glow. He couldn't see the face in the hood, only a dark shadow. Like what he thought he had seen looking into his airplane. Tony sat up. "What...what do you want? Who the hell are you?"

"I am Father Gorski. You must come to me. I need your help and you need mine. The enemy is fighting from a dimension that you cannot understand. Its army will attack you from all sides and your mind will fall into utter confusion and fear. I will show you what you must do to be strengthened in this other dimension. But you must set me free from the power of the Striga."

Tony sat in stunned silence. Finally he was able to speak. "What the hell is a Striga? What the hell are you?" he rubbed his eyes. "Are you real or, or you a hologram?"

"You will soon know this is all very real." The green glow seemed to envelop the small room. "The Striga is the Vampire of Paris. He is watching me. Find the Striga and you will know where I am. Yes, he is watching me. Come help me to die, and you will find the strength to fight the enemy—the strength to destroy the skull. But, beware, the enemy is in your midst."

Tony's body felt as if he were momentarily hit with a pulse of electricity and then the specter was gone. Tony sat staring at where the shape had been. He was aware of a movement in the overhead bunk.

"Damn! The son-of-a-bitch found us even under water," Mac said with a tremor in his voice.

"You saw him, too?" Tony asked.

"Hell, yes. Don't think we'd have the same frigging dream at the same damn time. Wants us to help him die? I'll help the son-of-a-bitch die right now given half a chance. What the hell is he and what the hell does he want with us?"

"I…I don't know…just don't know."

They sat in silence for a long time, staring into the darkness. Finally Mac jumped down from his bunk and turned on the light. "What the shit do we do next?"

He sat on the bunk next to Tony. "I don't like it, Tony. What does this Father Gorski want with us? We're not even Catholic. What the hell is this damn Striga? I don't want to go looking for a frigging vampire, but…hey, wait. What the hell. It's in Paris, right? I always wanted to go to Paris. We could get a couple of little Paris babes to help us. We could have a joyful adventure looking for the vampire, whether we find it or not. Wouldn't have to look too hard. The vampire might even be a beautiful Paris doll who wants to bite my neck and I could bite hers."

"Get serious, Mac." Tony was still shaken from the experience. That Mac, he thought. Always looking for the bright side when things get tough. How can he put up such a front? Wish I could do that. Can't believe he's not as scared as I am. He then said out loud, "We need to wake up the skipper and put in a call to Karl to have him set up a trip to Paris. We have to find out what's going on here before I go crazy." He stood up. "Someone's causing all this. Don't know who, how or why but we have to find out."

"Yeah, but we can't tell Karl about it. He might be the enemy. What'll we tell him?"

"He'll just have to trust us."

"That son-of-a-bitch don't trust us as much as we trust him."

"Maybe. We'll see."

It took forty-five minutes for the skipper to contact Karl Farmer. "Here you go," the skipper said tiredly. "When you leave, make sure the door to my office is locked. I'm going back to my quarters."

"Karl," Tony said when Karl's voice came on. "Karl, this is Tony and Mac. Something has come up and we have to go to Paris."

"Are you alone?"

"Yes."

"Okay, why do you have to go to Paris? What happened?"

"Can't tell you just now, but it's imperative we go to Paris. We can go while Sandra does her research."

"You're not trying to con me into a Paris trip, now, are you?"

Mac chimed in, "We wouldn't do that, Farmer, now would we?"

Tony interrupted. "Karl, this is very important. We have to get answers."

"Answers to what? I can't let you go unless you tell me why—and why can't you tell me?"

"Sorry," Tony said, "we can't tell you just now."

"Then I can't let you go."

"Look, Karl," Tony insisted. "It's so important that if we have to buy our own airline tickets, we will go."

"You're under my command. You don't do anything unless I okay it. Go to Paris and you get a court-martial. Is that understood?"

"Look, Farmer," Mac shouted. "Either let us go to Paris, or get us off this frigging ride! I want out of here! I've had all the fun I can stand."

"What can we do to convince you to let us go?" Tony said.

"You can tell me what this is all about."

"We will, but not just now. We have to sort this all out," Tony replied.

"It sounds like you've had some kind of harrowing experience. Maybe you need to wait until you get to Hawaii and discuss this with Dr. Slaughter."

"I don't think we should discuss this with Slaughter just yet." Replied Tony. "But I do think it's for the best that we go. What can I do to get your approval?"

"I'll give my approval on one condition, that Natasha goes with you."

It's too dangerous for her," Tony said.

"That's my ruling. If it has to do with the mission, then she has a vested interest and she goes, otherwise the deal's off."

"It's too dangerous. I don't want her to go," Tony insisted.

"She's my, or rather, the CIA's representative, and if she doesn't go, then the deal's off."

Mac broke in. "Don't be dumb, Tony. Let's let her go."

"That's the most intelligent thing I've ever heard you say," Karl said.

"Did anybody ever tell you you're an asshole?" Mac shot back.

"Yes, once or twice. Do you agree that Natasha goes with you, Tony?"

"It's against my better judgment, but all right."

When Tony and Mac were back in their room, Mac rubbed his chin thoughtfully. "Now why do you suppose Farmer insisted on Natasha going with us when we wouldn't tell him the reason for going to Paris?"

"Don't know. Unless he feels she'd blow the whistle on us if we're trying to con him."

"Guess we'll have to tell her. Shit, don't feel good about telling her, though," said Mac as he stretched and yawned.

Tony, who had been sitting on his bed, started pacing back and forth. "I trust her. Just don't want her to be in danger."

"Stop pacing. There's barely enough room in here for you to walk past me. Anyway, she's in danger just being on the project. We don't know when the shit's gonna hit the fan, but it will. If someone or something is trying to stop us, sooner or later they're gonna have to make their move. Maybe this damn Paris thing's their move."

"Yeah, guess you're right.

"Don't let emotions get in your way and cloud your judgment," Mac said as he pulled his shoes off and let them drop.

"Okay, we'll tell her about the Paris deal when we're in Hawaii. Don't know what her reaction will be. Myself, I'd rather lie out on the beach than go to Paris. But we do what we have to do. It's all so weird. Sometimes I wonder if I'm not dreaming or going crazy."

"You know, it might not be so bad that Natasha will be in on this Paris deal with us," said Mac. "She's pretty savvy when it comes to foreign things. She did a lot of traveling with her grandfather. Maybe she'll know what this frigging Striga is. She might be a big help in finding it. At least she might be able to tell us what it is or where it is."

"Yeah. She could be a big help to us, because I don't know where to start."

"I wonder if those Paris babes are as beautiful as they say. And relax, Tony. Stop pacing. Sit, boy. Stay."

"Yeah. Let's try and get some sleep. Don't have much time 'til morning."

"Shit. Don't know if I can, or even want to. That weird Gorski guy might come back," Mac said as he turned off the light.

CHAPTER 13

▼

HAWAIIAN INTERLUDE

"Dr. Slaughter would like to have dinner with the Brown party at seven in the dining room." The hotel clerk folded the piece of paper and handed it to Tony.

"So this is the Brown party. I guess you must be in pretty good graces with Farmer. How does it feel to be hot shit on a stick, Mister Brown?" Mac said sarcastically to Tony, stressing the words, Mister Brown.

He then turned to Sandra. "Well, Sandy Andy, you're soon going to meet the fabulous Dr. Slaughter."

"Great," Sandra answered as she signed her name on the register. "Don't know who the hell this Doctor Slaughter is but I hope he has more frigging couth than you."

"Who, me? Once you get to know me, you'll change your mind. To know me, is to love me," Mac said putting his arm around Sandra's waist.

"Sounds like a lot of bull shit to me," Sandra retorted as she deliberately pulled his arm away. "And as I said before, my name is Sandra, not Sandy."

"Okay, Sandy," Mac answered. "I'll try to remember."

"Natasha." Tony eased up next to Natasha and spoke softly into her ear. "Right after you check in, Mac and I have something important to discuss with you. Either your room or mine."

"All right. Your room."

After they checked in, Mac went to Tony's room to wait for Natasha. He let out a long, low whistle. "Hey, this is some place, Tony. One thing I can say about Farmer, nothing cheap about him. Everything is first class. If he weren't such an asshole, I could probably like him. From my window I can look out on Waikiki and see the bathing beauties lying on the sand. Why don't you and Natasha go to Paris and Sandy Andy and I stay here?"

"Not on your life. Don't think Sandra could take you. Besides, she has work to do."

"It's the night time I'm thinking about. She doesn't have to work at night, does she?"

"Don't know, but it's a moot point, 'cause you're going to Paris."

"Just rattling your cage, Tony."

There was a knock on the door. Tony let Natasha in and proceeded to tell her about the two apparitions, while Mac filled in all the details Tony left out. Tony then told her about the proposed trip to Paris. Natasha stared at Tony without uttering a sound.

"What do you say?" Tony asked. "Are you with us? Will you come to Paris with us?"

"I don't know," Natasha said, visibly shaken. She stood up. "How will this help us?"

"I'm not sure," Tony answered. "But the way things look like they're shaping up…well, just don't know. Don't understand it, but we have to find out—to protect ourselves." He scratched his head. "Must be some kind of telepathy. We have to find out who or what's behind it."

Mac, rubbing his chin as though deep in thought, said, "I'll tell you what it is. It's supernatural power—or maybe somewhere between natural and supernatural. Doesn't have all the powers of the supernatural but more than us. That's why they just can't appear and take the skull. But anyway, I do know this Gorski guy's from another dimension."

Tony looked down at his hands. "There's got to be an explanation. Somebody's trying to stop us. Maybe this Father Gorski can answer some questions. We can't find out sitting around here not knowing what to expect."

He turned and looked into Natasha's eyes. "This may even be the enemy, but we have to investigate. If it can help us, we need it, and if it's the enemy, we'll be on the alert. It might show itself. At least then, we'll know what this so-called enemy is."

He took a deep breath and slammed his fist into the palm of his hand. "Damn! I don't know what the hell to believe or what the hell to do!"

He felt like he was being torn apart. He was afraid but ashamed of what he was afraid of. He didn't want to believe in the supernatural yet he couldn't explain what was happening. He didn't want to get deeper involved yet the only direction was straight ahead.

"I'll go along with the trip, but I don't like it," Natasha replied, nervously shifting from one foot to the other.

"I'd rather you stay out of this mess," Tony said, taking her hand in his. "But Karl insisted. Don't worry. You'll be with me. I'll see that nothing happens to you."

Natasha smiled and squeezed his hand.

"Okay, let's cut the cute crap. We have a job to do," Mac said, tapping his fingers on the arm of his chair.

* * * *

"Right this way," the hostess said as she reached for some menus. "Dr. Slaughter is waiting."

Aaron Slaughter stood up. "Hello, I'm so glad to see all of you again. Is this Sandra? So good to see you, Sandra."

"Hi," Sandra replied. "Glad to meet you, too. I'm anxious to get to work. Understand you have a damn interesting theory. Looking forward to hearing it and working with you."

"I can't take full credit for the theory. Karl Farmer planted the seed and we developed the theory together. I'm happy that you have agreed to work with us, Sandra. I'm sure we'll get along just fine. It will be exciting for both of us. Oh, and by the way, just call me Aaron, and welcome aboard."

"Thanks."

Aaron clapped his hands. "Now, let's enjoy some good food and good company. Waiter, bring us a round of drinks."

"Hey, Slaughter," Mac asked. "How come you didn't change your name, too?"

"Because I'm not dead," answered Aaron. A smile slowly crossed his face.

After dessert, Aaron's mood suddenly changed. A dark cloud came over his features and he looked intently at Tony.

"I understand that you are going to Paris. Why?"

"I don't think we should discuss it at this time," Tony answered.

Sandra was startled. "Who the hell's going to Paris?"

"Tony, Mac, and Natasha," answered Aaron.

"Why," asked Sandra? "Shit, Natasha, you didn't tell me."

"I just found out a little while ago," Natasha said.

"Why are you going to Paris?" Aaron asked again. "What happened? Did something of a parapsychological nature cause you to decide to go? You can tell me. Maybe I can be of help."

"Hey, what makes you think something strange happened? And how'd you know?" Mac asked.

"So something did happen," answered Aaron. "That's the only explanation for your decision to do this so suddenly. Please don't think I'm prying, but I do want to help you. You know what my specialty is. I know that things of this sort can be very unnerving. Just remember, I am here to listen to you and to give you advice, if you request it."

"Thank you," Tony replied. "We appreciate your offer to help, but this is something we have to do by ourselves." Damn, he thought. Don't blow it, Mac.

Sandra looked perturbed. "What the hell's going on here? Is something frigging weird happening? What's all this spook shit? Parapsychological? Somebody clue me in."

Aaron touched Sandra's arm. "Don't worry about this. It has nothing to do with us. These people are off on a boondoggle. We have work to do and I'm really excited about starting."

"Shit, I don't know…. Hope I didn't make a frigging mistake," Sandra said hesitantly.

"Just bear with us," Tony said to Sandra. "This doesn't effect what you're doing. We'll explain it all at the proper time. In the meantime, you're doing what you do best. After it's over, you'll be able to research what you want to, and do it to your heart's content."

Sandra shook her head slowly. "Hell, I guess I can live with this as long as it doesn't get any weirder." She ran her fingers through her hair, pushing it back, and then shook it in place. She was silent as if thinking, took a deep breath, let it out and then said. "What the hell. Guess the end justifies the means and all that sort of shit—long as I get my money. Just hope it doesn't get too frigging weird or I'm out of here. I think you're all nuts, anyway."

"Well, just bear with us a little longer, okay?" Tony said getting up from his chair. He looked at Natasha. "Would you like to take a walk on the beach?"

"I'd love to," she replied.

"How about it, Sandy Andy? Like to walk on the beach with me?" Mac asked.

"Shit, no. Don't think so," Sandra replied. "I'd like to talk to Aaron about his theory and what the hell we want to accomplish."

"Want to come with us?" Tony asked Mac.

"No thanks. Three's a crowd. I'll just go to my room and watch television."

The full moon, reflecting on the waves, made them sparkle like a pirate's treasure chest of diamonds and pearls. Tony and Natasha stepped onto the soft sand. The breakers, as they curled over and turned to foam, were like silver chains stretched across the jewels. Natasha removed her shoes and Tony followed suit.

"Doesn't the sand feel good under your feet?" Natasha asked.

"Yeah."

The warm breeze was heavy with salt mist. Tony looked at Natasha. The soft glow of moonlight nestled in her hair.

She squeezed his hand without saying a word.

They walked along the sand, where it was neither land nor sea, letting each wave wash over their feet. Sometimes they ran laughing toward higher ground as a larger wave threatened to reach up and swirl around their legs.

After walking away from the lights and sounds of music from the hotel, Tony and Natasha stopped and stood looking at each other. The moonlight softly etched her face. Her eyes sparkled in the moon glow. Tony looked into her eyes. He hadn't felt this way since Sherri. He never thought he could love another woman, but here he was.

She moved closer to him. He took her into his arms and pulled her against his body. Their lips met in a long, tender kiss. She pulled away. Both were breathing heavily. He could taste the lipstick she was wearing.

"I love you, Natasha. I love you," but as he said the words his heart felt like it was being torn in two. He loved this woman who was warm and alive and tender, and yet, he still loved a woman who was no longer alive but whose memory still filled his heart. He had to move on, he told himself. Sherri was gone. Natasha was here and he loved her. Sherri would want him to love again. "I love you," he repeated.

"I don't know, Tony. I just don't know what to feel. Do I love you? But then, should I be allowed to love you? Our number one priority is the mission. We can't let anything take away from our full mind set to accomplish our goal."

"You're right. But then, love can only enhance, not take away."

He pulled her toward him and kissed her again.

Breathlessly, Natasha whispered, "I do love you, Tony. Whatever happens, remember, I do love you. But promise one thing."

"What?"

"Promise me we'll not let it interfere.

"I promise, but on one condition."

"What is it?"

"That when this is all over, you'll marry me."

She looked up at him without answering, her eyes filled with tears. Reaching up, she kissed his lips then whispered with a choke in her voice, "I can't answer that now, Tony. After it's all over—if you still want me—then ask me again."

He gently kissed her lips, and hand in hand they turned and walked back toward the lights and music of the hotel. The cool waves swirled around their feet and the music of the sea rumbled its serenade as the breakers curled and crashed upon themselves. The warm, salt air caressed their bodies. The moon bathed them in its soft silver light.

Finally Natasha broke the silence. "My grandfather thought he was doing right and died doing it."

"What do you mean?"

"Well, sometimes what appears to be evil may not be as evil as what appears to be good."

"What are you talking about?" Tony stopped and turned to look at Natasha.

"Oh, nothing," she said slowly. "Sometimes I just get carried away."

A wave rolled past their feet and they were ankle deep in water. Natasha reached down and in one sweeping motion splashed a handful of water in Tony's face.

"Race you back to the hotel," she said, laughing.

Later that night Tony lay in bed staring at the ceiling. He loved this woman and he knew she loved him. He wanted to marry her but the memory of Sherri still haunted him each time he looked at Natasha. I know Sherri would want me to marry again, Tony thought. But I can't make my mind accept it. What can I do? What can I do?

Chapter 14

VAMPIRE OF PARIS: THE ATTACK

"Ah, Paris," Mac gushed. "City of beautiful women and love just waiting for me."

"Okay, cool it. Let's check in," Tony said. He was tired from the trip and not in the mood for Mac's prattle.

"Yeah, let's check in," Mac answered. "Maybe a beautiful babe heard I was coming and she's waiting in my hotel room."

"Yeah Mac, maybe they read in the paper you were coming. Must be wonderful to be a famous lover like you," Tony said sarcastically.

Natasha laughed. "I don't know what I'm going to do with the two of you."

"What do you mean, the two of us?" Tony quipped.

"Tony's just jealous," Mac said with a laugh. Girls are just attracted to me. They can't help it. You're a girl, Natasha. Tell Tony"

"Like I said. Don't know what I'm going to do with the two of you."

After checking into the hotel and freshening up, they met at a cafe across the street for a cup of espresso. It had been a long trip from Honolulu to Paris, and Tony was trying to untangle two days of flying from his consciousness. At least, he thought it was two days, but at this point he wasn't too sure. Flying east toward the sun shortens the days. The only thing he was sure of was that he was tired. He wanted to relax some before going to bed and at the same time brainstorm a plan for the next day, but his brain wasn't working too well.

Mac leafed through a guidebook he had picked up at the hotel while complaining about getting gypped by such a small cup of coffee.

"Boy, they sure make the cups small around here."

"They're called demitasse," Natasha said. "It means half cup."

"They're kind of mixed up," Mac commented. "They give you a half cup and charge you twice as much.

"Hey! Now this is it!" he said as he turned the page. "Maybe we'll have time to do a little sight seeing before we leave Paris. I'd sure like to see this show at the Lido. Look at these babes!"

"They have beautiful costumes, don't they?" Natasha commented.

"Didn't notice," answered Mac. "I was looking at all the bare tits."

"That figures," commented Tony.

"If there's any possible way, I'd like to see the Louvre," Natasha said wistfully. "But first, we have priorities."

"I'm sure we'll find time to go," Tony answered.

"Hey, how about the Lido?" Mac asked.

"We have priorities," Tony answered with a grin. "First the Striga, then the Louvre and then the Lido."

"Damn it, the Lido should be first. Don't really relish the idea of finding the Striga," Mac said as he leafed through the book. "Wait! Here's the son-of-a-bitch!"

"Where?" Tony leaned over almost upsetting the table, while Natasha grabbed at the cups to keep them from falling.

"Right here. Says, up on the bell tower of Notre Dame are gargoyles and the Striga, the Vampire of Paris," Mac said as he handed Tony the book.

Natasha looked at the book with Tony. "Yes, now I remember reading about it once. Yes, I remember now," Natasha said thoughtfully.

"Hell," Mac said. "Just a stone statue sticking out from a ledge on the bell tower—an ugly son-of-a-bitch, but just a piece of stone. Here we were, worrying about a piece of stone."

"Don't be too sure about that," Natasha said in a low voice. "Didn't you say Father Gorski said he was being watched by the Striga?"

"Yeah," Mac answered. "But the book says it watches over Paris. Gorski's in Paris, so it's watching him."

"If that's true," Natasha mused, "why didn't he just tell us where to find him? The Striga fits in somewhere. Tomorrow we'll go to Notre Dame." She pushed her hair back behind her ears. "Maybe we'll get a clue. But we have to keep on our toes. We think this all somehow fits into our mission but we don't know how it fits. We don't know where the enemy is, or who the enemy is. For that matter, we don't even know what the enemy is."

She took a deep breath and let the air out slowly. "But to tell you the truth, fellows, I don't know if we should be helping this Father Gorski. We don't know what we might be freeing."

"That's right," Mac said, rubbing his chin. "Could be a trap. This weird Gorski guy could be suckering us in."

"Well," Tony added, "I really don't know what I'm doing here. If I hadn't experienced this apparition, or whatever it was, I wouldn't believe it. I still feel like it's some kind of Halloween trick."

He stopped and took in a breath. "But what else can we do? We have to find out what's going on. If our enemy is really supernatural, which I doubt, how can we protect ourselves from something we can't see? What do we fight it with?"

"Oh, you'll see it, all right," Natasha said. "You may not want to see it, but you'll see it. As for how to fight it, we'll have to find that out when the time comes."

"You know what?" Tony said thoughtfully. "If we see this so-called enemy it may be what we least expect it to be."

"Hell," Mac said with a shiver. "'It's all like a bad dream. Wish I would wake up and find myself in bed with a beautiful blond."

"Get serious, Mac," Tony said.

"I am serious. For once in my life, I'm serious. I'm very serious in saying I wish I had never gotten involved in this shit."

Natasha touched his arm. "We're all involved by circumstances. I most of all wish I'd never been involved. I wish this weren't true, but it is true, and much could hang in the balance."

"Remember," Tony said. "Father Gorski said one of our team was with the enemy."

"Yeah, but what if Gorski was the enemy and he told us that, just so we would be suspecting each other and we wouldn't have a united front?" Mac said as he thoughtfully rubbed his chin.

"That's true," Natasha agreed.

"Well, what the hell. Let's hit the sack," Mac said as he stood up. "It'll feel great to stretch out on a real bed. Let's meet early tomorrow morning for breakfast and then head out to Notre Dame to see the vampire." He was silent as if deep in thought and then continued almost under his breath, "Hope that weird Gorski guy doesn't come and pull our toes tonight."

* * * *

Tony was awakened from a restless sleep by the phone ringing. He reached over and put the phone to his ear.

"Hello," he said sleepily.

He heard Natasha's breathless voice. "Tony."

"What's the matter?"

"I'm scared. Something's scratching on my door."

"I'll be right over."

"Be careful. It's in the hall."

Tony dressed and eased open his door. He looked down the hall toward Natasha's door but saw nothing. Cautiously, he walked to Natasha's door and knocked.

"Who is it?"

"It's me. Tony."

Natasha opened the door. "Hurry in. I'm so glad you're here. Please stay with me the rest of the night. I'm sorry, but that scratching completely unnerved me."

Natasha went to bed and Tony sat in a chair. After a while there was a long scratching sound as if claws were being dragged from the top of the door to the bottom. Tony jumped up and ran to the door.

"Don't open it!" Natasha screamed.

Tony flung it open, dreading what he might see. Nothing. He examined the door. There were deep scratch marks on it.

Tony bolted the door and lay on the bed next to Natasha. "Go to sleep. I'm here with you."

She laid her head on his chest and soon fell asleep.

* * * *

"Well, let's hit the road to Notre Dame," Tony said as he took a last swallow of *café-au-lait* and wiped his mouth. "The Metro or a taxi?"

"A cab," Mac replied. "Farmer's paying, so let's not be cheap."

Tony was relieved when Natasha spoke fluent French to the taxi driver.

"I was hoping you could speak French. Sure will help out," Tony said to Natasha as the taxi rumbled along.

"My grandfather taught it to me. He could speak Russian, French, and Spanish, as well as English. We had lots of time on our expeditions for him to teach me. I can speak French, Russian and Spanish, but my Spanish isn't very good."

"I can speak English," said Mac.

"That's debatable," replied Tony.

The taxi stopped alongside the Square in front of Notre Dame Cathedral.

"Well, here we are," said Mac. "Let's get with it."

They bought tickets at the side of the church and started climbing the circular stairway.

"Man, a person could get dizzy climbing these things. All we do is go round and round. When are we gonna get there?" gasped Mac.

"Hang in there, Mac," Tony replied. "We must be almost there."

They soon stepped out into the light. A cool wind was blowing. "Burr," said Mac. "Should have worn my long-johns. Glad Farmer sprung for some warm clothes before we got here. This sure isn't Hawaii. Now where's the old stone son-of-a-bitch?"

"Here he is," Natasha exclaimed.

Extending out over the panorama below, was a figure that was different from the other gargoyles. It was of a semi-human having two horns on top of its head. With his chin in his hands, his teeth showed from a partly opened mouth, as he looked out over Paris.

"Don't know how this piece of stone could fit in the puzzle," said Tony. This is like trying to solve a murder mystery in a book, he thought. But this is real.

"He's supposed to be watching that weird Gorski guy," said Mac. "Maybe he's looking toward him."

"Yes! Maybe that's our clue," Natasha exclaimed.

"Where's he looking?" said Tony.

"Toward that building down there. The sign says Notre Dame Hotel. Maybe that's where this Gorski guy is," spouted Mac.

"Yeah, could be," agreed Tony.

"Yes," said Natasha. "Let's go to the Notre Dame Hotel and see if he's registered. It's worth a try."

"I'll bet that's where he is," said Mac. "Don't know if I want to see him, though. He's a scary son-of-a-bitch." He continued under his breath. "Shit, really don't want to see him."

"Well, we came this far," said Tony as he sucked in his breath. "Can't back out now. Let's check it out. There's got to be an explanation for this so-called supernatural stuff."

Slowly they ambled across the Square to the Notre Dame Hotel. The closer they got to the hotel, the slower they walked. Tony dreaded what they might find there, yet he wanted to get to the bottom of it.

"Okay," said Tony as they approached the hotel. "Let's be on our toes. This is where we might meet the enemy."

Natasha spoke to the hotel clerk in French. After an exchange of conversation, she returned to where Tony and Mac were waiting for her.

"There's no Father Gorski registered in the hotel," she said.

"Good. Let's go to the Lido," interrupted Mac.

"The clerk said there's a place for aged and infirm priests just up the street from here," continued Natasha.

"Well, let's go see if this Gorski guy is there, and then go to the Lido," Mac said.

Standing on the sidewalk at the doorway. Tony rang the bell. The door opened and a nun appeared. Natasha spoke to her in French, she answered then closed the door.

"Well, what did she say?" inquired Tony.

"She said there was a Father Gorski here but he was very old and she would ask him if he wanted to see us."

"I wonder if he's the same Gorski guy," said Mac.

"If that's the same one, he'll want to see us," Tony answered. He felt very uneasy, afraid of what he might find.

"Maybe," Natasha said half aloud.

A little later the door opened and the nun bade them enter as she spoke to Natasha.

"What did she say, Natasha?" Tony asked as they were ushered into a large dimly lit room.

"She said he would see the one named Anthony."

"Oh great," Tony mumbled under his breath.

"How did he know your name was Anthony?" asked Mac. "Must be the real one. Glad he wanted to see you, not me, so have at it. Burr, it's cold in here." He wrapped his arms around himself.

Tony really didn't want to go alone, but he couldn't let the others know he was afraid, so he took a deep breath and followed the nun down a long, dimly lit hall. The nun opened a door.

He stood in the doorway, filled with dread, while his eyes got used to the dim light. The curtains were drawn and only a glimmer came from around them. He could see the outline of a shadowy figure sitting in a chair next to a bed. Suddenly, he was aware of a crisp clear voice in his mind saying, "Come in Anthony and close the door."

What…? What is this? Tony, filled with fear, turned to leave, but the nun was standing behind him.

"Go in," the nun said in English. "He will not hurt you." The nun closed the door behind him.

Tony spun around and tried the door. It was not locked, so he cautiously walked to the chair. Tony was breathing hard and a cold sweat broke out on his forehead. He saw that the shadowy figure was wearing a long black robe with a hood. It's head hung forward. Tony tried to see the face but could only see a dark shadow inside the hood.

"What…what do you want with me?" Tony asked, in a whisper. He heard the voice within his mind again. "Come forward and sit with me."

Tony pulled up a chair in front of him and sat on the edge, ready to run at a moment's notice. "What do you want with me?" Tony repeated.

Tony was aware of the voice again which spoke and yet did not speak.

"I am Father Gorski. I saw him fall to earth. He is here among us. The battle is on. I have been waiting for you these many years. I will relinquish to you the commission. I am old. Very old and very tired. You must take over the battle. You and your two colleagues are soldiers. You must be strengthened to fight the battle."

"What do you mean?"

"You must take my place. My time is up, but I am unable to die until released from the Striga's power. My soul can leave my body but it must keep coming back until the silver cord is cut. It will be cut only when I am released. I made a costly error and have been paying the price ever since."

"No, I don't want to take your place." Tony tried to get the words out but they only came out as a hoarse whisper.

"Remember this. Face Evil and it will flee from you. I was afraid and I turned and tried to run. It attacked and I am its prisoner. You, Anthony, can set me free. Remember, also, that the power of the skull is in the fire."

Tony's breath was fast and shallow. Fear gripped at his chest. He wanted to turn and run but he was trained to swallow fear. He had to get to the bottom of this. He had to know what this was all about. Why did he only want to see me?

Tony swallowed hard. "What do you mean? The power of the skull is in the fire? Explain."

"You will understand when the time comes. I can say no more. But you must set me free."

"How? What do you want me to do?"

"I have been waiting for you since the day you were born. Now you must release me. Let me die."

"Wait a minute. Why should I do what you ask? How will it help me and my mission?" Tony's heart beat in his ears, but he was also starting to get angry. What was this guy trying to do?

"You will receive the commission. In freeing me, you and your soldiers will learn to face the Power of Evil and his minions. By doing so you will be strengthened for the battle."

"What battle? What do you want us to do and why did you choose me?" The drawn curtains moved and he felt a cold draft blow across the room.

"I did not choose you. I was told on the day you were born, that you would lead the soldier who will save the world from the power of the skull."

"What do you mean? Lead the soldier? Look, I need some answers. None of this is making any sense." His fear was subsided and he only felt anger welling up. "Damn it, I didn't volunteer for this. You don't make any sense. I'm out of here." He stood up and turned to leave.

As he did, he felt as if he had walked into a wall. He spun around. Fear again replaced his anger. He was powerless to oppose whatever this was. Was this guy a magician? How did he do all these tricks? But his common sense told him that no natural force could have done what he had experienced—the apparitions and now all of this. He resigned himself to the fact that he had to follow the directions of this man, or thing, whatever the outcome, and hope for the best.

"All right. What do you want me to do?"

"Sit by me, again."

Tony hesitantly sat in the chair.

"Go to the bell tower where the mother demon is eating her child and wait. Go today just before the doors are closed to the tower for the night."

Eating her child? The words echoed in his head. How much more of this can I take? Tony slowly stood up again, gauging the distance to the door. "What do you want me to do there?"

"Just go there with your two soldiers and wait. You will be told what to do. Please go now."

"Wait a minute. If I release you from the power of the Striga, how do I know it's not going to get me or my companions in its power?"

"If you face Evil, you need not fear. But if you let fear overwhelm you, and you turn to flee, it will conquer you."

Tony cautiously backed toward the door. When he got there, he stopped and looked intently at the figure in the black robe and hood sitting in the chair, its head drooping forward. It had not moved or talked, yet it had spoken to him by projecting its thoughts into his mind.

"Free me from the power of the Striga." The voice spoke again, crystal clear in his head.

Tony closed the door behind him and walked down the hall.

"Well, was he really the old weirdo? What did he tell you?" Mac asked as Tony entered the room.

Tony stopped, and stood staring into space. "He didn't say a word, yet he talked to me," Tony answered.

"What the hell are you talking about?" Mac asked.

"From now on we have to expect the unexpected," Natasha said slowly. "The physical world we know and are used to is just one window. There are other windows we're not aware of. We must be on guard. Not only look out for ourselves, but also for each other."

"Damn," Mac said. "I wish I knew what to be on guard for. Tony, tell us what the hell happened in that room with you and the old weirdo."

"Let's get a glass of wine. I need something. And then I'll tell you." Tony's voice was weak.

"Sounds like a winner," said Mac. "Let's go to one of those places where you sit at a table on the sidewalk."

* * * *

Just before five o'clock in the afternoon, Tony, Mac, and Natasha climbed the stairs to the bell tower of Notre Dame.

"Where are we going to find a demon eating her child?" Mac asked. "In fact I hope we don't find her. She sounds like a mean momma to me. I don't think I want to tangle with her."

"I think this is it," said Natasha, pointing to a gargoyle on the ledge across from the door to the belfry. The gargoyle had breasts like a woman but a face like a beast. She was biting into her baby as he was clawing into her arm. "Let's stand here and wait."

After a while the door to the belfry opened and people came out. A small gray-haired man stood in the door.

"I am sorry, monsieur. There are no more tours to see the bell. We are closing."

"Do you know Father Gorski?" Tony asked.

The little man stopped. "Are you the man named Anthony?"

"Yes."

"Then come in with your soldiers. I am Toutous."

They followed the little man into the belfry and he closed the door behind them.

"Look at the bell," he said pointing to a huge bell before them. "It is still rung on special occasions."

They stepped up to a raised section of the floor and walked over to the bell. It was a tremendous piece of metal about six inches thick.

"It takes eight men to ring it. Do you see the platform?"

Tony looked up to where the bell hung from a wooden shaft. A wooden platform connected to the shaft extended outward.

"Eight people must stand on the platform to start the bell swinging."

"We didn't come here to hear about the bell," Mac said.

"Oh…yes…come with me."

He led them past the bell to a door that opened into a small room. "Come in." The only light was through a tiny slit in the wall to the outside. "Come in and I will tell you what you must do."

They entered and Toutous closed the door and bolted it.

"We will need a strong bolt tonight."

"What do you mean, tonight?" Mac asked.

Toutous walked to a shelf and removed a bottle while wiping the dust from it.

"This is a bottle of holy water with seven drops of Father Gorski's blood. You must hide here until tonight and then you must throw the water and blood on the Striga. It is the only way to free Father Gorski."

"It doesn't sound like a big deal. Give it to me and I'll go do it now," Mac said boastfully.

"The one called Anthony must do the deed. Tonight the moon will be dark. You must wait until night."

"Wait a minute," Tony said, catching his breath. "Why me?"

"It is ordained that the one called Anthony must do the deed."

"That's okay, Tony," Mac said. "You and I'll go together. We'll get this crap over with, and then we'll go see the Lido."

"Why can't I do it now?" Tony asked. He did not relish the idea of waiting until night. "We could all go out now, do it, and then we could leave and not have to wait here tonight."

"No, it must be tonight, and you must do the deed alone."

"Wait! Why can't Mac and I go together?" Shit, Tony thought. What the hell is this?

"You must do the deed alone."

"Hold on here," Mac protested.

"Yeah," Tony added. Either Mac and I go together or I don't go."

"Anthony must do the deed alone, there is no other way. Tonight you will all see the face of the enemy. You must remain united and strong."

"Come on, Tony," Mac said. "Let's blow this joint."

He started toward the door and was knocked flat on his back by an invisible force. Tony hurried to his side.

"Are you okay?"

"Shit! What the hell was that?" Mac sat up and looked around.

"Expect anything," Natasha said, her voice shaking.

Mac got up and went toward the door again, and for a second time was knocked on his back.

Mac took a couple of deep breaths that ended with a low whistle. "Shit, Tony. Looks like whatever the hell that was is not going to let me go out that door. Looks like you're going to have to do it alone, old buddy."

I don't want to do this, Tony thought, his mind racing.

"We'll keep that damned door bolted. The son-of-a-bitch won't be able to get in here, and if he does, we'll cold cock the bastard," Mac said boastfully.

The little man smiled and said nothing.

As the shadows of evening closed in upon them, Toutous lit a candle. They sat on the floor and waited. It seemed like an eternity, waiting for the night, while fear clutched at Tony's heart. He felt ashamed to be afraid of a childish boogieman. But this was real. Didn't all these strange things really happen? He didn't know what to believe or what to expect. The icy feeling that gripped him was fear of the unknown.

Finally, Toutous looked toward the slot and said, "It is time. The one named Anthony must now do the deed." With shaking hands, he handed the bottle to Tony, and then opened the door to the belfry.

"Wait a minute." Tony hesitated. "All I have to do is throw the water on the Striga. Is that right?"

The little man smiled. "Yes, that is right."

"Good luck, buddy," Mac said in a whisper.

"Yes, good luck," Natasha also whispered. "Be careful."

Toutous went with Tony past the bell, to the door leading out onto the bell tower walkway.

"You must go alone from here."

Tony haltingly walked out into the night, not knowing what to expect. There was no moon and the blackness seemed to swirl around his feet. The lights of Paris spread out below him like a sparkling carpet, reflecting on the gargoyles. He wondered for a moment about the gaiety and laughter among all those lights. He tried to put thoughts of the supernatural out of his mind, but he was a little boy again, afraid of the darkness and what could be in it.

Cautiously he walked along the walkway, past the gargoyle that was eating her baby, past other gargoyles, toward the Striga.

As he approached the ledge where the Striga was, he heard a barely audible growl behind him. Whipping around, he saw nothing. A cold breeze made him shiver. A low growl again and then another and another. The back of his neck prickled as he realized that the growls were coming from the gargoyles. His breath quickened. He could hear his heart pounding in his ears. He felt like running. Anywhere. Just to get away from there. He forced himself to keep walking…slowly…toward the Striga.

When he reached the Striga, Tony stopped and started to uncork the bottle. As he did so, the growls grew louder. The Striga's eyes glowed red. A hissing sound seemed to come from its mouth. A sickening smell filled his nostrils. He gagged. A gripping horror swept over him. He had never felt terror like this before. He was wrapped in a blanket of dread that seemed to be squeezing the breath from his body.

Tony, soaked in a cold sweat, fought to keep his hands from shaking as he struggled to uncork the bottle. He pulled the cork out and let it fall at his feet. The growls of the gargoyles changed to a chorus of guttural sounds, and howls as if he were being surrounded by a pack of wolves. Drawing all his courage, Tony threw the contents of the bottle on the Striga. As the liquid washed over it, the Striga's hiss became a shriek. Then pandemonium broke loose. The gargoyles filled the air with howling, screaming, and growling. The sound swirled around him. It tore at his eardrums from every direction. The Striga hissed and shrieked. Red fluid that looked like blood puked from his mouth. The bell in the bell tower started ringing.

Tony yelled in terror. He ran toward the belfry. Stone-cold hands reached out. Grabbing at him. Tearing his shirt. He opened the door. Almost falling as he came to the raised floor. The clanging of the bell was deafening. He did not look up at the bell platform, dreading what he might see. He stumbled toward the door. Pounded on it. The door opened. He rushed in, falling to the floor. Toutous secured the bolt.

Natasha hurried to Tony and knelt at his side, rubbing his back. He lay on the floor breathing heavily. Fighting wave after wave of nausea. Trying to keep from throwing up the Evil he felt.

"What the hell is going on?" Mac asked. "Let's get the hell out of here."

"No." The little man was insistent. "We must remain in here until dawn. We must stay hidden. The police will soon come to investigate the noise and the bell."

After a while the sounds subsided and there was silence. Soon there were voices and footsteps as the police searched the area. They didn't find the room. The voices and footsteps faded away and all was quiet again.

"Well, guess we can go now," Mac said, getting up from the floor where he was sitting next to Tony.

The little man stood between the trio and the door. "No! You must remain here until morning. It is safe in here. Wait until morning. There is a hidden stairway that you will use. It enters into the choir loft where you can walk away and no one will suspect anything."

"What do you mean, safe?" Mac inquired.

"As long as the door is closed, they can not come through the door. Wait and be still."

Tony lay on the floor feeling too weak with fear to move. Natasha continued rubbing his back.

Soon there was a knock on the door. "Do not move," Toutous whispered.

No more, Tony thought. How much more can I take?

The knocking became louder and louder until it was an insistent pounding. They could hear hissing and growling while the door was raked with claw-like scratching.

Tony sat up, while Natasha huddled close to him. Mac muttered under his breath and then finally shouted at Toutous, "I think you suckered us into this—you and that Gorski guy. I think you're the enemy. Why are you making us do this?"

"No," Toutous answered. "The ones on the other side of that door, they are the enemy. You had to go through this to free Father Gorski from the Striga so that his soul could leave—so that the silver cord could be cut—so that he could die. But you will have to go through what is to come to strengthen your spirit for you to be able to deal with the spirit realm. You all must demonstrate that you can stand up to evil—that you can face evil bravely. You are not fighting flesh and blood but Dominions and Principalities. You have to deal with the minions of the Prince of Darkness.

"When you leave here tomorrow, you must go to Sacré Cour on Montmartre to refresh and heal your spirit after tonight. It will be a long night. You must be strong and not be afraid, for it is said, "face him and he will flee.'"

The hissing, growling, and scratching continued for what seemed like endless hours and then it was strangely quiet. The four sat on the floor of the small room huddled together, waiting for what might happen next. Both Mac and Tony had their arms around Natasha.

"Do you think they might have given up?" Mac asked.

"No," Toutous answered.

"Well, what the hell you think they're going to do next?"

"I do not know."

There was a soft knock on the door and a gentle voice spoke.

"Tony, it's Sherri. I've come back to you. Open the door, Tony, and let me in. I love you, Tony."

"Oh, no!" Tony gasped. "How can that be her? She's dead!" Hearing her voice hurt like acid pouring into an open wound. He felt as if a cold hand was reaching into his chest, trying to rip out his heart.

"Hold me in your arms, Tony. Kiss me. I'm back. Come to me, Tony. Make love to me. I love you. Please open the door and let me come to you. Please let me come to you."

"Oh, dear God," Tony gasped as he stood up, hesitated and slowly started toward the door.

Just then there was a more mature voice.

"Charlie, it's your momma. I'll bet you've grown up to be a fine young man. Open the door so I can see you. I'm sorry I missed your graduation at the Air Force Academy. Open the door, son. I want to see what an officer and a gentleman looks like. I am so proud of you, son. Please open the door for your old mother who loves you."

"Momma," Mac stood up trembling. "Momma, I miss you so much. Why did you have to go and die?" He stood up and also started toward the door but Toutous ran and stood blocking him.

"No!" he said sternly.

"Natasha."

"Grandfather."

"Bring me the skull so I can look at it one more time. It is so beautiful."

The voices pleaded in chorus, "Charlie, open the door, son." "Tony, kiss me." "Natasha, come to your grandfather."

"Let them in," Mac screamed at Toutous, pushing him out of the way. "Let them in."

"No!" the little man screamed. "Don't open that door!"

Tony, sobbing and trying to catch his breath, saw that Mac was trembling and breathing hard. He heard Natasha crying openly. Finally Tony managed to ask Toutous.

"Why are they with them? Are they in hell?"

"No, Anthony. The enemy knows all of the details of your lives. He can mimic anyone. He is a liar and there is no truth in him. Those are not your loved ones. Stand firm. Do not let him fool you."

After a while, all was quiet again. The four stood huddled together in the middle of the room. Tony held Natasha close to him, she was still sobbing softly. Tony gently kissed her on the cheek and felt the wetness of her tears. He wiped her face with his fingers and in the dim, flickering candle light their eyes met and seemed to give each other strength. No one said a word. They knew that another attack could come at any moment and dreaded what it might be.

A faint green glow illuminated the room. There was a flapping of wings and a large black bat squeezed through the slit in the wall and dropped to the floor. Tony felt a wave of fear wash over him. A second and a third followed. One after another, they squeezed through the slit, dropping to the floor and lining up in a row in front of them. Tony, Mac, and Natasha backed away from them until they were standing against the far wall. The black, squeaking line slowly crawled toward them, dragging their wings on the floor with a scraping noise. Tony felt a dread that filled every fiber of his body.

"No! Do not retreat! Face them unafraid! Walk toward them! Face him, he will flee!" Toutous screamed at the trio.

It was all that Tony could do just to keep from trying to run away, but there was no escape. His blood felt like ice water. How could he walk forward? How could he? He pulled Natasha close to him.

"Do it!" Toutous screamed at them.

Tony took a deep breath. "Now or never," he whispered, pushing Natasha behind him, he stepped forward and slowly started walking toward them. Mac stepped up to his side. Natasha followed. The line of bats jumped up and flew at them. Natasha screamed. The three flailed their arms at the attacking bats. Suddenly they disappeared.

"We can do this," Tony said weakly. "If we stick together, we can do this."

The words had no sooner left his mouth than he felt an evil presence. An unknown terror penetrated his being. The room became cold and clammy. An icy wind entered from the slit and blew out the candle. They were in total darkness. The three huddled closer together, shivering. Their arms around each other.

A low growl, hardly audible, came from across the room. Two red eyes glowed at them from the inky blackness—a low growl again and then a hiss.

"It's the Striga, the Vampire," Tony whispered, trying not to show the terror that was gripping at him. "Face him. Don't back away."

Breathing heavily, they faced the red, glowing eyes.

"You-son-of-a-bitch," Mac whispered through his teeth. He was answered by a hiss.

"Light the candle," Tony ordered Toutous.

Toutous struck a match but as soon as the match lit, a gust of wind blew it out.

Tony's foot touched something on the floor. It was the bottle that had contained the liquid he had thrown on the Striga. He had carried it back with him. Slowly Tony reached down, while still watching the eyes, and picked up the bottle. With all his strength he threw the bottle at the eyes. There was a scream. The crash of glass. Silence. The eyes were gone.

"Light the candle," Tony said once more.

Toutous struck a match and lit the candle. He held it up to survey the room. Shattered glass was scattered around the room.

"Look at the window!" Mac shouted.

Through the slit, Tony could see the first light of dawn in the sky.

"Morning is here," Natasha said with a sigh.

"We made it!" The three hugged each other. "We made it!"

The little gray haired man smiled.

Chapter 15

REVELATION AT MONTMARTRE

The trio climbed the stairs from the Metro, emerging into the sunshine of a Paris spring. They walked up a narrow street of shops to the bottom of the hill. Looking up, Tony admired the gleaming white Basilica of Sacré Coeur as it stood majestically on top of Montmartre.

"Well, this is where Toutous said we should come today," he commented, "to refresh our souls. I wonder…"

"Need more than my soul refreshed," Mac lamented. "Wish we could've slept a little longer. A couple hours aren't enough for a growing boy."

"Isn't it beautiful," Natasha said breathlessly, ignoring Mac, while gazing at the white Romano-Byzantine edifice at the top of what seemed like an endless number of white steps. "Did you know that Joan of Arc came here to pray?"

"Didn't do her much good, did it?" remarked Mac. "They burned her at the stake."

"We mustn't base our conclusions on what we observe," Natasha answered. "There's much more around us then what we can see."

"I don't get it," said Mac. "But then who am I to say. I saw a lot more crap in the last few weeks then I would like to even think about." He made noises like he was counting the steps. "We have to climb all those steps? Think I'll just stay down here and ride on that carousel."

"Dream on," Tony retorted. "You climb the stairs with us."

"Oh, what the hell. Just a good workout," said Mac, yawning.

As they started climbing the steps to the top of Montmartre, Tony chided, "Hey Mac. You can take the easy way on the left. The steps aren't as steep. For old folks like you."

"Bullshit! I'm in better shape than you. I'll bet I could out-climb you any day." Mac raced up, three steps at a time.

Arriving at the entrance to the Basilica of Sacré Coeur, the three hesitated, looking back at the city sprawling before them. What history these old buildings must have seen, thought Tony. Then, one by one, they entered the Basilica.

To their right was a rack with pamphlets written in English, French, and other languages. Tony took one, and was reading it, when he felt a tug on his sleeve. He looked down and saw a little girl of striking beauty. She appeared to be about six or seven years old. Long black hair cascaded down her back to her waist. She had an olive complexion, which was set off by a spotless white sheath that hung almost to the floor. It was secured at her waist with a crimson sash. But it was her eyes that captivated him. She looked up at him with the most beautiful, big brown eyes that he had ever seen. There was something about those eyes that made him want to keep looking into them forever. She smiled at him.

"Monsieur Anthony. Monsieur Anthony."

"What is it, little girl?"

She then started a long monologue in French. When she finished, she smiled again and skipped out of the front portal of the Basilica. Tony stood speechless, watching her until she disappeared into a group of tourists. Mac followed after the child. Natasha's face turned pale and she was visibly shaken.

"What did she say?" Tony demanded.

Before she could answer, Mac returned and said in a loud whisper, "What a strange kid. Don't know what happened to her. I followed her out the door and she was gone—nowhere in sight. She was really babbling. Couldn't understand a word she said. What did she say and how did she know that Tony was Monsieur Anthony?" he said looking at Natasha.

Speaking in a whisper, Natasha said, "Let's go where no one will hear us and I'll tell you."

They went into the knave of the church and found an alcove where they could talk in private.

"This is what she said. I'll try to translate as closely as possible: 'Monsieur Anthony, you are one of three soldiers that are commissioned to fight the forces of the Evil One. Because of what you did last night to the Striga, the evil power of the skull cannot harm you. The evil power of the skull can be increased a million times…'"

"How?" Mac interrupted.

"I don't know," Natasha continued. "The little girl said that the Feathered Serpent wants this to happen so he can fast spread his evil and his master can control the earth."

Natasha stopped, took a deep breath, and then let it out slowly. She was silent for a moment, and then continued. "She also said, 'remember, you are soldiers in a war. In a war there is danger and soldiers on both sides are killed. In this war, if our soldiers are killed, they are not dead. They just go home. The three of you are to be commended for your bravery last night in facing the enemy. Receive today, the peace. Let it fill your hearts and let it refresh your souls. It will give you added strength to face the enemy. Remember, the strength of the skull is in the fire.'"

Natasha took another deep breath. She let it out with a rush of air. "I can't believe I remembered every word she said."

When Natasha finished speaking, Tony held her hands in his, and looked into her eyes, then they slowly walked down the aisle and knelt before the altar. He now knew that it was real—that there was more than just the physical world. They had an enemy that would try to stop them from destroying the skull. But he now felt confidence and peace. Mac stood in the back of the church and waited for them.

The strength of the skull is in the fire. The words kept repeating in Tony's head. Father Gorski also said that. I wonder what it means?

*   *   *   *

Tony, Mac and Natasha sat in the first class lounge waiting to board the plane. "Boy, Farmer sure knows how to do things up right," Mac said as he stuffed a small pastry in his mouth. "Even though he didn't want us to come to Paris, he still didn't skimp. First class tickets, nice hotel, lots of spending money. Even though he's an asshole, he's not a bad kind of asshole."

"Yeah, but have you stopped to think, it's not his money? It's the taxpayer's," Tony answered.

"Well, maybe so, but General Stone sure was not a free spender with the taxpayer's money, except on himself."

Natasha blurted out, "I don't think we ought to tell Karl and the others about what happened here."

"Farmer will think we wasted his money," Mac answered. "Boy, will he be pissed!"

"How can we tell anybody? They'd think we went off the deep end. All three of us at the same time," Tony said. His mind was still trying to sort out the events of the last few days. It had all seemed so simple. Just destroy the skull. But now it had gotten so complicated. How will they try to keep us from destroying it? What did the little girl mean? War? What kind of war? Mac and I are trained for war, but what kind of war is this? Natasha's voice brought him back from his thoughts.

"We can tell him it's something we can't discuss at this time, but we'll tell him about it later," Natasha said.

"Mac and I already told him that," said Tony. "He didn't like it. That's why he sent you with us. I don't think he'll buy it."

"But what else can we say?" Natasha asked with urgency in her voice.

"Yeah, that's all we can do," said Tony. "I agree with you. I don't think we should tell anybody. If Karl gets mad, so be it. What's he going to do, fire us all?" Tony laughed.

"Well, I tell you one thing, I'm ready for whatever the enemy can dish out," said Mac, pounding on his chest. "I wonder what they'll hit us with next?"

"Remember our tactics class at the Academy?" Tony replied. "Find out the strengths and weaknesses of the enemy. Attack in the way they least expect it and in a way they're not ready to respond to. Do you think they'll try that?"

He was quiet as he mulled over in his mind what tactic the enemy might use. He took a breath and continued. "Our enemy knows we're not afraid of a direct attack, so I don't think that'll be their tactic for now. Maybe, for the time being, it will be not to attack at all. Keep us on edge waiting. Then when we're least expecting, come in for the kill, in a way that they think we're not ready for."

"You're right," Mac replied, "But Farmer will be pissed when we tell him all the sights we saw on his budget money. That Louvre was something. If some girl doesn't know what a naked man looks like before she goes in, she sure knows by the time she comes out. Never saw so many statues and pictures of naked people in all my life. I've seen porn that wasn't that bad."

"Damn, Mac. The Academy didn't teach you much class, did it?" Tony commented.

"It's art," Natasha said.

"Well, that's debatable," Mac answered. Then as if he suddenly remembered, "Hey! Speaking of art, we didn't get to go to the Lido," he declared with a wail.

"That's right," Tony replied. "Well, we were too busy trying to get all the sights in and too tired at night to think about the Lido. Sorry, old boy."

"No problem," Mac said with a sneer. "That's okay. One day I'll come back by myself and do what I want to do. I'll see every girlie show in town and become an expert on tits. I'll set up a data base and classify them."

"Time to board our plane," announced Natasha.

As they went past a tray of cookies, Mac scooped up a handful.

"Used to be a boy scout. Always be prepared. Never know when you might go hungry."

"Right, Mac," Tony replied. "Let me know if you ever get hungry on an Air France flight in first class. I'm still full from when we came over."

"Let's go start our eating orgy again," Mac replied. "I'll eat, then dream about all those tits I missed."

"Mac, you are disgusting," Natasha said.

"I'm surprised to hear you say that. You must not be representative of the female population of planet earth," Mac shot back.

"What do you mean?" asked Natasha, visibly annoyed.

"You just have to accept the fact that Mac is Mac," Tony interjected. "You'll get used to him. He isn't such a bad guy."

"Thanks, Tony. Can't help it if I'm a tit man. When I get rich, I'll have a mattress made of foam rubber tits to sleep on at night."

Chapter 16

PREPARATION FOR MOUNT MISERY

Dr. Slaughter, Sandra, Tony, Mac and Natasha sat around the table in the hotel conference room. Mac poured himself a cup of coffee, spilled some sugar from the packet as he tore it open and wiped it off onto the floor. Tony yawned and nervously doodled on a note pad. Natasha sat up straight and proud as if defying the world. Sandra twisted a strand of her hair while looking at her notes.

"Good evening." Aaron looked at the trio from Paris, and with a saccharine smile said, "Well. How was the Paris boondoggle? I understand that nothing was accomplished. Well, that's all right. I understand. While we were working, doing research here, you would have had nothing to do. However, I would rather have nothing to do in Hawaii than nothing to do in Paris."

"Wait a minute, there, Slaughter," Mac said, his voice rising as anger flashed like lightning across his being.

"Do you mean that you actually went there for a reason?"

"You're damned right. We didn't just screw-off."

Tony interrupted. "What Mac means is that we have nothing to report at this time."

That's not really what I meant, Mac thought.

"There's no reason to get angry, Mac," Aaron said. "If I offended you, I apologize. I didn't mean to say anything to anger you."

"That's okay, Slaughter." Mac was trying to control his anger. He hated for anybody to call him a slacker. "Remember, we are not screw-offs. That's one thing we're not."

"I understand, Mac. Just remember that you can look on me as a father figure. You can think of me as a kind of father confessor. Come to me and unload whenever you like. If the world doesn't treat you fairly, feel free to tell me all about it. I'm almost twice your age, and besides, my professional ethics require me to treat everything that you say as confidential." Aaron grinned and continued. "I won't tell Tony what you tell me."

"You know what, Slaughter?" Mac took a deep breath "…well, never mind." He suddenly felt an extreme dislike for Aaron and he didn't trust him.

Aaron laughed. "Please call me Aaron. I'm just one of the team." He paused and then continued. "While you were diligently doing your thing in Paris, whatever it was, the two of us were researching our theory. Sandra, I find, is outstanding in her field. We were very fortunate to add her to our team."

Sandra smiled and twisted her blonde hair tighter around her finger.

Mac felt a twinge of jealousy. He liked Sandra and didn't like her getting so cozy with Aaron. The bastard was too old for her.

Aaron continued. "At first we thought that the conditions at the magma interface we're looking for would occur on the Big Island of Hawaii, but it does not. After much research, it appears that what we're looking for is occurring on St. Christopher Island, also known as St Kitts, in the Caribbean. We think it is occurring within the crater of a semi-active volcano named Mount Liamuiga, colloquially known as Mount Misery." He smiled and winked at Sandra.

Mac felt anger flair up in him again. Mustn't let it bother me, he thought. Need to stay focused on the mission and be on the lookout for the enemy. Don't know what direction he may attack from.

"I know you must be tired after all the traveling that you've been doing," Slaughter continued. "So we will wait a few days to give you a chance to relax and enjoy Hawaii before we leave."

"Great," Mac replied. Time to get to know Sandra a little better, he thought.

"I think we ought to leave as soon as we can. Tomorrow, if possible," Natasha said.

"Loosen up, girl," Mac replied. "Relax. Let's enjoy a couple of days of fun in the sun. Enjoy life while you can." Can't she ever ease up, he thought?

"But we have a job to do, and I'm anxious to confirm that the research is correct."

Tony broke in. "Natasha, let's rest for a couple of days. We may need all our strength for what lies ahead."

"What do you mean?" asked Aaron.

"I guess you're right, Tony," Natasha said, ignoring Aaron. "But I would like to get this over with."

"What do you mean, 'we may need our strength for what lies ahead?'" Aaron inquired again.

"I...I mean if we have to climb Mount Misery, we'll need all our strength," Tony stammered. He nervously broke a wooden pencil in half that he had been fingering.

Shit, Tony, Mac thought. Cool it. Don't blow it now.

Aaron looked at Tony with an expression that said he didn't believe him. He was silent for a moment then continued, "Karl said we are to find this magma interface. After we verify that it is what we want, Tony, Mac and Natasha will obtain the object, transport it to the magma pool and dispose of it."

"Hey, that sounds like what I'd like to do," said Mac. "Climb a volcano in the Caribbean. Glad it's not in Alaska or the South Pole. We can do some diving while we're there."

"Yes, Mac." Aaron said. "I might join you. I'm a diver, too, you know. I have an advanced "C" card. So after we do the task that we've been assigned to, the six of us can enjoy some great diving at our leisure." He scribbled something on his note pad.

Good, thought Mac. Maybe I can drown you.

"The six of us?" Tony inquired. You mean Karl will be able to take time to come to the island and be with us when we do it?"

"Yes, he said he would."

"Good. Well, I'm tired," Tony said with a yawn. "Think I'll hit the sack. See you in the morning for breakfast."

"I think I'll go to bed, also," Natasha said.

"Well, what are we going to do, Mac, Sandra?" asked Aaron.

"Let's go for a walk on the beach," Sandra replied. "The sound of the waves at night is so relaxing."

"I'm game," said Aaron. "What about you, Mac?"

"Hey, that sounds like a great idea. I'll buy that. But Sandy, you sound different from the last time I saw you. Hawaii must agree with you. More relaxed."

"I love doing research, as long as some bastard doesn't screw around with me," Sandra said running her fingers through her hair. "So if you want me to stay relaxed, don't screw around with me."

"You underestimate my personality," Mac replied with a laugh. "I don't think you mean it."

"You really don't want to find out," Sandra said smiling while looking Mac in the eye.

The trio slowly walked along the beach, Mac kicking the sand with every third step, until they came to a concrete breakwater. They silently stood watching the white foam, which seemed to glow on the black surface of the waves as they churned against it. The smell of the salt air, and the rhythmic sound of the waves against the breakwater were almost hypnotic.

At long last, Aaron spoke up. "I'm curious, Mac. Why did you have to go to Paris? If it has something to do with the project, then it has something to do with all of us and we have a right to know."

"Yes, Mac," answered Sandra. "Don't bullshit us. I think you ought to tell us. If there's any frigging danger, then we need to know. Aaron told me about the skull. I know everything. Shit, don't be afraid to tell me."

"What?" Mac gasped.

The wind blew Sandra's hair and she shook it back into place. "You know I'm not chicken. Don't screw around with us. I won't back out if that's what you're afraid of. Besides, I think this is interesting."

That son-of-a-bitch. Mac caught his breath. "Slaughter, what the hell did you tell her for?"

"Look, I think if she is going to be working with us on the project, she has a right to know. Besides, if she knows the parameters, she can do a better job to help us get to the bottom line."

"Yeah, well…maybe you're right," Mac said slowly. "But don't tell Tony you told her. He'll be pissed." He rubbed his chin, thinking. *I wonder why he told her? It's too late now, and maybe it's better she knows. But why is she so calm about all this? I would have thought she would be freaking out and not believing it. Something is not quite right about this whole thing.*

"Tony's a reasonable man," Slaughter said softly. "I think he'd understand."

"Wouldn't bet on it. He's not level headed like me."

Sandra spoke. "Hell, Mac. You must have had a very important reason to go to Paris. I'm sure you wouldn't just up and go unless it was very frigging important. I know you're not a screw-off."

"Yeah, it was very important. You'd be proud of us if you knew what we did." Mac was proud of what they had accomplished in Paris and wished he could tell Sandra.

"I'm sure we would be very proud of you, Mac," Aaron answered. "I think you ought to tell us. If there is something you don't understand, maybe I can help you to understand it."

"No, Slaughter, I don't think even you could."

"So it was something of the supernatural. I knew that it had to be. Remember that this is my field of specialty. I would appreciate it very much if you would tell me all about it. Tony would never have to know."

"That's right." Sandra stood close to Mac and lightly rubbed her breast against his arm. "We won't tell Tony."

"Look, we're taking care of the situation. You have nothing to worry about. We'll tell you all about it after it's over."

Sandra backed away.

"If that's the way you feel about it, I won't press the issue," said Aaron. "I think I'll go to my room. I'll leave you and Sandra to watch the waves in the moonlight. Good night."

A cloud drifted across the face of the moon.

"Well, Sandy," Mac said as Aaron walked away, "We're finally alone together."

"Look, Mac. I like you, but let's just be friends."

"From the way you were rubbing up on me a while ago, it looked like you wanted to be more than just friends."

Sandra looked down and dragged her foot through the sand, making a small pile, then flattening it with her shoe.

"I get it," Mac said. "You were playing up to me, trying to get me to spill my guts."

"Look, there's no place in my plans for a relationship. Don't screw up my big chance. My family didn't have much money, and nobody ever thought I would be able to do what I've done—nobody, except my mother and father. They encouraged me and gave me confidence.

Sandra ran her fingers through her hair, fluffing it. "I worked my ass off through college and graduate school. It wasn't frigging easy, but I made it. I wanted to show them I could do it. I'm very interested in doing research my way, but there was always some son-of-a-bitch to screw things up. I never could get funded to do what I want to do."

She took a deep breath and let it out forcefully. "Now this is it. I can finally make a name for myself. I won't have room in my life for any frigging thing but my work."

Mac stood in front of Sandra. "Look girl. I can relate. You know, my family didn't have much, either. I was born on the wrong side of town. My dad died when I was in high school. He told me just before he died, 'Son, make your mother proud of you,' and I tried hard to do just that."

He looked down and kicked at the sand. "I made good grades in high school and got an appointment to the Air Force Academy by taking a test. My mother was to come to the graduation. I was really looking forward to her seeing me graduate."

Mac looked into her face. Then feeling embarrassed, looked down again and drew a straight line in the sand with the side of his shoe. "'My big boy,' she used to call me. She'd never been to Colorado and I was going to show her around, but she was too sick to come. I was the only one in the class who didn't have someone there at graduation. Went to see her after, but it wasn't the same…she died two months later. Why'd she have to go and do that? Why?"

"Too bad, but that's the way things go sometimes. Shit happens."

"Yeah, shit happens. Nothing I can do about it now."

"What'd you do after you graduated?"

"I thought, what the hell. I don't care if I die. So I went to flight school and did things with an airplane other people would have been afraid to do. In fact, I was so good that when I got my wings I went on to test pilot school instead of being assigned to a squadron. Made a damned good test pilot 'cause I didn't give a damn if I lived or not."

He kicked at the sand again. "But I tell you one thing. While I'm alive I believe in enjoying life.

"Now you take Tony. He had it easy all his life. Everything was handed him on a silver platter."

A wave rolled up the beach and went around his shoes. He jumped out of the way. "Went to a military prep school where all the rich kids go. Had a congressional appointment to the Academy."

He stopped and looked at Sandra. "I really like Tony, he's my buddy and there's nothing I wouldn't do for him. But he doesn't have the experience of having to fight for everything like you and me. Everything comes so easy for him. Why do some people have it so easy and others really have to struggle?"

He continued looking at Sandra. The moon came out from behind the cloud. The moonlight highlighted the gold of her hair. I'm beginning to really like this woman, he thought, and then continued. "But, like I said, I don't give a damn whether I live or die, so I believe in having a good time while I can. Let the good times roll."

"That's a great philosophy," Sandra said. "Hell, can't argue with that. But I do care if I die. I want to accomplish my goal so my mother and father will know they were right—that I could do it." She was silent as if thinking, and then continued. "Hate for them to think I'm dead."

"I'll tell you something I've never told a soul," Mac confided. "I lied when I told you I don't care if I live or die. I want to live because I want very much to be a hero—to finally have everyone look up to me. I want the president to give me a medal. I'm going to make it happen, too. I've put in for NASA. I want to be part of the manned mission to Mars."

"That's wonderful shit. Think you'll be chosen?" Then under her breath—"What a schmuck. NASA will throw rocks at him."

"What was that?" He couldn't believe what he thought he heard.

"I said, 'NASA has some great rockets.'"

"Oh. It sounded like you said…well never mind."

He kicked hard at the sand. "I'll tell you something if you promise not to tell a soul, especially Tony."

"Okay, my lips are sealed," she said with a smirk.

"Well, just before we left to go on this mission, I received word that I was chosen for the manned Mars mission. Haven't told Tony yet. Really don't know how to tell him we're going to have to break up our team at Edwards. Feel real bad, but this is something I want to do more than anything else. I'm going to be a hero."

He stood erect. "I'll be able to hold my head up high before the whole world, and everyone who thought I'd be a nobody will say, 'I know Mac personally.' Yeah, Sandy, I'm going to be a hero."

"That's wonderful shit, Mac," Sandra said with a yawn.

"You see, I clown around a lot," Mac continued. "Do it just to keep Tony from being too serious. Since he lost Sherri he's really been down. Don't want it to get the best of him. In our business, we have to keep our mind on what we're doing. Anyway, just want you to know I'm not really a clown. I'm really serious in what I do."

"Oh?"

"Soon as I get back to the base, I'm going to be transferred to Houston and begin training for the Mars mission." He swung his arms in an arc. "At least, the papers say I'm to report as soon as I'm cleared from my present duties."

"I won't tell a frigging soul."

"Well, anyway, I think you're pretty and I like you."

"You know, Mac, I really got to know Aaron while we were researching. That poor bastard's really a very lonely man. Never married. Devoted his whole life to his work. Damn, he needs friends. I think you should try to be more friendly to him."

"Hell, I'll try to be friends with him, if you really want me to. Only thing is, he's kind of nosy."

"He's interested in you, and all of us."

"Well, maybe so, but he's kind of weird, too. Well, anyway, let's you and I be friends. In fact let's you and I be very good friends."

"Okay." She gave him a kiss on the cheek. "Okay. Let's be good friends."

Chapter 17

THE VOODOO DANCE

As the plane rolled to a stop at St. Kitts, Mac said loudly to anyone who would listen, "Boy, that was one long trip." He yawned and stretched. "I'm off to the beach to take a nice nap in the sun."

He had been sitting next to a developer who wanted Mac to know all about his plans for a spa. Mac couldn't care less and finally just went to sleep while the guy was talking.

The sound of Mac's voice awakened Tony from a fitful sleep. He had been dreaming of Sherri, but it wasn't really Sherri, she was more like Natasha and was holding the crystal skull. He awoke filled with sadness and an overriding feeling of dread. He rubbed the sleep from his eyes and looked at Natasha who was sitting next to him.

She smiled.

Aaron stood up, opened the overhead rack and pulled out his carry-on bag. "Why don't we just relax until tomorrow morning? We can meet at breakfast and discuss our plans."

"Suits the hell out of me," Mac said as he rubbed his neck.

"Wish we could start right away," said Sandra who had been sitting next to Aaron on the flight.

"Damn, Sandy," Mac chided, as he stood and reached into the overhead rack. "You're as bad as Natasha."

"Damn, Mac. How many times I have to tell you, my name is Sandra. But then your feeble brain probably couldn't remember."

"Sure, Sandy. I can remember, but I think Sandy is a cute name, just like you," Mac said with a smile.

"You're an impossible asshole, Mac," Sandra said. "But how can I get mad at you. You're just Mac the asshole, and that's all there is to it."

Mac laughed.

"It'll take a day or two to make the arrangements for Mount Misery. We need the rest, anyway," said Tony.

"Tony's right," Natasha said. "We need to rest so we'll be at our best, both physically and mentally."

"I'll try to locate a guide to take us to Mount Misery," said Sandra excitedly.

"Have at it, babe," Mac said. "I'm going to relax and maybe have some fun tonight."

"Don't think so," said Tony as he handed Natasha her carry-on bag. "We need to get a good night's sleep."

"Damn, Tony. You're just like the rest of them. No fun," Mac retorted.

"Remember, Natasha's in charge of this little jaunt as per Karl Farmer's instructions, and what she says goes," answered Tony.

"Never thought I'd ever have a woman for my boss," mumbled Mac. "But, okay Tony, if it makes you happy, I'll do what the boss lady wants. But only because we're buddies." He turned and smiled at Natasha who ignored him.

What a character, Tony thought. But he knew that he could always count on Mac. He didn't know what the future would bring, but they needed each other if they were to defeat this unknown thing, or things.

After registering at the resort, they retired to their respective rooms.

"That chicken shit Aaron got a room all to himself," said Mac, as he and Tony entered their room and closed the door. "This is one time Karl Farmer screwed up. He couldn't get us each a private room."

"Would you rather room with me, or have a room all to yourself for now, but have Karl as a roomie when he comes?"

"Well, if you put it that way, I guess this is better. I wish they had assigned me to Sandy's room."

"You wish."

"I can dream, can't I? What a waste. Sandy and Natasha rooming together and you and I rooming together."

Tony looked out the sliding glass door to the balcony, nervously rubbing his hands together.

"What the hell's wrong with you now?" Mac asked curiously.

Tony answered, without turning around." I need to talk to someone."

"Well, I guess I qualify as someone. So talk away, buddy, I'm listening."

"Mac, I'm in love with Natasha. When this is all over, we're going to get married."

"That's great! Does she know it yet?"

"Well, yes and no."

"You're talking in parables. Did you ask her or not?"

"That's not the problem. No…just forget it."

"Okay."

"Well…I don't know why I'm telling you this. Maybe it's because you knew Sherri…but I don't know what to do. I'm in love with Natasha and I'm still in love with Sherri. I can't let Sherri go. It's like I'm still married to her and I feel guilty since I have these feelings about Natasha."

"Well, this is a switch. You asking me for advice," Mac said, while rubbing his chin.

"I feel stupid talking to you about this, but you knew Sherri and you're my friend." Tony still had his back turned to Mac.

"Okay, buddy. But I'm tired of hearing this shit. Get over it. So here's some advice from the world's greatest lover. Just don't get mad if you don't like my advice. You have to let go of Sherri. You have to let her go, you dumb shit. A window of opportunity has been opened. Don't screw it up.

"You can still love her memory, but you have to let her go. I know Sherri wouldn't want you held captive by her memory. She wouldn't want you to be alone if you could be happy with someone else."

"But how can I let her go?"

"Okay. Pick a beautiful flower and name it Sherri. We can go out in a boat and you can drop it over the side. As it drifts away say, 'Goodbye, Sherri, I love you.' You can still love her memory, but let her drift out of your life."

"Well…I'll be…I never knew you were such a sensitive person…I always thought that—"

"That I was just a big bumbling idiot?" Mac interrupted.

"No. I never thought that."

"Well, let me tell you something," Mac interrupted again. "Sometimes someone who wants love the most, but doesn't have it, knows more about it than someone who has a love in his life. I may not have one, but I know what makes love tic. You're lucky that you have someone you can love and I think she loves you, too. Maybe someday I'll have…"

Tony turned and stared at Mac, not believing what he was hearing.

Mac continued. "Well, enough of this baring my soul. Forget I said anything. I think I'll lie down a while before I go to the beach." He fell onto his bed and before Tony could finish unpacking was sound asleep.

After arranging his clothes. Tony lay on his bed and he too, was soon fast asleep.

It was dark when Tony was awakened by a knock on the door. He struggled to his feet.

"Who is it?"

"It's Sandra. Open up."

Tony unlocked and opened the door.

"Can I come in? I have something to tell you."

"Sure." Tony flicked on the light switch and Sandra saw Mac sleeping on his bed.

"Well, well. So this is the frigging mister ball of fire himself," she said smiling. "I thought he was going to let the good times roll tonight."

"He talks a good line," Tony said as he shook Mac. "Wake up. We have company." All he could get out of the limp body was a groan. "Wake up," he shouted.

"Here, let me try."

Sandra leaned over him and whispered, "Wake up, Mac. Wake up." There wasn't a sign of life. She blew softly in his ear.

As quick as a lightening flash, Mac grabbed her, pulled her down on the bed with him and was on top of her planting a kiss on her lips.

Sandra screamed and slapped Mac on the cheek. Mac got up laughing.

"Fooled you, didn't I? That'll teach you to blow in my ear."

Sandra stood up, smoothing her clothes.

"I see you don't know Mac very well," said Tony as he let go with uncontrolled laughter.

"Shit. I'm getting to know him a little better every day," said Sandra, who also started to laugh after getting over the initial shock. "Damn! That bugger is fast! I kid you not! Must be related to Speedy Gonzalez.

Came to tell you we're meeting right now on the balcony outside our room. Have some late developments to discuss."

"Okay," Mac said. "I'll be there right after I take a leak."

"Damn, Mac, you are so crude," Tony said in astonishment, yet not really surprised at anything Mac said or did. "We'll be there in a minute."

"By the way. Stop by the bar and get a drink before you come over. All the drinks are free, you know," said Sandra.

"Hey, that's a good deal," Mac said. "Who arranged it? Farmer?"

"That's the way it is at this resort. Everything is included except for what you spend in the casino," answered Sandra.

"I knew there'd be a catch to it," Mac mumbled. "Well, they won't get much out of me at the casino, I never win and I'm a poor loser."

"Well, in that case," said Sandra, "It might be a good idea to stay out of the casino."

"Maybe if you were with me my luck would change."

"Hell, I doubt it. See you in a little while—right after you take a frigging leak."

There weren't enough chairs so Tony leaned against the railing and Mac sat on it while both sipped their drinks.

Natasha started the discussion. "I hated to call you together tonight but, true to her form, Sandra has located a guide who's willing to take us into the crater of Mount Misery. But in order for us to make the ascent, descend into the crater and return before dark, we'll have to leave the hotel at six in the morning.

"I'm rested up, now," said Mac. "We could go tonight."

"Shit, don't be dumb, Mac," said Sandra.

The second floor balcony faced a small lagoon and across the lagoon were the pool, an outdoor bar, and a band. Music with a Caribbean beat floated up to the group.

"I saw on the event calendar that later on tonight there will be a Voodoo dancer," commented Aaron. "I don't know about you but I find that very interesting. I may want to talk to him afterwards. I would like to research the supernatural aspects of Voodoo."

"That kind of stuff gives me the frigging creeps," said Sandra.

"There's a lot of Voodoo in the Caribbean," retorted Aaron. "It's a fertile field for research into the supernatural. It may give me a new insight."

"It's evil," Natasha commented. "You shouldn't deal with evil. We have enough of it to contend with without looking for more."

Aaron replied. "All so-called evil is one. It may have different faces, but all is one. I am researching the supernatural. Who is to say what is good and what is evil."

"What a profound statement", said Mac sarcastically.

"What do you say we go down and get a Piña Colada, Natasha?" asked Tony.

"Aaron and I are going to go down and listen to the music," said Sandra.

"Well, hell. I think I'll go walk along the beach," said Mac.

"Did you know there are two beaches," Sandra said. "One is the Caribbean beach and it's black sand. The other is the Atlantic beach and it's white sand. You can walk to either one. Isn't that neat?"

"Yeah, I guess so," said Mac dejectedly.

Tony carried two Piña Coladas to where Natasha waited for him by the pool. They had changed to their bathing suits in anticipation of going for a swim, but decided not to. Tony handed Natasha one of the drinks and sat in a deck chair beside her. A soft blue glow shown from the underwater lights in the pool. The music softened as it filtered through the foliage behind them. Millions of twinkling stars spread like a blanket across the black velvet sky.

"Isn't this beautiful?" Tony said wistfully. "I wish all of this were over and we would be here together. Just the two of us."

Natasha squeezed his hand.

"I love you, Natasha." Even though he meant what he said, and he did love her, the words sounded hollow to him.

"Aren't the stars bright? It is beautiful here." Natasha mused, ignoring the statement he had just made.

"Let's get another drink and go for a walk on the beach," said Tony. It hurt him that she had ignored his profession of love to her.

When they got to the Atlantic beach, they kicked off their thongs and walked across the soft white sand.

"Don't forget where we left them, Tony."

"Don't worry."

"Look how the moonlight reflects on the sand. I don't think I've ever seen the moon so bright."

The two walked hand in hand along the moonlit beach, sipping their drinks. Once in a while a wave washed across their feet. Finally their footsteps took them to where the beach ended and the waves came crashing upon large boulders.

Tony took Natasha's glass from her hand, put the drinks on a rock, and took her into his arms. He loved this woman and he couldn't let this moment pass without expressing his love for her. For the moment, the memory of Sherri vanished and there was only Natasha. She tried to push him away.

"Please, Tony."

His lips smothered her words. This time she didn't resist. Her arms tightened around his neck and she returned his kisses with fervor. Tony ran his hands up and down the curve of her thighs. It had been so long since he had felt a female body. She had on a two-piece bathing suit and his hands moved lightly across her soft bare skin. He felt for the clasp on the back of her top and unsnapped it. She stopped kissing him and looked up into his eyes.

"Tony!"

The top fell to the beach leaving her breasts exposed in the silver moonlight. A cloud covered the face of the moon and darkness surrounded them. Tony pulled her close to him, bare skins pressed together. Passionately their lips met.

"Tony! Is that you?" The voice was unmistakably Mac's.

Natasha grabbed for her top and Tony helped her as Mac came running up.

"What the hell are you doing?" Tony snapped at Mac.

"I had to tell you. I saw Farmer walking on the beach."

"You're crazy! He'll return with us when we transport the skull here. 'Till then he's up there guarding it."

"No. I was walking along the beach and this man came toward me. I couldn't see his face 'cause he had on a big hat and his face was in the shadow. When he passed me he said, 'Hello, Mac,' and kept walking. I stopped when I heard his voice 'cause it was Farmer's voice. I said, 'Farmer?' He didn't answer and kept walking. I ran after him and when I got to him he said, 'Stay away'. So I stayed the hell away."

"Are you sure it was Karl?" Tony asked.

"Didn't see his face, but I'd know that voice anywhere."

"It might be the enemy," Tony said. "They may be trying to get us to be suspicious about each other—to drive a wedge between us. To split us up."

"How do we know Karl isn't one of them?" asked Mac.

"He may be. But think about this," answered Tony. "If he were one of them why would he raise your suspicions by walking by you and then telling you to stay away?"

"True, unless he's trying to confuse us.... Well, I'm not staying out on the beach alone," continued Mac. "It's almost time for the Voodoo act. Let's go back to the hotel and watch it. You know, I'm getting tired of all this crap. I'll be glad when this is all over and I can relax and enjoy myself."

Natasha stood quietly throughout the conversation, her mouth slightly open.

"Are you all right?" Tony asked her.

"Let's not say anything about this to the others," she said.

After going to their respective rooms and dressing, Tony and Natasha went to the open-air stage.

"Over here. We've saved a place at our table for you." The voice was Aaron's.

"Where's Mac?" Tony asked. "He left with me but I stopped at Natasha's room. I thought he went on ahead."

"Don't know," replied Sandra. "We had a fifth chair at the table but somebody took it when we weren't looking. Guess Mac lost his seat. Shoulda been here sooner."

"Hey guys! Here you are! Been looking all over for you." Mac came barging through the tables and chairs. "Hey! Where's a place for me to sit?"

"We're sorry, Mac," Aaron said.

"That's a hell of a deal! Guess I'll have to sit by myself."

"You see another table?" asked Tony. "Natasha and I'll sit with you."

"Don't see any empty tables. So long, gang. I'll stand off to the side. Better view from there, anyway."

"Natasha, I'm going to stand up with Mac, if you don't mind. Let's meet after the show for a nightcap," Tony said apologetically.

"I'll go with you, too," Natasha replied. "Sandra, Aaron, see you in the morning."

"Okay," replied Aaron. "Sorry you couldn't stay with us."

"See ya," said Sandra.

The three filed through the tables until they reached an open spot near the stage where they could have a good view.

"Thanks, buddy, but I could have stood here alone," said Mac.

"Well, what the hell," Tony said grinning.

"Yes. You, Tony and I, we're like the three musketeers," said Natasha. "We need to stand by each other until this mission is over."

A bare-chested black man walked up to the drums, sat down, and started a slow, rhythmic beat.

Another black man, barefoot and bare-chested, with white pants, walked onto the stage and gyrated slowly with the beat. The voices of the drums reached out into the warm, tropic air as the beat increased. Flickering torches that ringed the stage were the only light.

The drums increased in volume as the rhythm increased to a frenzy. The dancer—black skin glistening with sweat—gyrated and spun in time to the drums. He appeared to be in a trance. His eyes were glazed as a dead man's. Picking up a small torch, he lit it from one at the edge of the stage, and then twirling it, ringed himself in fire. He threw the torch, spinning in the air, catching it again and again. Without missing a beat, he picked up a bottle and put it to his mouth. Holding the torch below his chin, he spit out a column of flame. Dancing to the side of the stage where Tony, Mac and Natasha were standing, he again raised the bottle to his lips. Looking directly at Mac, he blew a column of fire toward him. Mac jumped back.

"Son-of-a-bitch! That son-of-a-bitch tried to burn me up!"

The beat of the drums increased. The dancer furiously whirled and bobbed. Foam dripped from his mouth as a screaming jumble of sounds came forth. But, through the gibberish, clear as a bell, somewhere between the conscious and the subconscious, Tony heard words:

"Fuck you wimpy bastards! You are all dead! Fuck you Mac, you fucking son-of-a-bitch! Eat shit, Mac! We will drown you in shit!"

Suddenly, the drums stopped. The dancer dropped to the floor and there was silence. The three looked at each other, stunned.

"You heard that, too?" Tony gasped.

Mac just nodded his head. In the flickering light, Natasha looked pale.

When the applause started, Natasha said, "Let's go". Not a word was said as they walked back to their rooms.

Later, Tony and Mac stood together in silence on their balcony staring out into the night. A squall was approaching, and lightning flashed across the sky. The strains of Caribbean music drifted on the warm, moist air, punctuated by the distant roll of thunder. Mac finally broke the silence.

"I don't understand. Why me? Why have they singled me out?"

"I don't know. I just don't know."

"I'm scared. Tony. For the first time in my life, I'm really scared."

Chapter 18

MOUNT MISERY

The Land Rover bumped along the dirt road through sugar cane fields, as they climbed to the foot of Mount Misery. Looming ahead was the mountain, an emerald cone rising into the deep blue, cloudless sky. The cool morning air was a mixture of smells. A potpourri of tropical flowers, fresh morning dew and soft breezes from the sea. At the edge of a thick, green jungle, the Rover came to a halt with bump and a jerk. The guide, a Scotsman with a flaming red beard, got out of the vehicle and started gathering the equipment, which he placed in a backpack. He handed a canteen of water to each of the five, and strapping the backpack to his shoulders, took a rope from the tailgate, putting his arms through the coils.

This is all so beautiful, thought Tony. Yet, he was filled with foreboding. It's hard to believe that among all this beauty, evil could be lurking.

"There's a gang of monkeys that live on the slopes. Watch for them," said the guide as he started through the thick underbrush.

The slope was not overly steep and there were so many beautiful and interesting things to see, that no one complained of being tired.

At first Tony was afraid that Aaron would have trouble because he was not as young as the rest of them, but Tony was soon amazed at the elder man's stamina.

At one point, the guide stopped and pointed out some fluorescent orange seeds that were on the ground. They looked like glowing eyes.

"The natives won't come on this mountain," said the guide. "They think that spirits live on these slopes. They call these seeds the spirit's eyes."

Mac stooped to pick one up.

"Don't touch them!" the guide said sharply.

"Why?" asked Mac.

"They're very poisonous. Besides, why tempt fate?"

"Good thinking," Mac said as he stood up.

"Before we go on," the guide said, "Try swinging on this vine." He grabbed a large vine and swung through the air, coming to rest on a rise about thirty feet away.

"Hey, let me try," said Mac, giving out with a Tarzan yell.

"Come on," Natasha called to Mac. "We don't have time for this."

"Killjoy," Mac called back.

As the day wore on, the climb became progressively more difficult. At long last they arrived at the rim of the volcano's crater. A cool wind was blowing, and now and then they were shrouded in clouds.

"We'll rest here before we descend to the bottom of the crater," the guide said as he took a cloth from his backpack and spread it on the ground. "Here's some sandwiches. You'll need the strength."

The crater was about a mile across. Clouds covered the opposite rim. Seven hundred and fifty feet below, the jungle covered the floor of the crater like a green carpet. In several places, steam wafted up through the thick foliage.

"The magma pool is somewhere down there," Sandra whispered.

"How do we get down there?" asked Mac.

"Remember the coil of rope?" answered Tony.

"Hell, that looks like work," Mac commented.

"This isn't Disneyland. There's no ride to the bottom," Tony retorted.

"Does everyone feel they can make the climb down and back up?" the guide inquired. "Remember, if anyone gets hurt we may not be able to get you out."

"Hell, let's do it!" Mac yelled. "Come on everybody! Let's go!"

The first part of the descent was without ropes, holding onto roots and vines.

"Always hold onto two things so that if one gives way, you will still have something to hold onto," the guide warned.

"Don't fall on me, Sandy," said Mac. "If you do, maybe we can do a fast one before we hit the bottom. Just as soon take advantage of the situation."

"Maybe I could frigging castrate you on the way down. Just as soon take advantage of the situation," answered Sandra.

"Get serious, Mac," said Tony, "and watch what you're doing."

After they had descended about halfway, they came to a ledge and rested while the rope was tied off for them to begin their descent. Tony happened to look toward Mac and saw a large, deadly banana spider crawling up the back of Mac's shirt.

"Don't move, Mac," Tony said quietly and with a quick swipe, knocked it off.

"What the hell was that for?"

"Just a banana spider."

"Shit! Those things are poisonous," Mac gasped, almost loosing his balance. "Thanks, buddy."

One by one they reached the bottom and planted both feet on level ground. Wisps of steam rose from the floor of the crater. A thick green jungle loomed before them. There was a strange silence here. On the way up to the crater, the call, the chatter and the screams of many birds could be heard, but there was no such array of wildlife here. This was a lush, green, world, where only plant life grew in wild profusion.

"What is it you want to find, now?" the guide inquired.

"My calculations and research indicate there will be a lava pool here on Saint Kitts," Sandra replied. "This is the only damned logical place on the island for the occurrence. This is the only volcano. Strange, though, I don't smell any frigging sulfur."

"I don't recall, in all my years of exploring this mountain, of ever seeing any lava. I could have missed it, though. I'll take you to some places where the steam is coming from the ground in abundance."

"Okay," Sandra said, "let's go."

Sandra smelled, dug into, and poked with a bamboo pole every likely place that they came upon. Finally the guide spoke up.

"That's all the steaming places. I don't think we missed any."

"Are you sure?" Sandra asked with a twinge of anxiety in her voice.

"I'm afraid so, lass."

"Damn!" Sandra said in a whisper. "Shit! I don't see how I could have made a mistake. Everything pointed to the balanced magma interface being here. Damn!"

Aaron put his arm around her shoulders. "If your calculations show that it occurs here, than this is where it is."

"But it's not frigging here."

"It's got to be here. I'll tell you what we'll do. We can come back and bring sleeping bags and a tent and we can grid this whole crater. That way we won't miss a spot."

"Thanks, Aaron," Sandra said as she touched his arm. "Thanks."

"I can bring you here and come back for you in three or four days. You name it. But I won't stay with you," said the guide.

"That's fine," Natasha said. "When can you take us back?"

"Not before the day after tomorrow. I'll arrange for the sleeping bags and tent. It'll take you that long to get the soreness from your bodies, anyway. But I don't think you'll find what you're looking for. There's only steam seeping up through the ground. Any lava will be deep. Only heat here. You smell no sulfur, do you?"

"We'll find it," said Aaron. "If Sandra says it's here, then it's here. This is one woman who knows her business."

Sandra took his hand in hers. "Okay, let's go. We can come back later."

"Yeah, let's go," said Mac with a sneer as he looked at Aaron.

Going down the slope was much harder than it had been climbing up that morning. The disappointment and fatigue were beginning to take their toll, but walking down a forward slope was very unwieldy. This was best accomplished with the help of a stick but there were still gullies to negotiate and rocks to climb over. Everyone was relieved when they came to the trail through the tall reeds that led to the Land Rover. They collapsed on the grass next to it.

"I don't think I have the frigging strength to get up again," said Sandra with a sigh.

Tony felt the same way, but he didn't want to admit it.

"Here, this will give the lot of you the strength to get home." said the guide as he opened an ice chest. "There are Cokes in here and a bottle of rum."

He was right. The rum and Coke gave them the added boost to get them on their way. The ride back was quiet with few words spoken. After they arrived at the resort, and arranged for the guide to return two days later, they dragged their weary bodies to their rooms.

"Damn," Mac said as he fell onto his bed. "What a wasted day. I'll bet tomorrow I'll find muscles I didn't know I had and each will be hurting. I'm afraid Sandy doesn't know what she's talking about and that old son-of-a-bitch, Aaron, who's old enough to be her father…. Well that bitch is eating it up. He's slick and she's falling for it. Probably won't be long before she's crawling in bed with him. That old bastard."

"Sounds like you might be just a tiny bit jealous," said Tony.

"Hell no. Not me. Right now I'm so tired that I'm going to just lay here and go to sleep. You guys can grid that steamy ass crater. I'll just stay here and wait for you."

"Whatever. But when Sandra blinks those big blue eyes at you, you'll go." Tony noticed that Mac wasn't listening and was staring off into space.

"You know what?" Mac said. "I don't think that spider was a coincidence. Remember the Voodoo guy said they'd get me."

"Maybe it was and maybe it wasn't. Don't start getting paranoid on me."

"It wasn't a coincidence." Mac said as he undressed and slid into his bed, pulling the covers over his head. "Keep an eye out for me. You're always saving my ass. Keep it up, buddy."

"I'll do the best I can. We have to look out for each other and we both have to look out for Natasha."

He was answered by a snore.

Tony crawled into bed and soon, he too, was snoring.

Tony was up early the next morning. "Wake up, Mac. It's time to rise and shine."

"Don't think I can move a muscle. I'm sore from the top of my head to the bottom of my feet and my teeth itch. Just going to stay in bed."

"Okay. I'm going to breakfast. Sure am sore, too. Guess we used muscles we weren't used to. And we're supposed to be in top shape, as America's fighting men."

"Screw the fighting man shit. If we were being attacked right now I'd just let them kill me. It would be the easy way out. Feels like I was shot at and missed and shit at and hit. I now know what Doc meant when he would say on the morning after he had gotten all drunked up, that he felt like he had been hit in the face with a blivit bag—a one pound bag with two pounds of shit in it."

"See you, Mac."

Tony walked out to the open-air breakfast area and was hailed by Sandra and Aaron.

"Tony. Over here," Sandra shouted.

Tony acknowledged with a wave, and after filling his plate with tropical fruit, sat with them.

"Tony, Aaron has something exciting to tell you," said Sandra who was all smiles as she twisted a strand of blond hair around her finger, "Go ahead, Aaron."

"Sure. I went for a walk early this morning—"

"Man! That is exciting!" Tony interrupted jokingly. "How could you go for a walk so early? Aren't you sore?"

"I'm fine."

"Let him go on." Sandra said. She sounded agitated.

"Okay. Sorry."

"Well, I went for a walk early this morning. I met one of the natives and started asking him about the history of the island. He said his grandmother had told him that many years ago, before the ships came from Europe, a strip of land joined St. Kitts to Nevis, another island about a mile away. An ancient city was built on this strip of land and in this city was a temple to the fire god. In this temple was a pool of fire that came from the nether world below. Once a month, when the moon was full, a human sacrifice was thrown into the pool of fire in honor of the fire god." Aaron wiped his mouth.

"One day there was a great earthquake and the city sank beneath the ocean. The native said it's about sixty fathoms below the surface of the water. On days when the sea is calm and clear, you can make out the shapes of columns and arches in the depths. He also said that at night, when the moon was dark, you could sometimes see a glow they say is from the temple of the fire god."

"Don't you see?" interrupted Sandra excitedly. "Don't you see? This could be our magma pool!"

Aaron continued. "The natives say that it is sacred and will not let anyone dive there. However, with a little persuasion and the aid of some green stuff, I was able to find a native who was willing to put his scruples aside and bring us there tonight under cover of darkness."

"Shit, isn't that wonderful!" Sandra said breathlessly. "Damn, don't you see? This is the magma pool!" She grabbed Aaron's hand and squeezed it. "This man is frigging wonderful in more ways than you can imagine. You know, he's not even sore this morning? He's taught me a few things, too, that I didn't learn in school."

"I don't want to hear it," Tony said.

"No, it's not what you think," Aaron interjected. "I've learned a lot about life and I'm teaching her about life and death. About what is perceived and what is not."

Sandra smiled at Aaron.

"Sixty fathoms," Tony said thoughtfully. "That's about one hundred eighty feet. Pretty deep for scuba. We'll have to work out a dive plan and decompression time on the way up.

"Morning, Natasha," he said as she joined them at the table. "Looks like we get to go diving sooner than we planned."

At that moment the sky opened up and a rainsquall blew through. Mac came running through the downpour.

"Son-of-a-bitch! It waited 'til I stepped out of my room to start pouring."

"The rain is early today," observed one of the resort workers.

Tony took a deep breath. The rain smelled fresh and clean.
"Hope it's clear and calm tonight," said Sandra.
"It will be," said Aaron. "It will be."

Chapter 19

TEMPLE OF THE FIRE GOD

The rickety shuttle bus to the Caribbean beach had stopped operating for the day. The only alternative was to carry the dive gear the half mile or so from the hotel.

"Those people thought we were crazy," said Mac as he struggled to carry both his and Sandra's gear.

"Yeah," answered Sandra as she bounced along next to Mac. "Shit, they seemed surprised we were going on a night dive. Don't think night dives are common in this frigging place."

"I understand that when you make arrangements for a dive here, you agree to a time and go to the beach and wait. If the operator feels like it he may show up around the time agreed to, or he may not show up at all," Aaron said.

"Well, I sure hope he shows up tonight," said Tony.

"Oh, he will," said Aaron, pulling something from his pocket. "I have half of a hundred dollar bill here. The native has the other half. He'll show."

"Good thinking," Tony said approvingly. "That's real good thinking."

"Shit, he's really got it all together, doesn't he?" Sandra said with admiration.

"I don't think that's such a big deal," Mac answered.

"Don't you want me to help you carry your gear?" Tony asked Natasha as she struggled to shift the weight of her bag.

"I'm quite capable of carrying my own gear, thank you." Natasha answered.

"Okay. Just thought I'd ask."

"I've carried more stuff than this through worse places."

When the five arrived at the beach, they dropped their bags of gear and their fins on the sand and scanned the dark water for any sign of a boat.

"Well, it's almost time and I don't see a boat," Mac said.

"Give him time," Aaron said. "He'll be here. I'll guarantee that."

"Well, he'd better. After I had to carry all this gear out here," Mac said.

"Does everyone have their underwater flashlights?" Sandra asked. "Check to see if the battery is okay."

"Too frigging late if they're not," said Mac.

"Are you uneasy about a night dive?" Tony asked Natasha.

"Well, after getting to that sub at night, this ought to be a piece of cake. But, yes, I am a little nervous. I'm worried about diving so deep."

"Don't worry. I'll be right by your side," Tony assured her. "Just do what we do and you'll know when to decompress. We'll time it." He was concerned about Natasha. She wasn't experienced enough, he thought.

"Hey, is that light out there a boat?" Mac asked.

"Yeah, I think so," answered Tony. In the distance, a light was moving slowly toward them.

"That's him," Aaron said. "I'll bet that's him."

Slowly the light moved across the water toward the beach.

Aaron signaled with his flashlight and the boat stopped just off shore.

They splashed to the boat, threw their gear on board and climbed over the gunwale. There was plenty of room to move about the boat because it normally carried twelve divers with two tanks each. They were only four.

"I have only one tank for each of you," said the native who was operating the boat.

"That's okay. We'll find out what we need to know on one dive," Sandra said as she squirmed with excitement.

"How far is it?" asked Aaron.

"It is around the end of the island," the native said as he arranged some of the equipment. "Between St. Kitts and Nevis where the Atlantic and the Caribbean meet. It will be calm tonight and the moon will be late in rising, so we may see the light of the fire god."

The native looked at them. "Please do not anger him. It has been many years since he shook the land and took his people with him beneath the waves. Sometimes even now, the fire god shakes the land but it is not in anger. He is only moving in his sleep. Please do not wake him and anger him."

"That's very interesting," said Aaron. "Do you know why the fire god shook the land and took his people with him?"

"I do not know, unless the people angered him. Please do not anger him."

"We will be very reverent toward him. Don't worry," Aaron replied.

"We will not have lights on the boat, so no one will see us and know where we are going," the native said as he flipped a switch and the running lights went dark. The sound of the engines changed from a throaty blub, blub, blub, to a low roar as they headed away from the beach.

The boat plowed through the water, its wake glowing white as it disappeared behind them. Now and then the water flashed brilliant green phosphorescence. The night was dark and the starlight reflected off the surface of the water—a soft, pale glow that was not quite light and not quite darkness. It seemed to surround them, and come from everywhere and from nowhere.

Tony sitting at the stern, opened his bag, and when he thought no one was looking, slowly reached into it and took something out. In the dim starlight, he hoped no one would see that it was a flower. He kissed it and dropped it over the side of the boat into the water. The flower tumbled in the wake of the boat, then floated into calm water. The starlight, for one brief moment, made the water surrounding it sparkle like a thousand diamonds being tossed into the wind, then the flower became a shadowy shape that disappeared into the darkness. "Goodbye, Sherri," Tony whispered. "I love you." His throat tightened and a tear rolled down each cheek.

No one noticed except Mac. He smiled and laid his hand on Tony's shoulder.

Tony went to where Natasha was sitting and sat down beside her. He put his arm around her and she turned and looked into his eyes. "I love you, Natasha," Tony whispered. "When this is all over we'll never be apart."

"When this is over…" Natasha whispered. "When this is over…" she sucked in her breath. "I do love you." Their lips met in a long, gentle kiss.

"We are over the city now," the native said as he throttled back on his engine. Slowly he circled while he looked down into the blackness of the water.

Sandra was breathing hard with excitement.

"It'll be there," Aaron said, putting his arm around her. "It'll be there. Don't worry."

"We're in luck. There it is," the native said as he put the engine in neutral.

They looked down into the black abyss. Very faintly, diffused by the rippling of the water, was definitely a glow from somewhere in the depths. It flickered for a while, disappeared, and then reappeared again.

"Shit! That's it!" Sandra bubbled excitedly.

The native shut down the engine. The little group was enveloped in silence. Only the lap of the waves against the side of the boat could be heard as they fixed their eyes almost hypnotically on the blackness of the water, waiting for the flicker to reappear.

"Look, there it is again," Mac said, in little more than a whisper.

"I'll be glad when it's all over," Natasha said with a hint of anxiety in her voice.

"Okay," Tony said. "Before we gear up, we're an uneven number so we can't use the buddy system. We need to stay close together and keep each other in sight. We each have a chemical light stick." He looked at Natasha. "Just before we go in the water, Natasha, break the capsule."

"You see, Natasha," Mac said, looking at her. "The stick will stay lit long enough for us to make our dive. All we have to do is count the light sticks now and then to make sure that every one is accounted for."

"I'd like to add something," Sandra said. "If there is a temple, we must be careful when we enter. We don't know the physical condition of the structure. Also if we find that gases have replaced the water inside the structure, these gases will probably be hydrogen sulfide and sulfur dioxide, both of which are frigging poisonous. Do not breath it. Keep breathing through your regulator. Also, as we approach the temple, let me lead."

"All right," Natasha said. "Let's gear up. Tony, will you help me?"

One by one, the five stepped off the stern of the boat into the blackness of the deep. Tony was the last to enter the water. He wanted to be sure that everyone was floating on the surface with their light stick glowing. "Okay," Tony yelled, just before he stepped off. They had agreed that this would be the signal for them to let the air out of their buoyancy compensators and descend together, after which Sandra would take the lead.

As the dark water closed over Tony, the cold wetness poured down his neck, filling his wet suit. The only sound that he could hear was the compressed air filling his lungs as he breathed in, and the bubbles of air leaving his regulator as he breathed out.

Tony looked around for the glowing light sticks and swam toward the group huddled together—an island of green light surrounded by blackness. A swarm of little blinking lights that looked like fireflies swam by. Tony wondered what they were.

For anxious moments they waited for the glow of the fire god's temple. Finally, deep below them, a flickering appeared. Sandra immediately started swimming toward it with the group following closely behind.

As they got closer to the glow it appeared to get brighter and keep flickering. Tony thought how moths and other night flying insects are drawn to a candle flame, only to be burned to death. He wondered if the insects were drawn to the candle by the beauty of its brightness. Or maybe they were they compelled to fly into it because they believed it to be a portal into a brighter world of sunshine. A world where there were no spiders or bats to beware of, and only good things would happen there. He wondered if maybe they were like the night flying insects and were drawn from the blackness toward the light of the fire god's temple. He wondered if they were not being drawn to their destruction.

Tony could see that they were now approaching a domed structure. The whole area was lit by an eerie glow that emanated from an opening at the base. There were ruins around the dome that reminded Tony of the ruins of ancient Rome or Greece. Several columns and arches still remained standing, and all but the dome were encrusted with coral. The whole scene was ethereal. Sea fans and soft coral waved among the ruins with each surge of the sea. A forest of black coral filled the bottom of what appeared to be a large amphitheater. All around were pink, orange, and red coral branches. To Tony, it seemed unreal, like a dream just before it turns into a nightmare.

Something moved in the flickering light. A dark shape, with slowly undulating wings, approached them as it weaved through the ruins. Natasha grabbed Tony's arm. Larger and larger the shape became until Tony recognized it to be a very large devilfish, like the one they had seen in Australia. It must have been about thirty feet from wing tip to wing tip. Slowly, it approached the group who had stopped swimming and were now huddled together watching this monster of the deep in awe. Circling slowly, it looked them over, and then with an easy gracefulness, swam away into the blackness. As it swam away, as before, a cold current surged over Tony.

Sandra continued again toward the opening. At the entrance she hesitated, looked in, then swam through the opening. One by one they followed—Tony keeping up the rear.

As Tony entered, he stopped in awe. The water inside was filled with a light that made it look as if it were molten gold. There was a sparkling surface above him and he knew that the dome must not be completely filled with water. Together they swam upward.

Bobbing to the surface, Tony looked around. The inside surface of the dome reflected the eerie light. White stone steps led from the water to a terrace. From the terrace were more steps leading to another terrace. Tony could not see what was on the second terrace, but the light was coming from somewhere on the top.

The five swam to where the steps came out of the water. They sat to take off their fins, leaving the regulators in their mouths so they could keep breathing air from their tanks. Negotiating the steps toward the first terrace was difficult with the heavy tanks on their backs and they had to crawl on their hands and knees. Finally, all safely on the first terrace, they lay down exhausted.

Suddenly Aaron took the regulator from his mouth and said, "We can never make it to the top with our tanks on. If this atmosphere is poison gas, we'll soon know. If not, than we can climb to the top without our tanks."

Tony was horrified. Sandra kept shaking her head and making sounds like, "Urnmro ummm."

Aaron breathed in deeply and exhaled. "This is good air. It doesn't even smell sulfur in the least."

They watched. Tony waited for him to fall over at any moment. Then one by one, they cautiously took the regulators from their own mouths.

"You dumb shit," Mac said in astonishment. "You could have killed yourself."

"Wait a frigging minute!" said Sandra. "As far as I'm concerned, Aaron is a hero. Ready to sacrifice his life for the mission. Shit, if anything, he should get a medal."

"I don't understand this at all," said Tony. "This air is fresh. Where is it coming from?"

"Don't know, Tony," Mac said. "Maybe when we get to the top of the steps we'll see. Okay, Sandy. You want to lead the expedition?"

The five slipped off their BC's and lay their tanks down. Sandra was the first to start climbing the second set of steps to where the light was coming from.

As they reached the top, they stopped. What an awesome sight, Tony thought. The terrace was flat, constructed of black volcanic rock, extending to the wall of the dome. Three quarters of the way to the back wall was a white stone altar. In front of the altar was a golden post with a golden serpent wound around it. In front of the golden serpent was a hole in the floor, about fifteen feet in diameter, from which emitted a bright light. The light slowly changed from a brilliant white, to orange, to red, to pink, and back to white again.

When the light became red, the altar looked as though it were soaked in blood. Natasha gasped.

"You okay, Natasha?" Tony asked.

"I'm okay," she answered.

Sandra slowly approached the hole. "This is it. This is it." She kept saying. When she got to the hole, she stood looking into it while the light reflected on her face.

The rest of the group followed.

Looking down, Tony saw a caldera of boiling white-hot magma. As he watched, the boiling stopped and started to cool. It became a glowing orange, changing to red, which pulsated like a living heart. When the pulsing stopped, a bubble of white-hot magma burst through, pulled the cooler material down, and then boiled white hot again. It then began its cycle anew.

"Shit! I did it! I did it!" Sandra screamed, her voice echoing in the dome.

"You did it!" Aaron added his voice to the echoes in the dome.

"Well, I'll be a son-of-a-bitch. Look at that," Mac mumbled to himself.

Tony and Natasha stood silently looking at the boiling magma, their arms around each other.

"It'll soon be over," Tony whispered to Natasha. She snuggled against him.

"I really don't understand it, Tony," Mac said as he rubbed his chin.

"What?"

"I don't understand how the fresh air gets here unless over the years oxygen was released from the water. That means there's a finite amount of oxygen in here. So we don't want to outstay our welcome or our oxygen. But then, I don't understand why the magma doesn't fill this dome with poisonous gases."

Aaron walked over and stood next to Mac. "Maybe it's just an illusion," he said in a low voice.

"Bullshit. I know what's real. This is solid stone under my feet," Mac replied in a loud voice while stamping his feet on the hard, stone floor. The sound of Mac's voice and his stamping echoed in the dome.

"Maybe it is and maybe it isn't. Things aren't always what they seem."

"Bullshit."

"All right. Let's see how real this magma is," said Natasha, taking a rock from a bag tied to her waist. "This rock is about the size of the skull."

She walked to the edge of the caldera and tossed the rock to the middle of the boiling liquid. The rock floated for a second, then a large bubble of magma tossed the rock toward the edge of the pool and the current pulled it under.

"Well, I guess this is it," said Natasha. "Let's go back to the resort and make arrangements for Tony, Mac, and I to transport the skull here. I want to get this over with. The sooner the better."

"What's the big hurry?" said Aaron. "I would like to do some experimenting with the skull. We're too close to such metaphysical power to just throw it away. There is much to be learned."

"Sorry," said Mac, "but our mission is to destroy the skull, not play with it."

"We'll see about that," said Aaron. "Farmer promised me that I could study the skull."

"It's nothing to play with," said Tony. He couldn't wait to complete the mission so his life could return to normal with Natasha at his side. "We've been commissioned to destroy it and that's what we're going to do—as soon as we can."

"I don't think that's fair," said Sandra. "Aaron has every frigging right to study the skull before it's destroyed. Shit, after it's destroyed it'll be lost to mankind for all time." She looked into the magma.

"That's the whole idea," Mac said sarcastically.

Natasha looked Aaron in the eye and spoke up defiantly. "Aaron, you have no idea what evil that skull is. My grandfather died to save the world from it. Time's growing short. It must be destroyed before the Feathered Serpent returns."

"How do you know the time is growing short?" asked Aaron with a sneer. "We may have a thousand years before he returns."

"We know differently," answered Natasha as she looked into the magma pool. The glow reflected red on her face.

"We'll talk about it," said Aaron smiling. "Let's not argue here. We need to go back to the resort where we can bask in our success and plan our next move."

"I don't really want to leave this frigging place," said Sandra, looking hypnotically into the magma pool. "My theory was correct! Shit, I could just stay here and look at this magma forever!"

"Well, you can stay here forever, but we're going to the boat," said Mac as he started down the steps. He stopped, and looked back at Sandra.

"Come on, Sandy!" he called.

She didn't move or acknowledge.

"Shit, Sandy," Mac mumbled as he climbed up the steps, grabbed her by the arm and guided her down the stairs.

"Come on. Let's get out of here," Tony said. He really wanted to get out of the temple and get the show on the road.

They put on their BC's and air tanks and slipped into the water. Tony looked back toward the pulsing glow just before he slid beneath the surface. *I wonder* what the enemy will try to do when we return with the skull. The closer we get to the end of our mission, the more desperate they'll be to try to stop us. I wonder if there will be any casualties? I wonder how this will all end up?

When they returned to the hotel, Sandra was beside herself with excitement. "I proved my theory," she kept whispering over and over.

Natasha, Tony, and Mac agreed that the three of them would meet secretly in Tony and Mac's room when they got back, to discuss their next step. So when Sandra excitedly suggested that they all have some drinks to celebrate, they pleaded exhaustion and said they wanted to go to their rooms.

* * * *

Natasha knocked on the door and Tony let her in.

"I don't know how we could have managed this meeting if Sandra hadn't wanted to stay up and have a few drinks with Aaron to celebrate," said Natasha as she walked in. So in case she suddenly gets tired and decides to retire, we better make this fast."

"Don't think we have to worry," said Mac. "The way she was playing up to Aaron, she'll probably retire to his bed."

"Speaking of Aaron," said Tony. "I don't like what he said down there."

"Yeah," Mac shot back. "Sounded like a threat to me. You think Farmer made him that promise?"

"I don't know," mused Natasha. "I can't imagine Farmer making him a commitment like that."

"But then," Tony said, "what is Aaron supposed to be doing on the team? He hasn't contributed to anything except to bolster up Sandra."

Natasha pushed her hair behind her ears. "Maybe Farmer thought we might not be able to handle the idea of the supernatural and Aaron was the logical choice to counsel us. He is a psychologist and also well versed in the supernatural."

"Yeah, you're probably right," Mac replied. "But I think he could be dangerous if he wants the skull as badly as he let on." He was silent and then said. "Shit, we should have grabbed a drink before we came up here."

"Well, let's get on with the business at hand," Natasha said, as she reached into her purse and pulled out a slip of paper. "Karl Farmer said to call this telephone number back in the States. We're to say a code phrase, which he gave me, and leave it on an answering machine at that number. The code phrase, Madam

Pele is hungry, will clue him that we've found the magma pool. Madam Pele, by the way, is the Hawaiian goddess of fire that is supposed to reside in the volcano."

"We know that," said Mac impatiently, "but this isn't Hawaii."

"Karl knows where we are. He checks the machine daily and when he hears the code words, he'll dispatch a military jet to come pick up the three of us," Natasha continued, ignoring Mac's comment. "The jet will fly us to the air base. We pick up the skull from the underground bunker and Karl flies back with us. Arrangements have been made with the British Government to enter the air space on the island."

"Well, one thing is certain," said Mac. "If Farmer is flying with us, he'll make sure we're safe. That's for sure."

"Tony, could you make the call later tonight without Aaron and Sandra knowing?" asked Natasha. "We'll tell them tomorrow that we notified Karl."

"Sure," said Tony. "We'll ask the management to use the phone."

"Okay," said Natasha as she gave Tony a peck on the cheek. "See you tomorrow. Thanks."

"See ya," said Mac.

"Wait a minute," said Tony to Natasha. "Come back here."

Natasha turned around to face Tony and gave him a long kiss. "Love you, Tony."

"That's better. Love you, too. Be careful."

After Natasha left, Mac looked at Tony and smiled. "She's a sweet girl, isn't she? You sure are lucky. I'm glad for you."

"Yes, she is, and thanks."

"Wish I had a girl who loved me."

"Hang in there, big guy. You will, some day."

"Not to change the subject, Tony, but I'm kind of worried about that Aaron character. He could cause us all kinds of trouble and he's got Sandy on his side. I think she'd do anything for him. I'd like to show her what a phony he is, then maybe she'd go for me instead."

"You're right," Tony agreed. "In the frame of mind he's in, he might do anything to get his hands on the skull. You think he really wants it for experimenting, or is he working for the enemy? He's complicating things. We'll have to keep an eye on him as well as keep an eye out for the enemy, unless, of course, he is the enemy." He walked to the balcony and looked out. A warm breeze was blowing. It smelled of salt and seeweed.

"Yeah," Mac replied. "We'll also have to keep an eye on Sandy, 'cause she'll help him get whatever he wants. I'll bet she gives him what he wants tonight.

That old son-of-a-bitch. If she only knew how good I was, she'd leave that old bastard alone and come to papa."

"Come on, Mac," Tony said with a laugh. "Come on. Let's go make that call."

CHAPTER 20

THE DECIDING BATTLE

The airplane carrying Tony, Mac, Natasha, and the skull touched down on the darkened runway. A four-plane fighter escort stayed with them until just before they landed on St. Kitts.

The flight had been uneventful, but Tony wondered what the fighter escort could have done if the enemy had really wanted to cause trouble during the flight. He also wondered why Karl had requested an escort. Surely he knew the power of the supernatural. Maybe it was strictly political. He felt very uneasy because everything was going too smoothly. Why hadn't the enemy made its move? What was it waiting for? One thing was certain, there wasn't much time left. The enemy would have to make its move soon.

During the flight, Tony had time to think over the past events. It still didn't seem real to him. His mind could handle the most sophisticated, highly advanced technology, but it couldn't fully accept the supernatural aspect. He kept trying to find "logical" explanations, but there were none.

Natasha sat next to him on the plane. The leather satchel, which contained the drawstring bag, which in turn contained the skull, had been on the floor between them. It was the original satchel and bag that Natasha had carried out of the jungle. She wouldn't touch it. She told Tony she couldn't bear to look at it because of the memories it invoked. Soon after takeoff, she told him to look under it and he had held it up high enough to see the underside. It was stained reddish brown, which looked like blood. "That's from when it was placed on the altar at the pyramid," she said.

Before the three left the base, Karl brainstormed with them on the strategy to complete the mission. He seemed surprised when they told him about what Aaron said, and assured them he made no such promise to Aaron. Karl was miffed when they wouldn't tell him why they had gone to Paris, but accepted the premise that if it were for the good of the project, he would not press the issue.

To Tony's surprise, Karl told them that he would not be able to accompany them back to St. Kitts. He said that something had come up which demanded his complete attention and stated, "I'm confident that the three of you are competent to be able to complete the mission."

As the trio boarded the plane, he shook hands with each of them, thanked them on behalf of all humanity and said he would probably never see them again. He also told them that after the mission, they would be returned to pick up their lives where they had left off. Tony, Mac, Natasha, and Sandra would be brought to a deserted island off the coast of Australia to be "rescued" by the Australian Authorities.

He had assured them that Sandra had a trust fund set aside in her name so she would be able to continue her research. Tony and Mac would return to Edwards Air Force Base. Aaron would return to his research group, adequately compensated, while Natasha would return to whatever life she wanted to live.

It all sounded so simple, Tony thought. We would return to the physical world after defeating the Feathered Serpent of the supernatural world.

Did Karl actually believe it would be so simple? Or did he not grasp the full significance of the whole mission, or of the power of the supernatural? He also assumed they would win over the enemy. But what if the enemy won? The realization of the moment swept over Tony, and he felt a wave of fear well up within him. The final battle still had to be fought. What would it be like? How would the enemy attack and how could they fight back? After it was all over, would they be able to continue their lives as if nothing had happened? If they survived, they would never be able to tell their story. After all, who would believe them anyway?

He looked at Natasha, smiled at her and she smiled back. How he loved her. Let's get this nightmare over with and begin our life together, Tony thought.

The plane rolled to a stop. Tony looked out of the window. All he could see was the blackness of the tropical night. He thought with pride of the technology the Air Force possessed. How the aircraft could land on an unfamiliar landing strip in total darkness.

"All right," the copilot said as he opened the exit door then pressed a button. There was a whirring sound and Tony knew that a ladder was being extended from the plane.

"Where are we?" Mac asked as he walked to the opened door and looked out into the blackness.

The pilot appeared from the cockpit and answered. "At the far end of the runway. You're on your own. Somebody will come to meet you. We're out of here. Goodbye and good luck."

"Let's go, Natasha," Tony said as he felt for the 357 Magnum in his shoulder holster. He picked up the leather satchel and went to the open door. Natasha followed.

Mac, his pistol drawn, was already climbing down the ladder. He stepped off onto the runway and peered into the darkness for anything that might seem suspicious.

"All right," Mac said. "I got you covered. You can come down now." Natasha negotiated the ladder. Tony followed.

As soon as the trio were on the runway, the whirring began again, indicating that the ladder was being retracted. The door was closed and sealed and the aircraft taxied away, leaving them in the dark, alone. Soon, Tony heard the sound of the jet engines increase, as the aircraft started down the runway toward them. Airborne, it sped over their heads, and roared into the dark night sky toward the sea.

"Well, there they go," said Mac.

The words no sooner left his mouth, than a blinding flash pierced the blackness of the sky. A few seconds later, came a noise like a clap of thunder, and the distant sound of the jet became silent.

"What the hell was that?" Mac asked.

Tony gasped. "My guess is, somebody didn't want anyone to know what happened here tonight. That we were brought here and left."

"Son-of-a-bitch! That damned Farmer's playing for keeps! Those poor bastards! He didn't have to do that. I wonder what happened to those guys giving us a fighter escort? Hope he didn't wipe them out, too," Mac said.

"Natasha, you all right?" Tony asked.

She didn't answer.

"Are you all right?" Tony asked again.

"Yes…yes, I'm all right," she said with a tremor in her voice. "But I'm getting nervous standing out here. I'm glad there's no moon, but I wish there were some trees or bushes close by for us to hide in."

"Yeah," Mac replied, turning slowly around, pointing his pistol into the darkness. "I don't like this. What the hell's going on here?"

"What's that?" Natasha asked as she strained to listen. A dark shape was coming down the runway toward them.

"Get over here off the runway and lie down flat 'til we can see what it is," Tony commanded.

Soon he could see that it was an automobile, slowly approaching, with its headlights turned off. It stopped when it went off the end of the runway.

"Anybody out there?" Aaron's voice came from the car.

"Yeah, we're here," Mac answered as he approached the vehicle.

Tony strained to see, and as he got closer was able to tell that Aaron was driving a taxi and Sandra was sitting in the seat next to him. "Where'd you get this, and where's the driver?" asked Tony.

"Hurry and get in," Aaron said nervously.

They got into the car. Tony put the satchel on the floor between his feet.

"Do you have it?" Aaron asked.

"Yeah. We have it," said Mac laying his pistol on his lap.

No one spoke as Aaron turned the car around and very slowly drove down the runway. Finally Sandra spoke.

"Shit! You won't believe this, but Aaron stole it. Hit the frigging driver over the head. Maybe dead. Or worse, gone to the cops." She was breathing hard and heavy.

"I don't think we have to worry about him," said Aaron.

"What is this?" Natasha asked angrily. "You may have ruined the whole plan. What if we get arrested by the police?"

"You dumb shit!" Mac said. "What if you killed the poor bastard? We could all be arrested for murder. If he's not dead then he knows what you look like."

"I don't think he will remember what I looked like. In fact, to tell the truth, I don't think he will ever wake up."

"Holy shit! Why did you do it?" asked Tony. He was trying to process all that had happened and was feeling very vulnerable.

"Karl called me today," Aaron said, clearing his throat. "He told me he wasn't coming and I was to meet you when the plane dropped you off. He said I was to hire a taxi but the driver must not know about meeting you here." Aaron cleared his throat again. "He said that I understood the importance of the mission and what was the significance of one life compared to what would happen to all of humankind if the project failed? I agreed with him." The taxi went off the side of the runway and Aaron swung it back on with a bump.

If the project failed, Tony thought? What Aaron did, certainly endangered it.

"Wasn't there another way to do it?" Natasha asked. She was silent and then continued. "Well, it seems that Karl doesn't put much value on human life."

Yeah, Tony thought. Aaron doesn't either.

"What do you mean?" asked Sandra.

"The airplane we arrived in exploded as it flew away," Natasha answered.

"That explains the flash that we saw. We thought that it was lightning," said Aaron.

"Shit! I'm scared," said Sandra, half to herself. "Damn! What if Karl doesn't want any of us around after this is done."

"Don't worry," Aaron said with a laugh. "Do you think he would have set up that trust fund in your name if he didn't want you to come away unscathed? Also why should he worry if we blab this to the whole world? Who would believe us? We would all be put into an insane asylum for a study on mass hallucinations."

"How are we to get out of the airport?" Mac asked.

"The airport is closed for the night," answered Aaron as they approached the hangar. "There is no one around."

As they turned the corner at the end of the hangar, the beam of a flashlight blinded them. A guard stood in their path.

"Stop!" the guard shouted.

Aaron accelerated and hit the guard, knocking him over the top of the car. He then backed up, ran over him, and then ran over him again as he went forward.

Both Natasha and Sandra started screaming hysterically.

"Shut up," Aaron yelled.

"Why did you have to do that?" Mac yelled at Aaron.

"Did you want to get arrested?" Aaron replied as he drove out of the airport gate and switched on the headlights. "If the police come after us before we have a chance to hide this taxi we'll have to shoot it out. But then, I don't have a gun. I hope you do."

Sandra sobbed hysterically. Natasha tried to catch her breath while Tony sat in silence, not believing what had just happened.

"Let's hurry and dump this thing," Mac said. "It's got blood on it from the guard. Damn, you asshole! You sure got us in one hell of a spot. They'll get us for stealing a taxi and two murders. How do they execute here? Hanging or firing squad?"

When they were close enough to walk to the resort, Aaron drove into some brush well off the road.

"Okay, let's go," he said as he opened the door.

Mac put his arm around Sandra, who was still sobbing softly.

"Are you all right?" Tony asked Natasha.

"Yes," she whimpered.

They abandoned the taxi and cut across the resort's golf course.

"What the hell are we going to tell 'em when we come in at three in the morning?" Mac asked.

"Let's go to the beach and hide in the rocks until people are up and around," said Tony. "Then we can go into the compound and not be noticed."

"Good idea," replied Mac.

"I've arranged for the dive boat to take us to the temple at nine in the morning. We'll just have time to eat breakfast, get our scuba gear, and leave again," said Aaron.

"You sure seem to want to get the show on the road," said Mac. "You given up about wanting to research the skull?" He rubbed his chin.

Aaron laughed. "We'll see."

Tony sat on the sand with his back against a rock, holding tightly to the satchel's handle, his pistol in his lap. He had to keep shaking his head and biting his tongue to keep awake. Natasha sat next to him. She would nod off every once in a while and wake up with a jerk.

Mac stood holding his own 357 Magnum, while keeping an eye on Aaron and Sandra.

In spite of everything, both Tony and Natasha dozed off. Tony didn't know how long he had been sleeping when he awoke with a jerk. He felt for the satchel with the skull in it. It was gone! He jumped up. Natasha jumped up also.

"What's the matter?" Natasha stumbled over her words.

"The skull! It's gone!" Tony exclaimed.

"Oh, no!" Natasha mumbled.

"Mac's gone too! Where are Aaron and Sandra?" Tony couldn't believe that he had let himself doze off.

"Don't get excited. Calm down. I'm right here." Mac's voice came from behind him.

Tony spun around.

"I took it when you dozed off," Mac said with a laugh. "You needed the rest, so I let you sleep."

"Sure gave me a scare," Tony said as he bent down and picked up his pistol.

"What's going on?" Aaron said as he sat up. He and Sandra had been sleeping on the sand.

"Time to rise and shine," Mac answered.

The eastern horizon began to take on a pinkish glow and the water reflected the glow back to the sky.

"What are we going to do with our pistols?" Tony asked. "We just can't walk in with guns in our shoulder holsters."

"Just hide them in these rocks and cover them with sand," said Aaron.

"Oh, no," replied Mac. "Not on your life."

"I have a big purse," Natasha said as she dumped its contents on the sand. "Put them in here."

Mac and Tony took off their shoulder holsters and flung them far into the water then handed their pistols to Natasha.

"Okay," Tony said. "It's light enough now. People are starting to move around. Let's go to the resort, freshen up and go meet the boat. If anybody questions us, we can say we went for an early morning walk along the beach. Don't feel like it, but we have to eat breakfast so as not to arouse suspicion."

"Right on," said Mac. "Let's get this over with so we can get on with our lives. I haven't had my chance to tame the Black Widow. She ought to be ready for us by now. I miss old Doc's boilermakers, too. I could use one right now. Hell, tonight we celebrate. I'll teach these damn people how to make a boilermaker."

After freshening up, they went down for breakfast. Aaron and Sandra were already there. Tony, Mac, and Natasha sat with them. No one was hungry and they just picked at their food. Finally Mac stood up.

"Let's put on our bathing suits, get our gear and head for the beach."

The others stood up as one. Tony noticed that the activity of the night before was starting to take its toll and their weariness was beginning to show as they slowly walked back toward their rooms.

"Aaron. Looks like you've been out all night," said one of the people at another table as they walked by. "What did you find here that was interesting enough to stay up all night?"

"Hell," said Mac. "We got up before dawn to see the sun rise on the ocean. It just feels like we've been up all night."

"Was it worth it?"

"Hell, no. Would rather have stayed in bed. Don't let anyone talk you into it. Believe me."

A resounding chorus of laughs answered him.

"Hi," said Sandra as she walked by.

"Who the hell were they?" Mac asked. "They sure were nosy."

"Just some people Aaron and I met while you were gone," Sandra answered.

When the door to their room was closed, Mac let out a deep sigh. "Son-of-a-bitch, Tony! We are in deep shit! Do you think those people were suspicious?"

"Suspicious of what?" replied Tony. "What would they be suspicious of? They just commented that we looked tired."

"Guess you're right. Getting paranoid. It's just that we could all get hung for what that stupid bastard Aaron did last night."

There was a knock on the door. "It's me, Natasha."

"Okay," said Tony as he walked toward the door.

"Wait one damned minute," said Mac as he hurriedly stepped into his swimming trunks, pulling them up while tripping and fumbling around the room. "Wait one damned minute. I'm standing here with everything I've got swinging in the breeze and you're gonna let Natasha in."

"Calm down. Don't have a shit fit. I won't open the door until you've secured all your equipment," said Tony as he started to open the door.

"What's all the commotion about?" Natasha asked as she walked into the room.

"Just Mac. He gets excited easily."

"I was just thinking," Natasha said as she pushed her hair behind her ears. "I don't think it's a good idea to bring our pistols with us. The three of us will be going into the water and we'll have to leave the pistols with Aaron and Sandra."

"Well, I agree with you but not for the same reasons," said Mac as he rubbed his eyes and stretched. "What the hell can they do to us if we're in the water? Besides, Aaron wants the damn skull before we go into the water. What I'm afraid of, is that the police will become suspicious and search us. If they find guns on us, shit, we've had it, even though the killings were not with a pistol."

"Maybe so," said Tony yawning, "but the police have no reason to be suspicious."

"On the other hand, suppose they search our rooms and find them here," said Mac.

"Why would they be searching our rooms?" said Natasha. "What would they be searching for?"

"That's right," said Mac. "Damn. They're not looking for anything. Guess I really am getting paranoid."

"Look," said Natasha. "Let's make an agreement. If we're threatened by the police and the project is in jeopardy, one of you will have to use the power of the skull to destroy the police."

"Can't do it," said Mac shaking his head. "Sorry, but I couldn't kill anybody."

"What's the difference whether you kill with an airplane or kill with the skull?" Tony asked.

"With an airplane, it's like a video game. You don't see their faces. If I have to kill the cops, I'll see their faces. They'll be real human beings. I'm sorry, but I can't do it."

"Okay," Tony replied, rubbing his face. "I'll do it if it has to be done."

"Let's go," Natasha said as she picked up her bag of diving gear and headed toward the door.

The trio arrived in the lobby ahead of Aaron and Sandra. There seemed to be a lot of activity going on. Four policemen were talking to a group of people. Tony, Natasha, and Mac stood nervously waiting for Aaron and Sandra. When they finally arrived, Tony mumbled under his breath, "Just walk by them as if you don't notice them."

As they walked past the group, Tony noticed that they were the same people who had made the comment about them looking like they had been out all night. The man who had made the comment said something to the police and pointed to them.

"Don't panic," Tony whispered. "Keep cool. Just keep walking." Tony tried to control the panic that was welling up within him.

"Excuse me, sir," one of the policemen said. "Excuse me, sir. I would like to talk to you."

They stopped and Aaron said, "What can we do for you?"

"There were two murders committed on the island last night. We would appreciate it if you could give us any information that might help us."

"That's terrible. If we hear of anything, we certainly will contact you," replied Aaron.

"You sure look like you've been out all night. Your eyes are red," the policeman said.

"Yours would be too if you'd been to the party in my room last night," said Mac.

"Where are you going?"

"We're on our way to diving your beautiful reefs," Mac continued.

"If you partied that much, maybe you shouldn't be diving today," the policeman said.

"No problem," Mac said as he picked up his bag of diving gear and started toward the door. The others followed.

The shuttle bus had just left so they started walking down the road toward the beach.

"Damn! That was close," Mac said.

"Yes," said Sandra, trembling and visibly shaken. "Oh, hell. Don't look now, but a police car is coming toward us from the resort."

The car pulled alongside the group. Two policemen were inside.

"Excuse me," one of the policemen said as the police car stopped next to the group. He stepped from the car and put his hand on his holster. "Come with us to the station. We would like to question all of you."

"Why do you want to question us?" Aaron asked.

"The taxi driver didn't die right away," the policeman said. "Now get in the car, all of you."

Tony put down his bag of scuba gear, still holding the satchel that contained the skull.

"Get in the car," repeated the policeman, drawing his gun. Tony hesitantly put one hand on the side of the satchel. He felt the hard round shape of the skull. Slowly he slid his other hand down from the handle until it too felt the skull. Tony could feel the power starting to surge through him.

"Drop that bag!"

The words had no more then left the policeman's mouth then both policemen disappeared in a flash of light. Smoke curled from where they had been. Tony forcibly pulled his hands away from the satchel and it fell to the ground. Aaron lunged toward it but Mac blocked him with his shoulder and sent him sprawling.

"What the hell are you doing?" said Mac as he picked up the satchel.

Aaron slowly picked himself up as he rubbed a skinned knee. "I was just getting it for Tony."

"Stay the hell away from it. Come on, Tony," Mac said as he held the satchel out for Tony to take.

Tony stood dazed for a few moments, and then slowly took it from Mac. He then picked up his bag of diving gear and started walking down the road.

Looking around to see if anyone had seen what happened, Mac saw Sandra still staring at the police car. "Come on. Sandy." She didn't respond so Mac went back and took her by the arm. "Come on. Sandy. Everything's gonna be all right."

No one spoke for the rest of the way. When they arrived at the beach they silently stood on the sand watching for the boat. The beach was deserted except for two other divers standing about fifty yards away. Finally Aaron spoke.

"Thanks, Tony."

Tony didn't answer.

"I hope the boat comes soon. We don't want any more confrontations with the police," Aaron continued.

"What the hell would they charge us with?" Mac asked. "Vaporizing two police officers? There's no bodies. Nothing except two burnt spots."

Sandra starting sobbing.

"Don't be stupid. Control yourself," Aaron hissed at her. "Do you want to attract attention?"

Mac put his arms around Sandra and she buried her head on his shoulder and sobbed.

"It's okay, Sandy," Mac reassured her. "It'll soon be over and everything'll be all right."

"Is that our boat?" Natasha asked.

Mac looked up. "I think it is," he replied.

Finally, thought Tony. Let's hurry and get this over with. He felt as if all the energy had been drained from his body and his mind.

"Well!" A loud obnoxious voice cut the air as the two other divers approached. One was a fat, bald, middle-aged man and the other was a bleached blond woman with a string bikini. "Well," continued the fat man. "The boat's finally going to come. We've been waiting since eight o'clock. These people here need to be educated on how to read a clock. If I had anyone like them working for me back home, I'd fire them. Are you from America? Where are you from?"

The woman walked up to Sandra. "What's the matter, honey? Your man made you cry? My man makes me cry sometimes, too."

The fat man continued in a loud voice. "Do you know where we're diving today?"

"I'm sorry," Mac answered. "But this is a private party."

"Like hell it is," the fat man retorted. "We're all going diving."

"I'm afraid this is a private party," Aaron reiterated.

"Hell, they won't mind two more," the fat man loudly proclaimed.

"If Joe says he's going diving, then he's going diving," the woman yelled in a screechy voice.

The boat nosed into the shallows and stopped, its motor still running.

"Okay. Let's go," said Mac as he picked up his bag and starting walking toward the water. He looked back at Tony. Mac dropped his bag and went back to where Tony was.

"What gives, Tony, old buddy? You okay? You're just staring into space."

Tony looked at Mac. His mind was still in shock. "I'm okay. It's just…well, you know."

"Yeah, I know, buddy. Let's go and get this frigging thing over with and we can get on with our lives."

Tony and Mac walked together toward the boat. The couple had hurriedly gone to get their bags and were splashing alongside Tony and Mac. Aaron, Natasha, and Sandra had already climbed on board. When Tony and Mac got to the boat, they handed their diving bags to Aaron.

"Let me have the satchel so you can climb on board," said Aaron.

"Keep your frigging hands away from that satchel," said Mac as he pulled himself on board. Tony handed Mac the satchel and climbed over the side and into the boat.

The couple threw their bags on board and the fat man lifted the woman over the gunwale loudly demanding, "Hey! Give me a hand."

"Tony," Mac said. "Here comes another cop car."

"What do the cops want?" asked the woman.

Mac grabbed the woman by an arm and a leg, picked her up, threw her screeching into the water, and kicked the fat man in the face just as he was pulling himself aboard. The man grunted and fell backward into the water while Aaron threw the couple's gear after them. Mac pushed the driver aside and put the boat in reverse. He revved the engine and the boat jerked away from the beach.

"What are you doing?" the native asked.

"You don't want those strangers coming with us where we're going today, now do you?" Aaron questioned.

"No."

After they were in deep water, Mac put the engine into forward gear, turned the boat away from the beach and accelerated to full power just as the police arrived at the beach. Mac gave the controls back to the native and went to where Tony and Natasha were sitting. Aaron and Sandra stood next to the driver.

"Well, Tony, Natasha, the end of our mission is at hand." Mac said with a smile as he sat next to Tony. Tony didn't answer. He just clutched at the handle on the satchel and stared into space. His mind felt numb.

"It's okay. Tony," Natasha said softly. "It's going to be over soon. Thank you for what you did back there."

"Yeah," Mac added. "Thanks a lot for what you did back there."

Tony looked at Mac. He put his arm around Mac's shoulder. Letting go of the satchel, he pulled Natasha close to him with his other arm. "Either one of you would have done it if you had to. It's strange, we're in the business of killing, but when you vaporize two people in a flash of light with a power you don't understand…well, hell. I can't spend the rest of my life thinking about it. We've got a job to do so let's do it and get it over with."

He was quiet as he took deep breaths, and then continued. "We still have to figure a way to get off this island after we do it."

Natasha snuggled against Tony. Then she sat up straight, and solemnly looking at both Tony and Mac said, "Look, I want you to know I love both of you. Mac, like a brother, and Tony, I love you more than you will ever know."

"We're all three going to come out of this okay," Tony said. "Natasha, you asked me to wait to ask you, but I'm asking you now. As soon as this is over, will you marry me right away and come back to the base with me?"

"Yes," she answered. "As soon as this nightmare is over, if you still want me."

"Of course I'll still want you. Why wouldn't I?" Tony said as he pulled Natasha to him and kissed her.

"I'll be the best man," Mac said.

"Well, looky here." The voice was Sandra's as she saw Tony and Natasha kissing. "What the hell have we got here?" she said yelling over the sound of the engine and the wind.

"Don't have to answer her," Mac said. Lowering his voice he continued. "Look. We have to watch both of them. Don't know how Sandy will react in a choice between him and us. Don't think she's one of them but we can't take any chances. That Aaron guy seems to have a lot of influence over her."

"Just the three of us will go down. Aaron and Sandra will stay up here," Tony replied.

"How will we get them to stay up here?" Natasha asked.

"Don't know. We'll have to think of something," said Tony. "Aaron is the one we'll have trouble with. Watch him carefully. He's not going to give up easily. He seems too confident. He has something planned."

Just then the boat made a turn to the right.

"Hey! Where the hell are we going?" shouted Mac. "We're supposed to be going the other way." He got up and walked to where the native was piloting the boat.

"Why are you going this way?" Aaron asked the native.

"I am sorry sir, but I cannot take you to the sacred city. I should not have taken you there before. It is not good. I am sorry. We will dive at a beautiful place that I know of where there are many black coral."

"You're sorry? You sorry son-of-a-bitch!" Mac shouted. "You're going to take us where we want to go. Not where you want to go!"

"Just a minute, Mac," said Aaron calmly. "We need to reason with him. I'm sure that we can convince him to take us where we want to go. Sandra, get me your small bag."

Sandra handed a bag to Aaron. By then Tony and Natasha had joined the rest of the group.

"What's going on here?" Tony asked.

"We are about to reason with the driver of this boat," said Aaron as he reached into the bag and pulled out a pistol. He handed the bag back to Sandra. "Take the other, Sandra, and cover them. I will take care of getting us to the right destination."

Sandra took the other pistol from the bag. "Okay, just go back to where you were and sit calmly. Everything will be all right."

"The pistols!" Tony gasped, looking at Natasha. "How did they get the pistols?"

"My purse," Natasha stammered. "I...I must have left it on the bed."

"Well, we're in one hell of a mess now," said Mac as they went back to their seats. The boat made a one hundred and eighty degree turn and continued on. "But, at least we're going in the right direction, now. Don't know what the hell he's going to do but he's at least getting us to the right place."

"I...am...so...sorry, Tony," Natasha said slowly drawing out each word. "I am so sorry. It was stupid of me to be so careless."

"It's okay," Tony answered. "We all make mistakes." He was silent and then continued. "Looks like the enemy is starting to make its move, and right now he has all the cards."

"Wrong," Mac interrupted. "We have the ace. The skull. You can vaporize them if you want to."

"Mac, Tony," Natasha said softly. "I didn't tell you this before, because I didn't think it was necessary, but the power of the skull will not harm it's own."

"Shit!" Mac said in a hoarse whisper. "Anything else you'd like us to know. It's just our lives you're screwing with."

"Wait," Tony said. "They don't know or they would've killed us and taken the skull. We can bluff 'em."

"Don't know about that," replied Mac. "Why aren't they concerned about us having the skull? My guess is that they know the skull can't hurt 'em and they're just playing along with us. But why don't they just kill us and take the skull? Wish I knew what their game is."

The engine idled and the boat came to a stop. Sandra leaned over the side of the boat, looking into the water.

"I can see something. Yes, this is it," she said, but there was no excitement in her voice.

"Okay. Throw out the anchor," Aaron said, pushing the driver.

The native boatman untied the anchor from its place on the bow and threw it into the water. It hit with a splash and the rope played out from its coil. When the rope stopped, he tied it off and the boat slowly pulled against the taunt rope until the anchor set, giving a slight jerk, then it slowly came around until its bow faced into the current.

"Check to see if the anchor is secure," Aaron barked to the brown man in cut-offs.

"It's secure," he answered.

"Damn you. Go back and check to make sure."

"All right, but I know it's okay."

The man turned and crawled out on the bow. He reached over the side and pulled on the rope. As he did so, Aaron pointed his pistol and a sharp crack resounded over the water. The native stiffened, shuddered, and then dropped into the water with a splash.

"Shit! You son-of-a-bitch! Why'd you have to do that?" Mac jumped up from his seat and screamed at Aaron.

Sandra raised her pistol, pointing it at Mac. Her hand trembled. "Keep it cool, Mac. Sit down until we tell you to get up."

"Sandy, you're not into all this killing shit, are you?" Mac asked. Sandra didn't answer.

Tony was stunned, but not surprised. Damn, he's playing for keeps, he thought. What will his next move be?

Aaron shut down the engine. The only sound was the lapping of the water against the side of the boat.

"Sit down, Mac," Aaron said as he waved the pistol in Mac's direction. "This way, Sandra doesn't have to wait in the boat to keep the native from taking off and leaving us here."

"Oh, no. You're frigging crazy if you think I'm going in," Sandra said rather weakly. "His body's ringing the damn dinner bell. If you're going down, you better shit and get. Ever see sharks in a feeding frenzy? The water churns with red foam. I'll stay the hell here and wait for you."

"You dumb shit!" Mac shouted to Aaron. "Now we're all gonna be shark food."

"Not if we hurry," Aaron said with a smile. "Sandra keep the gun on them while I suit up." He looked at Mac and smiled again. "Better hurry. We don't want to be eaten, now do we? And by the way, Mac, you don't have to shout at me. I can hear very well."

"I'm sick of your disgusting smile and tone of voice, Slaughter," Mac said, while emphasizing each word. "I hate you and you hate me. So cut the crap."

"You have me all wrong, Mac," Aaron said still smiling. "I don't hate you."

"Yes," said Sandra. "Just work with us. We can all be friends. Why are you acting so shitty?"

"Screw both of you!" Mac answered as he sat back down.

Tony sat in stunned silence. Then after regaining his composure, he leaned toward Natasha and Mac and whispered, "Don't inflate your BC. Don't come to the surface. Stay below and wait for me. He might try to shoot us."

"No whispering. Don't plan on any heroic measures," Aaron spoke softly. "We are all in this together, aren't we? We have a job to do. Now let's work together and get the job done."

"You bastard," Mac said half aloud. "We'll have your ass."

"Okay, Natasha," Aaron said matter-of-factly. "You go in first, followed by Mac. Tony you go in last. You're carrying the precious cargo. I wouldn't want anything to happen to it. Oh, and by the way, inflate your BC's. We need to all dive together."

Natasha stepped off into the water followed by Mac.

"Hold on to that satchel. Tony old buddy," said Aaron grinning.

Tony didn't inflate his BC and as he stepped off boat, he yelled, "Go! Go! Go!"

Natasha and Mac began deflating after their BC's as soon as they hit the water and were able to dive, but the satchel pulled Tony back to the surface. Damn, air in the satchel! He partially unzipped the bag, and as it filled with water, dove again. As he was submerging, he heard a sharp report. A searing pain ripped into his right arm. He almost dropped the satchel. Quickly, he grabbed the handles with his left hand. He looked at his arm. A thin cloud of blue was coming from it. Blue—the color of blood under water!

As Tony looked at the blood coming from his arm, he saw a dark shape surrounded by thousands of silver bubbles enter the water. Here comes Aaron, he thought. Mac and Natasha were waiting below for him.

When he reached them, they continued together. He couldn't go as fast as they could because of the satchel's resistance and the pain in his arm. Looking back, he saw that Aaron was gaining on them.

What the hell is he going to do now? he thought. Then he noticed Aaron holding something. It looked like...yes it was! A compressed air spear gun! He must have told the boat operator to bring it! He wanted to warn the others but couldn't catch up. Using his knife handle, he tapped on his tank. The sound of metal on metal pinged through the water. They turned.

Tony thought quickly. Maybe we can surround him, and before he can reload, we can attack and stab him with our knives. He can only kill one of us at a time.

Tony motioned for Mac and Natasha to spread out.

Aaron stopped, trying to guess their strategy.

Tony faced Aaron waiting for his next move.

Aaron didn't see the dark shape rocketing toward him from the purple gloom—the gray, torpedo-shaped body of a huge shark. Just before its massive body hit Aaron, it rolled onto its side and its eyes rotated back into its head—two huge white saucers. Aaron was hit with such force that his tank flew off his back. The shark circled, still holding Aaron in its huge jaws, clamping its mouth and shaking its head. Finally, the body broke into two pieces. The shark grabbed the top half while the bottom half slowly drifted down with entrails following like huge tentacles. Blood, like blue smoke, floated from the open body cavity.

Shit! Tony thought. We better get the hell into the temple before the sea is churning with sharks. Especially with blood coming from my arm. Using all the strength he could muster, he headed toward the temple portal.

Natasha and Mac were also swimming as fast as they could toward the domed temple. They arrived at the portal and waited for Tony, then they went in together.

Surfacing at the steps, they pulled themselves out of the water. After catching their breath, they shed their BC's and tanks.

Mac saw the blood on Tony's arm. "What happened, Tony?" he asked anxiously.

"Son-of-a-bitch shot me. Don't think it did any real damage. Salt water makes it hurt like hell, though."

"I don't have anything to wrap it with," said Natasha.

"It's not an artery. Bleeding should stop when it dries off," replied Tony. "Won't bleed to death. I was worried about sharks…That poor son-of-a-bitch…But, he had it coming. Wanted to kill us."

The adrenalin was surging through Tony's body. He wanted to finish the job before the enemy could block them. He looked at Mac and Natasha. They seemed ready to tackle whatever came their way. He was proud of them. The three made a good team.

"Let's hit it," Tony said.

"Sure you're okay?" Mac asked.

"Yeah. Let's go."

The glow of the magma reflected on the ceiling of the dome, from white, to orange, and then red, as they climbed to the top of the steps. The reflections seemed to transform the dome into something alive, pulsating rhythmically as if it were a living heart.

Reaching the top of the steps, they stopped to catch their breaths. Tony looked across the flat terrace. The glow from the caldera reflected on the golden serpent wrapped around the golden post, making its eyes glow a fiery red. Looking past the post, he saw the white, stone altar, but as his eyes became accustomed to the dim light, he knew that something was not right. "Hold it," he said softly almost under his breath.

"What's the matter, Tony?" Mac responded in a whisper.

"What's that in front of the altar?"

"Don't know. Can't see very well in this light, but from here it looks like a person."

"It's all right, gentlemen." A voice echoed in the dome. "I've been waiting for you. You two men and Natasha have done a fabulous job. You have served him well."

"Hey," Mac said. "It sounds like Farmer."

"You are right," the voice replied.

"How did you get here and what are you doing here?" asked Mac.

"How I got here is beside the point."

Shaken, and trying to comprehend, Tony asked. "What are you, and why are you here?"

"Do you remember when Aaron told you about the patient he once had that was ninety years old and had what seemed to be superhuman powers? Well, I am that man."

"You're crazy, Farmer," Mac said. "You're not ninety years old."

"Karl Farmer is not ninety years old, but then, I'm not really Karl. Aaron introduced me to Karl three years ago, but poor Karl met with an unfortunate accident the same day we met. I traded bodies with him. He didn't need his body and I did. I was then able to leave the mental hospital. My old shell was left behind for them to bury, or whatever they did with it."

The magma pool flickered.

"Aaron knew who I was and was fascinated with the prospect of being with me and studying me. I used him to keep me informed of what the other members of this team were doing and thinking. With his psychological and metaphysical expertise he was very useful. He let me down about why you had gone to Paris, though, but that's a moot point. You're here now, and that's all that matters."

Tony was breathing hard. His heart pounded in his ears.

The entity continued. "I told Aaron about the power of the skull. I promised him, if he helped me, I would let him experiment and do research on it before it was destroyed. Poor Aaron. He really expected me to let him touch the skull. I had to send our little friend to dispose of him. He was getting rather bothersome."

"You son-of-a-bitch," Mac said, his voice quivering, sounding as if he were about to explode into a burst of fury.

"Keep calm, Mac," Tony said touching Mac's arm and feeling the muscles flex.

"You know, Mac," the voice continued. "We really didn't expect you to pass the test when you held the skull. We fully expected to have to kill you. Then Tony would have been very fervent in wanting to destroy the skull, and would have worked even harder for our cause."

"You frigging bastard. You wanted to kill me." Mac's voice trembled in anger.

"Stay calm, Mac," Tony said slowly. He was also trying desperately to restrain himself. "Don't let blind anger play into his hands."

Then Tony continued, speaking to the entity at the altar. "What the hell do you mean, work harder for your cause? I never have and never will work for your cause. Destroy the skull? Yes, we're going to do that. But work for you? Never! You son-of-a-bitch."

"You stupid..." the entity on the alter replied. "You stupid, pathetic mortal. How could you be so stupid? You still don't see it, do you?"

After pausing a few moments to compose himself. Tony asked the entity, "Who the hell are you?"

"My master is Quetzalcoatl, the Feathered Serpent. He sent his minions to retrieve the Crystal Skull. They found the pyramid empty. Natasha's grandfather had retrieved it, and so the skull was conveniently delivered into my hands. Now that we have found the temple, I will be the one to deliver it to my master, one of the chief princes. I will be given power and prestige."

"Did Natasha's grandfather know who you were and why you wanted the skull?" asked Tony still holding tightly to the handle on the satchel while his other hand pulled Natasha closer to him. At the same time, the three of them walked slowly toward the caldera and the magma pool.

"No. All he wanted to do was destroy it."

"Well, that's exactly what we're going to do," said Mac.

"Come here and give it to us," said the entity, his voice changing as he spoke so that he sounded as if a chorus of voices were speaking.

"Screw you, you son-of-a-bitch," shouted Mac. "We can destroy you. We can vaporize you as we did those two guys on the island."

The figure at the alter laughed with the chorus of voices. "The skull cannot hurt one of its own. You cannot hurt me with its power.

"Natasha, faithful servant of Quetzalcoatl, bring the skull to me."

Tony dropped his arm from around Natasha and stepped back. Words choked in his throat.

"Natasha, are you one of them?"

"Listen to me, Tony."

A chill rolled over Tony's body. His throat seemed paralyzed. In utter disbelief he looked at Natasha while trying to catch his breath. Finally he was able to get the words out. "You…you made believe…you loved me…to sucker me in?"

"Tony, listen to me. I do love you. I do love you, Tony."

"No…no…no…" Tony's voice trailed off into silence.

"Please Tony. Please listen to me. When my grandfather died I didn't want to destroy something as beautiful as the skull. My grandfather had given his life for it. Karl told me that the power of the skull could do so much good. In the hands of Quetzalcoatl it could keep the world from ever going to war again. It would be able to cure disease and stop hunger in the world."

"Yeah. Right," interrupted Mac, who had up to now been listening in shocked silence.

"Tony, we had to make you believe we wanted you to destroy the skull," continued Natasha, "so you would help deliver it into the hands of Quetzalcoatl. His temple had a fire pool in it. We needed you to help us find his temple. We needed you to help us deliver it to him, because there were forces trying to stop us."

"Damn, Natasha!" Mac said, slamming his fist into the palm of his hand. "Damn! You suckered us in and Tony loved you."

"Tony, listen to me," pleaded Natasha.

Tony's lips were moving but no words were coming from his mouth.

"I believed him until we went to Paris. I realized then, the skull was evil and its power could never be used for good. It was then I realized I was on the wrong side."

Natasha sobbed and continued, her voice trembling. "Don't you remember? You, Mac, and I were confirmed while we were in Paris as the three solders to fight against evil. I love you, Tony. I really do love you."

In the flicker of the pool, Tony could see tears glistening on her cheeks. "Why…why didn't you tell me before?"

"I was afraid you wouldn't love me."

"Wouldn't love you?"

"Why did Farmer bring us here?" Mac asked. "Why go through all the trouble to bring us to the brink of destroying the skull? All we have to do is throw it into the caldera and it's gone."

"I don't know," Natasha answered wiping her eyes. "I don't know."

"You are a traitor, Natasha," the voices spoke from Farmers mouth. "Enough of this. Because you have been unfaithful to the Feathered Serpent, you must suffer. You will see your lover die."

The entity lifted a spear gun and let fly a spear toward Tony. Before Tony knew what was happening, Natasha threw herself in front of him and the spear embedded itself deep into her chest with a hollow thud. Tony dropped the satchel and grabbed her as she sank to the ground.

"Natasha," Tony screamed.

"I love you. Tony," she whispered. There was a gurgling sound and she lay limp in his arms.

A flood of anguish, disbelief, hopelessness, and horror tore through him, drowning him in its bottomless depths. A sound left his lips—the sound of a soul in utter despair. It echoed and swirled within the confines of the dome. "N0000000000…"

Mac stood watching, and then his body trembled with rage. "You son-of-a-bitch! You fucking bastard!" he screamed. "You'll never get this skull, you son-of-a-bitch!" He ran to where Tony had dropped the satchel and scooped it up.

The voices laughed, each seemingly trying to out laugh the other. Diabolical laughter filled the temple, echoing, swirling and rolling around the dome.

"Try and stop me, you fucking bastard! I'll destroy the skull and then I'll come over there and kill you!" Mac screamed.

"Go ahead," answered some of the voices, while the rest continued laughing.

Just then Mac stiffened. "The power of the skull is in the fire," he whispered.

"Wait!" he said in a loud voice. "How could I be so stupid? The power of the skull is in the fire! That's why Farmer wanted us to find a lava pool to throw the skull into. He knew this temple was around somewhere and he sent us to recruit Sandra to find it."

"You are very intelligent," the entity interrupted. "You are correct. This is the temple of the Feathered Serpent. When the skull is thrown into the lava it's power will be increased a million fold. The temple will rise above the water and this is where the Feathered Serpent will make his home."

Laughter swirled around the temple again.

The voices continued. "From it Quetzalcoatl will rule the world as one of the princes. This altar will become a throne, directing the power of the Feathered Serpent's thoughts to the skull which will fill the lava pool and derive its power from the inferno."

The lava pool flashed and flickered brighter as the entity spoke. "He has lost one battle with Michael and has been cast from his rightful domain, but he is claiming the earth. He will rule through the Feathered Serpent."

The voices laughed and screamed in a cacophony of sound and then they became silent. A sound like a howling wind filled the dome.

The entity continued. "Here he will assemble an army. The Feathered Serpent has already returned and is waiting. He is already gathering his faithful who will rule with him when he comes into his power."

The pool belched a bubble of white-hot lava. "You cannot cause the skull to hurt me, so you might as well throw the skull into the fiery pit."

Mac stood motionless, listening to the entity. Then, he slowly opened the satchel and removed the skull. His hands closed around it. "Maybe it won't hurt you but I can make it hurt itself. Gonna focus the power of the skull on itself. It's gonna short circuit. Get out of here, Tony! Run! Dive into the water and get out of here! Hurry, Tony!"

Through the haze of grief, Tony heard Mac as though he were far away. He realized what was happening but he had lost all will to live. His body and soul were numb. All he wanted was to hold Natasha, to never let her go.

Mac held the skull close to his face. "Kiss your ass goodbye," he whispered to the skull. The skull started pulsating with a bright, blood red glow, harder and faster as a heart filled with terror.

"No!" The voices screamed in horror. "No! No!"

Tony felt himself being lifted through the air. He felt the cold water close around him. He was propelled toward the exit and pushed through the portal. Air expanding in his lungs boiled from his mouth as he was thrust toward the surface. His body screamed for oxygen. There was a blinding white flash and then oblivion.

Chapter 21

THE AFTERMATH

Tony tried to focus his eyes. He was in a bed in a small room. Someone was seated in a chair next to him. Straining to see, he recognized Sandra. "Where am I? What happened?" The words came out in a throaty whisper.

"It's okay. You'll be all right. Been a volcanic eruption. The damn boat was blown in the air." Sandra made an upward motion with her hands. "It sank. Saw you floating. Shit, thought you were dead, but slipped my life jacket on you. I swam and swam, dragging you along. Finally, somehow we were washed up on the beach."

She smiled broadly. "Should be given a medal, shouldn't I? Saved your ass."

"Anyone…anyone else?"

"Nope. Not even bodies."

"They're gone." Tears filled his eyes.

"I'd better get the nurse. They told me when you came to, I was to call them."

She got up to leave the room then stopped and came back to the bed. "The crystal skull. Did you destroy it?"

Tony tried to answer her but was too weak to form the words.

"Can't understand you. If you destroyed the skull, just nod your head."

Tony slowly nodded his head.

"Good! Mission accomplished! Can't wait to start collecting my damn trust fund. Guess I'd better get the nurse so we can get you well. The sooner we get your ass well the sooner I can start my research," Sandra said as she started to walk out of the room. She stopped at the door and looked back. "Don't worry about the frigging police. They're really confused. You know, the disappearance of the two cops with burnt spots and the volcanic eruption. They wouldn't know who to charge with what." Sandra left the room humming to herself.

Tony lay quietly, too weak to move. All he could do was breathe and even that was an effort. As his head began to clear, the memory of that day in Paris, when he and Natasha and Mac stood in the vestibule of the Basilica of Sacré Coeur on Montmartre, came back to him. The memory was so vivid that he could almost feel Natasha's hand in his.

"Why? Why did this have to happen?" Tony mumbled. He remembered the "little girl" as she jabbered to Natasha in French. He recalled the words that Natasha had translated for them. "Because of what you did last night to the Striga, the evil power of the skull cannot harm you." A sudden realization came to him. How could I have been so stupid? he thought. That's why I didn't get the bends when I came up. I could have done what Mac did while they stayed behind. I wouldn't have been killed and they would have been safe. What a stupid fool I am.

Tony sobbed uncontrollably.

When he was able to think clearly again, his mind wandered to a statement that the entity had made. He wondered what it had meant when it said that if Mac had been killed I would have worked harder for the cause?

Of course! I would have tried harder to find the magma pool and throw the skull into it to avenge Mac's death. I would have worked for the entity without realizing it.

How did our lives get so tangled up in all this? Tony thought. We all came from such different places and circumstances. Yet our lives all intersected at one point in time and space.

I must have been the backup for Father Gorski when he turned and tried to run from the enemy. He was captured by the Striga and I was recruited to free him from its power. Mac must have been the back up for me as I dropped the skull when Natasha was dying. I guess all good strategy for wars must have back up contingencies.

Then Tony remembered what Father Gorski said to him, "You will lead the soldier who will save the world from the power of the skull."

I didn't have to lead him. Mac took the lead. I wonder if maybe Mac was Father Gorski's backup and not I. Why wasn't Mac chosen to do the deed that freed Father Gorski?

When push came to shove, Mac did what he had to do. Mac was a hero…but who will ever know?"

It seemed as if he could hear Natasha's voice as she continued the translation that day on Montmartre. "Remember, you are soldiers in a war. In a war there is danger and soldiers on both sides get killed. In this war, when our soldiers are killed, they are not dead. They just go home."

Montmartre, Tony thought. Doesn't it mean mountain of the martyrs? Natasha and Mac certainly were martyrs.

Tony realized that Natasha and Tony were really gone and a wave of grief surged over him. "I'll miss you, Mac, old buddy," he whispered. He took a deep breath. "I love you, Natasha."

He seemed to hear Natasha answer, "I love you, too." Grief surged over him again like a monstrous breaker, cresting and crashing down on him, tossing, shaking, and rolling his soul in agony. His body couldn't find the strength to sob any longer. In his exhaustion he closed his eyes and drifted into a dreamless sleep.

CHAPTER 22

RETURN TO THE ISLAND

The submarine skipper handed Tony a white canvas bag.

"These are the bathing suits you wore the night you were picked up in these same waters", he said. "An expert with the CIA chemically aged them to look like you had been wearing them in the elements continuously since then."

Tony loosened the drawstring and looked inside. He pulled out a pair of briefs, recognized them as Mac's and dropped them back. Pulling out a women's top, he handed it to Sandra. Groping around, he located the matching bottom. "Here, this is yours." He pulled out another—the one Natasha had worn. Holding it tenderly, he slowly felt it between his fingers, then dropped it back into the bag and pulled out his own trunks.

"Change into them and meet me topside," the skipper continued. "We'll have a Zodiac boat ready to take you to the island. It's been arranged for a fisherman to call the authorities tomorrow and say he saw someone on the island waving for help. A helicopter will be dispatched to pick you up."

As Tony climbed out of the hatch, a warm, moist breeze was blowing. The air tasted fresh and good after the stale air of the sub.

The skipper followed through the hatch. He held out his hand to Tony. "Good luck. Don't know what your mission was, but thanks."

Tony grasped his hand. "Don't thank me. Thank the ones who didn't come back."

Sandra grabbed the skipper's hand smiling. "Mission accomplished," she said excitedly.

Tony and Sandra climbed down the ladder into the rubber boat. The crewman gunned the motor and headed toward the island, which appeared as a dark shape across the surface of the water, underlined with a white ribbon of sand. Moonlight, reflecting on the whiteness of the sand, made it seem as though it were glowing by its own light. As they passed through a breach in the barrier reef, white breakers crashed on both sides. The boat glided smoothly through the lagoon and soon slipped onto the beach with a scratching sound.

Tony and Sandra stepped out of the raft and pushed it back into deeper water. The crewman turned it around and sped away, leaving a white trail of phosphorescent foam in its wake. "Thanks," Tony yelled after him. The drone of the motor faded into the distance. They were left with only the rumble and boom of the breakers crashing on the reef, and the soft swish of the waves as they advanced and then retreated on the shore of the moonlit lagoon.

Tony turned and walked toward the dense vegetation of the island. He stopped at the edge of the sand. "Well I guess we'd just as soon make ourselves comfortable. We have all night."

"Tony, come sit out here in the sand where we can see around us. It's too frigging dark there. Scares me."

"Okay, but what would you do if the moon sets?"

"Don't think it will tonight."

Tony walked to where Sandra was and sat next to her. For a long time he silently watched the moonlight dancing on the water of the lagoon and the white line of breakers crashing on the reef. Finally he breathed a deep sigh and said, "Sandra, I'm sorry about Aaron. I know you liked him."

Sandra laughed.

"But, I thought you liked him."

"I played up to the old bastard 'cause he knew a lot of people worth knowing in the academic world. Could have done me a lot of good. Also used him to find out what was going on and to keep me updated on things. You damn guys would never tell me a frigging thing. Had to have sex now and then to keep him in the right damn frame of mind. Could have done me a hell of a lot of good, but guess I'm on my own again. Well, I have the finances now. That'll be a frigging big help.

"You know," Sandra continued, "Mac wasn't such a bad guy, but he couldn't help me. Besides, he came on too strong. But I know something about Mac even you don't know."

"What?"

"Mac told me he always wanted to be a hero. Wanted it so much he put in for the manned Mars mission. Well the son-of-a-bitch was accepted."

"What?"

"He was gonna wait 'till the last minute to tell you 'cause he felt like shit about breaking up the frigging team. Was supposed to report to NASA as soon as he completed this mission."

Tony was silent for a long time, staring into the dark sky—at a star that twinkled with a reddish light. "Mac was a great guy…He would do anything for me…and I for him." He was silent again and then continued. "He even gave his life to save me."

"Come on, now. I don't buy that shit. Nobody would give their life for someone else."

"You have a lot to learn, Sandra…You have a lot to learn."

The two sat silently, watching the moon glow twinkling on the waves. A soft breeze rustled the leaves behind them.

"Isn't it beautiful, Tony—just the two of us alone on this island in the moonlight? She was silent as she tried to adjust the strap on her top. "Well, how about that? The strap on my top broke. They really aged it and now it's rotten. See if you can do something." She slipped it off and handed it to Tony.

"I don't think I can do anything with it."

"Well, I just won't wear a top then." She looked down, the moonlight caressed her breasts as she threw her shoulders back.

"Think I have nice breasts?"

"You have a beautiful figure, Sandra," Tony said, rather embarrassed.

"I'm getting cold without a top. Could you put your arms around me?" Sandra said as she moved closer.

Tony put an arm around her.

She gently rubbed her breast against him, and then kissed his bare chest.

Tony looked down at her and as she lifted her face to him, met her lips with his. Tony felt her soft smooth skin as he held her. Her tongue flicked into his mouth like a serpent's. He pulled back.

"What's the matter, Tony baby?" Sandra asked.

"I'm sorry…I lost my best friend and the woman I loved…I couldn't…It wouldn't be right."

She moved away from him, visibly agitated by his rejection.

"I'm sorry, Sandra," Tony said again.

"I thought you were a man."

"Maybe I was raised different from you, but there are certain times for certain things…and this is not the time."

Sandra sat in silence for a long time and then said almost under her breath, "It's just a shame to let such a romantic setting go to waste."

She picked up several handfuls of sand, each time throwing them as hard as she could. Not looking at him she said, "Tony, do you think we'll ever meet again?"

"Probably not. You'll go your way and I'll go mine."

"We've been through a lot, haven't we?"

"Yeah."

"You know? I probably could have gone for you."

"You're a beautiful woman, Sandra. Maybe given different circumstances—a different time, a different place—we might have fallen for each other. Who knows? But we're very different, you and I."

"Yeah, you're damn right, we're different." Sandra started laughing—a wild, uncontrollable laugh.

"What's the matter? Why are you doing that?"

"So, you wouldn't screw me? That's really funny, because now you're the one that's screwed."

"What are you talking about, Sandra?"

"Sandra is dead. She drowned."

Tony started to get up but a strong hand pulled him back.

"You're not going anywhere."

"Wha…what the hell's going on?" Tony stammered.

"The blast destroyed Karl's body. Sandra drowned and I was able to use her's. Always takes a while until it becomes me. In the meantime, the brain with the original personality and memories has control. It's never taken this long before. Now that I'm me, I'm gaining my strength back. Sandra was weak."

The thing laughed. "She sure had a hot body, though. I really wanted to screw you, Tony baby." It laughed again.

Tony couldn't believe what he was hearing. He tried to get up again but once more was pulled down. He tried to pull away but Sandra's small hands had incredible strength.

"What…what do you want?"

"I want your body. Sandra served the purpose, but now I want to be you."

Fear poured over Tony like an icy rain. This was a dead body holding him in its grip. Sandra was dead! Karl, or whoever it was, was now her. "Why…why do you want to be me?"

"I'd have access to military secrets that could help the cause. I need to redeem myself to the Feathered Serpent."

Tony's mind raced, trying to think of a delaying tactic. *Maybe if I could stall until the helicopter arrives…*

"You said Sandra had a hot body." Tony forced the words out. "Let's have sex." His words belied the disgust in his soul.

The thing laughed. "Why the sudden change, Tony baby? Did you just realize that this is your last chance to screw before you die?"

"Look, give me one last request, Karl, or whoever you are," Tony said. "I've always played straight with you. I thought you were my friend. Give me a chance to have a little pleasure before I die. There's just you and I on this romantic beach. You have a woman's body and I'm a man. I'm sure you'd really enjoy it."

"Okay, Tony baby, but you better be good. Kiss me."

It flicked its tongue in and out. In the dim light, it looked to Tony like it was forked.

It brought its mouth close to Tony. He drew back.

"What's the matter, Tony baby? You're the one who suggested it."

Tony drew on all of his courage and kissed it, trying not to gag.

The thing held Tony in its arms, squeezing him tightly against its bare breasts. It reached down, and in a single motion ripped off Tony's bathing suit.

"It doesn't feel like you can do me any good. Tony baby."

The thing rolled over on top of Tony, pinning his arms down. "I don't think you're enjoying this, Tony baby."

Tony tried to break away but its strength was too much for him.

"Enough of playing games. I have to kill you so I can have your body. But I don't want to damage it. I'm going to slowly squeeze your throat until you can't breathe. I'll be careful not to hurt you, though."

It held Tony's neck in both hands and slowly tightened it's grip.

Tony tried desperately to pull the hands from his throat to no avail. He tried to throw the thing over. It held firm. He kicked it with his feet. Pounded it with his fists. Nothing fazed it.

The thing laughed. "Death is inevitable, so relax and enjoy it." It laughed again. The entity loosened its grip a little and let Tony gasp some air.

"Please. Why do you have to be me?" He hoarsely pleaded.

"Don't fight it, Tony baby. Just let your body relax, and it'll be over before you know it," the thing said as it slowly tightened it's grip again.

"It's now or never," Tony thought. With one hand he grabbed the back of Sandra's head. With the other hand he forced two of his fingers into her eye sockets. He felt the soft pop as his fingers punched into the eyeballs.

Surprised, the entity released it's grip momentarily. Tony tried to escape, but the grip tightened again. It groaned in pain. After taking a few sharp breaths it was able to speak.

"It's all right. You can damage my body. I'll soon have yours. Can't see you but I can feel your neck. That's all I need. I'm going to make you die slowly now, to punish you. You've been a bad, bad boy," it hissed.

The dawn was starting to break and Tony could see the thing clearly, now. Blood and fluid dripped from Sandra's empty eye sockets, as they looked down at him, unseeing.

It slowly squeezed his throat as Tony fought for every breath. Then, waiting until Tony wheezed a breath out, the thing closed off his windpipe.

Tony felt as if his lungs would collapse. His whole body screamed for air. He desperately flung his body, trying to dislodge the thing. He pulled on its hair and beat on its arms with all his strength. It only laughed.

As he pushed his hand on the sand, trying to force himself over, he felt a piece of round coral. With his last ounce of strength, he grabbed it. Swinging his arm as hard as he could, he slammed it onto the side of the thing's head—again and again. Finally, the hold on his throat was slowly released, and he was able to breathe.

Tony threw the thing over onto the sand. He kept hitting it with all his strength until the head became a mush of blood and brains. Yellow hair stained red. The sand became crimson, as blood flowed from the prostrate body, pooled, and then disappeared into little rivulets below the surface.

Tony gasped for air as he tried to support himself on all fours.

A dark, shadowy wisp, like smoke, came from the body and dissolved into the air.

Tony let himself go and fell onto the sand. Exhaustion overwhelmed him. He gasped for every breath.

After gaining strength, he raised himself to his knees. What once had been beauty was now a hideous, grotesque, bloody, mass.

"It's morning," Tony thought, panicking. "The helicopter will be coming soon."

He found a large shell and starting scooping out a hole in the sand. "Got to hurry," he kept saying over and over to himself. "Got to hurry. They'll be here soon."

The shell wasn't fast enough. He scrapped the sand out with his hands until his fingers were raw and bleeding. Finally the hole was large enough to lay the body in.

He grabbed the body by the feet and dragged it to the depression in the sand, hastily covered it and smoothed the sand over the area.

Tony ran away. He ran as far as he could before collapsing on the sand at the water's edge. His body shook as if it were a mass of jelly with no bones or fiber. He threw up, retching and gasping. A wave washed over him.

From the distance came the wop, wop, wop of a helicopter.

Chapter 23

THE REPLACEMENT

Is it over? Is it really over? The thought lingered in Tony's head as he felt the aircraft leave the runway. He secured his landing gear and slowly pulled back on the stick to gain altitude and took a heading toward the testing area.

He had barely checked back into the base when Colonel Martin had him in the air again. I guess this was the best way.

It seemed as if it was all a dream—as if he would wake up and things would be as they were before. How could his life have changed so much in so short a time? He was a test pilot and was used to things going wrong. He had flown in combat and fought an enemy that was flesh and blood, people much like himself. But this…. He had never before believed in the supernatural, but now, how could he not believe? His mind was confused—in turmoil. And there was this vague lingering fear—an emotion that a test pilot must never have.

It took weeks for his mind to finally accept reality after he was picked up from that deserted island.

Thinking back on everything that happened and what led to it all—the Feathered Serpent, Father Gorski, the Crystal Skull, Karl Farmer, Natasha—he had written on a piece of hotel stationery: "Sometimes, seemingly unrelated events, weave a web across time and space. A web, which unless broken, can ensnare millions of souls."

Standing on the hotel balcony in Hawaii, he had held the page in his hand. Closing his eyes, he had let the warm sun kiss his face as he thought of Natasha.

Then he tore it piece by piece, letting the wind carry it away, and as he wiped a tear with the back of his hand whispered, "Is the web broken?"

"Come in, Tony. This is blue base."

He was now in the testing area. *I wonder if they've improved this baby since the last time I tested it?*

"Roger, blue base. Tony here."

"Take it on the elevator. Straight up. Full throttle."

"Roger, blue base. Beginning the ascent now."

Tony pulled back on the stick while easing the throttle forward until he had one hundred per cent thrust and was standing on his tail.

"What'd you guys do to this baby? I already broke Mach one and it's still moving on out."

"When you get to Mach 1.5, start into a zero G arc and ease back to sixty per cent."

"Damn! Already there. This baby goes like a scalded cat. Think we've really got something here."

"Tony, this is Colonel Martin. Bring it around and come on in."

"So soon. Colonel? Just got up here. You send me up here soon as I check in, now you want me to terminate?"

"Wanted you to climb back in the saddle as soon as possible. It's better that way."

"Thanks, Colonel."

"General Stone wants to see you in his office soon as you land. Don't keep him waiting. When he's finished, I'd like to see you in my office."

"Roger—if I can get this equipment to go home. It's like a wild horse."

After landing. Tony hurried to the general's office.

"Go right in. He's expecting you."

Tony walked into the office.

"Come in, Captain Thompson. At ease. Have a seat."

"Thank you, sir."

The general looked at Tony with his steel gray eyes. "Can you tell me what happened to Captain Charles MacPherson?"

"Only what you see in the official report, sir. While on leave, he disappeared while scuba diving at night near Heron Island, Australia. His body was never recovered."

"I see. Can you tell me if he died in the line of duty?"

"Yes sir, he did. Very much so. But that's not for the record.

"I understand." He stood up and Tony followed suit. "Well, you are now officially off TDY and back under my command. You have a lot of work waiting for you so don't mess around. Colonel Martin is waiting for you in his office to get you back in the swing of things. We need you here, so don't be going on any of those extended exotic leaves any more."

"Yes sir. I mean, no sir," Tony answered, saluted and turned to walk away.

"Just a minute, Captain." The General walked around his desk and approached Tony. "One more question. Was the mission a success?"

"Yes sir."

"Judging by the level from which the request was made, it must have been damned important." The general extended his hand to Tony. "Thanks," he said. "Now let's get back to normal. I don't want to lose any more of my test pilots." And then, almost in a whisper, "Guess I'll have to advise NASA."

"What was that, sir?"

"Nothing. You're dismissed"

Tony walked slowly out of the office. He knew what the general had said.

He was tired and he just wanted to go to his room and rest but Doc and Bob had made him promise to meet them at the Officer's Club for a few drinks.

The colonel was talking to someone in his office when Tony arrived. "Hi, Tony. Come in. I'd like you to meet someone. This is Lieutenant Cedric Norman. Lieutenant Norman, Captain Anthony Thompson."

"Hi, pleased to meet you. Just call me Sid." He smiled broadly as he looked at Tony, then continued, "Haven't we met somewhere before?"

"No, I don't think so," answered Tony.

The colonel continued. "Lieutenant Norman just graduated from test pilot school. Had the highest all around score in his class. He'll be your new partner. Be working with you in the XXF program as well as the CYBER program with Doc and Bob. Still gung ho, so it shouldn't be hard to teach him the ropes. No combat time, but almost a thousand hours flying time."

He laughed and then he became serious. "Last week Lieutenant Norman had a flameout on takeoff. Survived a crash that by all rights should have killed him. In fact, when the crash crew got there, they thought he was dead, but he surprised them. He wasn't even hurt. He's ready to go again."

"Should I call you Sid or Lucky?" Tony laughed. "I'm on my way to the club to have a cool one with Doc and Bob. Would you like to meet them?"

"Sure. Why not?"

As Tony and Sid walked to the Officer's Club the desert breeze began to blow.

"You can get pretty thirsty out here," Tony commented.

"Yes, I think a cold drink would taste very good right now, sir."

"Look, Sid. Just relax. Don't call me sir. We're going to be a team. I'm sure the colonel briefed you on the two projects we'll be working on, but he probably didn't tell you much about Doc and Bob. They're both real nice guys. You'll enjoy working with them."

"I'm sure I will."

"Well, here we are," Tony said as he opened the door for Sid.

"Hey! Over here!" came a voice from a table in the corner.

Tony and Sid walked over to the table. "Doc. Bob. I'd like you to meet Sid. He's going to be my new partner."

"Well, they sure didn't waste time getting a replacement for Mac," Bob said.

"Okay, Sid. Have a seat and I'll introduce you to one of my famous boilermakers," Doc said as he reached under his chair and picked up a brown bag. "We're celebrating the return of a famous test pilot and commemorating the loss of another. Here comes the pitcher of beer."

"That's a hell of a way to introduce Sid to the team," Tony said. "He's gonna think we're a bunch of drunks. I sure as hell hope we don't have to fly tomorrow."

As the pitcher of beer was placed on the table, Doc pulled a bottle of clear liquid from the bag and held it above the pitcher with a flourish. "Just watch how a real artist makes a boilermaker."

"What's in the bottle?" Sid asked.

"Only the very best medical grade ethyl alcohol," Doc answered.

"Holy shit. Doc!" Tony objected, "Not the hundred ninety nine proof! That stuff will zap us for sure."

"On the contrary. This alcohol is the very purest," Doc answered.

"Well, I don't know. I'm not much of a drinker," Sid said as Doc handed him a glass of the mixture.

"You'll like it. Just chug-a-lug," said Bob.

"No, Sid! You'll be on your ass," Tony warned. "Doc's boilermakers will drop you on your ass before you know it. Better take it easy."

"Tony, heard you already checked out the new and improved Black Widow," Doc said. "How'd you like her?"

"Fine as wine," Tony answered. "Don't know what they did to it, but they sure souped it up."

"You know, Sid," Doc said very pompously. "The last time Tony tangled with the Black Widow, it almost got his ass."

Sid managed a nervous halfhearted laugh. "You mean the XXF? Why do you call it the Black Widow?"

"You'll soon find out, son. How do you like my boilermakers?" asked Doc.

"Okay, I guess."

"Okay, then," Doc said as he topped off everyone's glasses. "Let me tell you some of the tales of my profession. I'll begin by telling you about the time when I was on duty in an emergency room one Saturday night in Houston before I got on at NASA. This guy brings in his buddy with a light bulb up—"

"Nooo, Doc. Not the light bulb story again," Tony moaned.

"I never got to hear how the story ended. What did the good doc do about it?" said Bob.

"Wait a minute, fellows," Sid broke in. "I'd like to ask a question."

"Ask away," Doc answered.

Sid went on. "I want to learn to be one of you, so I'd like to understand. The three of you lost a good friend. Don't you feel some remorse?"

Tony took a swallow from his drink. "Yeah, we loved Mac. But in this business, death is part of life. You accept it and go on living. Don't get too attached to anyone."

"Let me tell you something," Tony continued. "If you want to be a good test pilot, remember this. The equipment you'll be testing is, for the most part, unproven and untried. Every time you strap yourself into that cockpit, death is sitting on your shoulders. You have to look at death in a new way. He's your constant companion."

He heard Sid mumble under his breath, "I know death very well."

Tony was silent as he looked at Sid, and then continued. "You can outwit him for only so long. If you stay in this business long enough, one day he'll probably win." Sid smiled and nodded his head.

There was a long silence around the table and then Doc lifted up his glass and said, "Here's to Mac, a great test pilot and a very good friend."

"Hear, Hear," they said in unison as they lifted their glasses.

"Too bad he had to die like that," Bob lamented. "Poor son-of-a-bitch had to go and die in a scuba accident—to die in a screw-up? Or maybe eaten by a shark."

Tony swallowed hard, choking back the words that wanted to come screaming from his mouth. He was quiet for a moment, then held up his glass and softly said, "To a hero."

There was another long silence, and then Doc spoke up. "Guess we better hit the sack. Don't want Sid to be too beat on his first day on the job. We'll have time some other night to really test my boilermakers."

The four got up together and walked out into the moonlight. The desert night was cool and refreshing. In the distance came a sharp staccato of barks, then a long lonesome howl. It was answered by another, and then another.

"What was that?" Sid asked.

"Coyotes, son," Doc answered. "Yeah, this is the wild west," Bob chimed in. They arrived at the officer's quarters and started to go in.

"Wait, Tony," Sid said. "Don't go in just yet."

Tony turned and looked at Sid. The moonlight reflecting on his eyes made them look as though they were glowing.

Sid smiled. "Just want you to know I'm glad I'll be working closely with you. Sleep well, Tony baby. Sleep well."

THE END

AFTERWORD

A battle was won, but not without its costs. Other webs will be spun and other battles will be fought before the final battle is waged.

0-595-34803-3

Milton Keynes UK
Ingram Content Group UK Ltd.
UKHW042212010923
427918UK00003B/146